THE **BABY** CHRONICLES

What an inspiring and amazing story to read! *The Baby Chronicles* helped me gain awareness and gave me answers to questions I have had for a very long time. God bless us. Thank you again.

—**Baheya Aysheh**, Author, Colorado

I am so proud of the work Beatrice Bruno has done with her first work of fiction, *The Baby Chronicles!* I wouldn't be surprised if *The Baby Chronicles* made the bestseller list and then to the Big Screen. I loved it! Personally, I would love to see it made into a movie!

I was very proud of one of the main characters, Margarette Ann, for standing up to her father, Albert, as she was leaving to join the Army!! You'll have to read the book to find out why! I could actually see the scene playing out as I read.

This would be a great read for someone who is a non-believer. I have some friends to whom I'm going to recommend *The Baby Chronicles*. I can't wait to read about these women and their lives in the US Army!

Thank you so much, Beatrice, for allowing me to be one of the first to experience the journey of Beverly, Joyce, Margerette Ann, and Emmaline from before birth up to enlisting in the Army!

—**Lavada Price**, Author, Texas

The Baby Chronicles will captivate your mind, the truth will touch your heart, and the wisdom will change how you view the potential of your life. Beatrice Bruno has crafted a masterpiece destined to ignite our hearts to fully live the Gospel.

—**Cheryl Townsley**, Author, Wisdom Coach, Colorado

The Baby Chronicles is AMAZING! God has really used Beatrice Bruno in a wonderful, fun, and exciting way! I finally got a chance to read it on the plane and could not put it down! *The Baby Chronicles is v*ery thought-provoking and directs your thoughts to God and the unseen spiritual realm. I can't wait till it comes out in audio and the movies!

—**Jacqui Clay**, Retired Army CSM and Assistant Principal, Arizona

THE
BABY
CHRONICLES

Where You Were Before You Were

BEATRICE BRUNO

NEW YORK
NASHVILLE • MELBOURNE • VANCOUVER

THE BABY CHRONICLES
Where You Were Before You Were

Published in New York, New York, by Morgan James Publishing. Morgan James and The Entrepreneurial Publisher are trademarks of Morgan James, LLC. www.MorganJamesPublishing.com

The Morgan James Speakers Group can bring authors to your live event. For more information or to book an event visit The Morgan James Speakers Group at www.TheMorganJamesSpeakersGroup.com.

Shelfie

A **free** eBook edition is available with the purchase of this print book.

CLEARLY PRINT YOUR NAME ABOVE IN UPPER CASE

Instructions to claim your free eBook edition:
1. Download the Shelfie app for Android or iOS
2. Write your name in **UPPER CASE** above
3. Use the Shelfie app to submit a photo
4. Download your eBook to any device

ISBN 978-1-68350-082-7 paperback
ISBN 978-1-68350-084-1 eBook
ISBN 978-1-68350-083-4 hardcover
Library of Congress Control Number:
2016907882

Cover Design by:
Megan Whitney
megan@creativeninjadesigns.com

Interior Design by:
Bonnie Bushman
The Whole Caboodle Graphic Design

In an effort to support local communities, raise awareness and funds, Morgan James Publishing donates a percentage of all book sales for the life of each book to Habitat for Humanity Peninsula and Greater Williamsburg.

Get involved today! Visit
www.MorganJamesBuilds.com

Dedication

To the men and women I had the privilege of serving with in the US Army and Military Forces. To everyone who has ever been born, these are our chronicles. This is how we came about and why we do what we do!

God is faithful!

Foreword

The Baby Chronicles is a divine revelation from Christ Jesus given to Beatrice Bruno, The Drill Sergeant of Life.

Although the Drill Sergeant of Life has written a biblical fiction, she has proven through scripture (I Peter 1:20; Titus 1:2; I Corinthians 2:7; II Timothy 1:9; and Ephesians 1:4) that before there was gender (male or female), race (Jew nor Greek), social class (slave nor free), we were in Heaven with God (see Galatians 3:28).

Our eternal purpose cannot be explained nor put in human terms. Too much of our Christian life is spent living in the natural instead of the supernatural. Where we came from, our parents, our ethnicity, economic status, etc., are barriers *we* have put as barriers to success in life. Not God.

Beatrice Bruno has eloquently written a treatise that describes our beginnings as spirit beings that only want to be with our Father God. With the closeness of His presence and the beauty of Heaven, none of us wants to come to an Earth filled with despair, hatred, uncaring, unbelieving, and so on and so forth.

The Baby Chronicles is truly an amazing work of the Holy Spirit. The way in which Beatrice goes into a spiritual realm is very descriptive of our longing to never leave the Father. Then, He gives us to our parents and the world as a gift for an eternal purpose. Unfortunately, we get so easily distracted and the same "spiritual" being that never wanted to come here to an ugly world changes and never wants to return to the Father.

But thank God for His eternal purpose through Christ Jesus for His predestined plan of salvation. The Drill Sergeant proves, even in fiction, that "*God has chosen the foolish things to confound the wise and the weak in the world to shame the strong*" (I Corinthians 1:26).

This book will change the way you view your life, God, and why you were sent here! After finishing this book, you will see yourself the way our Father, Abba, sees us. You will no longer allow any natural barriers to affect your supernatural purpose.

May the Lord bless Beatrice Bruno, called to be an Apostle and fulfilling her destiny as the Drill Sergeant of Life, for this book! And may you the reader be forever changed!

—**Pastor Norman Chase**, Living Disciples Christian Center, Denver

In the Beginning . . .

Prologue

My Son," said Almighty God. "The universe is too vast; it has nothing in it. Why don't We create something We can sit back and enjoy—for Our pleasure?"

"Yes, Father, We can do that," answered the Son. "What do You have in mind?"

"Well, I had hoped You would come up with something. Here's what I was thinking," said God. "Down There, all We have is this dark space. To be truthful, I can't even see My hand in front of My face Down There."

"Yes, Sir, I agree. I had considered that Myself," admitted the Son.

"Well, Son, I believe I've come up with something. How about this: Let there be light!" God the Father commanded.

Instantly upon giving the commandment, an explosion shook the Heavens. The angels stood still and eternity stopped. A brightness emanated from beneath they hadn't seen before—not from Down There.

All the angels wondered what God was going to do with *There*, the space beneath their dwelling place. A universal divide had always existed between Heaven and *There*. *There* was dark, a void. The angels had been hesitant in venturing out of Heaven, especially since God hadn't told them to venture out. But now, *There* had light.

"But," God told His Son, "something is still missing Down There."

3

"Father, do You see that thing Down There, that mass of nothing? It appears to be formless, nothing occupies it. Hmmm, I never really noticed it until now. May I try something?" asked the Son.

"By all means, Son, please do. Three Minds work better than One," God the Father gave the go-ahead.

"Well, Father, Let's try this. First, Let's give it a shape," the Son said, working His hands around the thing. He shaped it, then shaped it some more until it formed a perfect circle. "Ah, this is good. What do You think of that, Father?" He asked.

"What are those designs You're making on that—what are You going to call it, Son?" Almighty God paused, considering the creation in His Son's hands.

"Since I Am forming it out of the dust of the atmosphere, I think I will call it 'Earth,'" answered the Son. "I Am creating these designs so everything doesn't appear the same. See, Father, this part of the Earth will be different from that portion."

"Well, My Son, I understand. I Am sure You will make it more plain as We continue to create this new thing."

"Spirit," God Almighty asked. "What are You doing?"

The Spirit of God answered, "I Am moving upon the face of some substance I don't recognize."

"What does it look like?" asked the Son.

"It's clear but has ripples. As You mold the orb You call Earth, this substance moves, flows into the pockets You've created for it," the Spirit of God said to the Son.

"Hmmm," pondered the Son. "What can I name that substance and what is the purpose of it?"

"Son, I think I have an idea. Now, You're creating this place called Earth, correct?"

"Yes, Sir."

"Let's think on this a moment, Son. On this Earth, You will have dry land, correct?"

"Well, yes, Father, because it is made of dry land, but…"

"Well, on the dry part, You will have living things like plants such as We have here in Heaven and animals. They will need a liquid substance to sustain them. This is the liquid substance and We can call it 'water.' Look at it. It is a living organism in itself and gives and sustains life," said God the Father, triumphantly.

"Father, that's brilliant! I understand Your logic. So if I make pockets in various places on Earth, this water substance will flow into those pockets and provide life to everything it touches in those areas, right?" asked the Son, fully comprehending. He grew more excited as He spoke things out. "Spirit, what do You think about this?"

"I see what You mean, Father and Son. But there seems to be a bit more of this water substance in this part over here. Look at how the orb is almost overcome by it. What shall We do?" questioned the Spirit of God. "What if We . . ." the Spirit said as He shifted the Earth until it was suspended between two bodies of the water substance.

As He suspended the Earth, He allowed it to bounce on the bodies of waters for a moment. As it did, a spray of the substance sprinkled on the parts of the Earth that were not near the large bodies of waters.

God the Father saw it and said, "Spirit, what did You just do?"

The Spirit of God thought He had done something wrong.

"Pardon Me, Sir. I allowed the orb to drop down a bit. When it touched the two bodies of waters, it caused a spray to sprinkle back over the Earth."

"No, Spirit, I'm not upset. I just have a better idea," God the Father said. "Son, do this. Create a firmament, an arch, over Your Earth. Now, the area above the firmament closest to Us will be called the Heavens since it is an extension, an expansion, of where We live. We will provide these waters to the Earth because the waters in the Earth need a source. We have the source right here in the Heavens."

"OK, Father, I understand what You're doing. Because We are the Creators, We will provide for Our creation from here so it will have everything it needs. Good idea," acknowledged the Son.

God the Father, His Son, and His Spirit stood back to look at what They had created so far. They were pleased with what They saw. The Master Artists continued to create this new thing, the Earth, in the atmosphere beneath Their Heaven. As They molded and shaped the orb and the world it encapsulated, the seraphims and cherubims surrounding the Trio of Creators wondered about this new thing.

Meanwhile, Archangel Lucifer, the leader of the singers, showed great interest in this new place being created. He had quickly grown tired of being in the shadows in Heaven. He wanted to expand.

Almighty God knew his thoughts and turned toward Lucifer, fierceness in His countenance. Lucifer stepped back into the shadows of the other angels.

"I will bide my time, Almighty," he thought. "I will bide my time."

One

Father, there is no color, no life on Our Earth. Everything looks so drab in black and white Down There. What if We add color to it?" asked the Son.

Looking at the black, white, and gray world beneath Them, the Father considered His Son's query. He wanted the Earth to be a reflection of His wonderful Heaven—colorful and full of life.

"Yes, Son, do what is in Your heart," God granted permission to the Son.

The Son looked around Himself in Heaven at the master copy He would follow as He created the Earth. Hmmm, grass, herbs, fruit trees—yes, that was what the Earth needed.

"Father, look," said the Son.

The Son worked on the huge palette of the earth-mass as He created what was to be on Earth as it was in Heaven. As He created what He received from the Father, the Spirit of God moved across the face of the Earth waving His hands. Tiny seeds of color fell over the land as He sowed the power of God's commandment to bring forth grass, herbs, and fruit trees on the Earth. The Spirit of God conducted as a musical maestro as living things sprang forth from the newly-created land mass.

Grass sprouted from its seed, herbs sprouted from their seeds, and wonderfully multicolored fruit trees sprouted from their seeds. The Son poured out of Himself all things to be created on the Earth to the pleasure of the Father. It pleased the

Father that the Son had everything within Himself to create all things on the Earth, causing it to be a direct reflection of Heaven.

"*Magnificent!*" exclaimed the Father in awe. It was a duplication of what He observed around Himself in His Heavenly abode.

"*Hallelujah!*" exclaimed the Archangels, Gabriel and Michael. Immediately, the seraphims and cherubims took up the wave of '*Hallelujahs*,' rejoicing at the creation they observed beneath them. All the angels with the exception of one . . .

The Creators descended to walk upon the face of the Earth. They were very pleased with Their creation so far. *Beautiful! Magnificent! Awesome!* were only three of the superlatives They used to describe Their creation to this point.

"Let's get back to work," God the Father advised excitedly as They ascended into the Heavens, elatedly making plans as They went. The Son returned to His palette as the Spirit of God stood by to carry out the will of God.

"You know, Son," said the Father, "We should equip the Earth with times and seasons. Even though the Earth will be a direct reflection of Heaven, the Earth is also in an atmosphere quite different from Heaven. As a result, there will be a day and a night as well as four seasons to allow plants and other life forms to know when and when not to bring forth."

"Umhmmm," contemplated the Son. "So if We hang the Earth on an axis only We can see…like this," the Son said, moving His hand over the Earth, "then the Earth can rotate on that axis. And, Father, I had a thought. To tell the difference between night and day, let Us hang these two lights above the Earth in the atmosphere between Heaven and Earth. One will be called the sun and will provide heat as well as light during the day on the Earth. It will be the stronger of the two lights . . ."

As the Son paused, the Spirit illustrated everything as it was thought out. He went about His task of setting into motion what the Son said.

"Then," the Son continued, "We can place the other light called the moon in the same atmosphere as the sun. Now, although it will provide light during the night, it will not shine as brightly as the sun. These two lights will divide the light from the darkness, the day from the night. After this, Father, the universe will never experience this much darkness again," the Son concluded.

"I agree, My Son. This light, it is good," agreed Almighty God. "Let Us also add some lesser lights to the Heavens. We shall call them stars. They will also be used to show times and seasons and provide direction as well as light. Look in Your hands."

The Son looked in His hands and saw the twinkling particles the Father called stars. There were so many of them! Throwing them out into the cosmos, they sparkled brightly in the atmosphere, surrounding the moon and the sun.

God the Father, His Son, and His Spirit observed that these things were good.

"Father God," said the Spirit. "I've been thinking. The Earth is full of living things—the grass, herbs, and trees. But, there is no life. Look around Us." He pointed. "There is life everywhere in every corner of Heaven. There are songs being sung, noises, laughter. You have created so much up here. But what about on the Earth?" the Spirit of God entreated.

"Umhmmm," pondered God the Father. "I have contemplated that very thing, Spirit. You are correct. I have created the angels to inhabit the Heavens. There does need to be life and living on Earth as it is in Heaven. What shall We do?" He asked His Son and His Spirit.

"Let the waters bring forth abundantly the moving creature that has life, and fowl, birds that may fly above the Earth in the open firmament of Heaven," commanded God the Son. As He commanded, thunder clapped and lightning flashed in the Heavens. Time stood still as this new thing came forth in the Earth beneath.

In the water substance, They glimpsed a huge creature. This creature had a hump on top of it. In its head, the creature had a hole that spouted water as he swam on top of the water and then dove under the surface.

"I have created whales, fish, and other creatures that can live in and under the water," explained the Son. "These creatures will provide food for each other and also for these creatures." He pointed to the flying creatures hovering nearby. "Those are birds. They will live on the Earth and make their homes in trees and bushes."

"Let the Earth bring forth the living creature after his kind, cattle, and creeping thing, and beast of the Earth after his kind, and it was so."

The Trio observed these new creatures: big, small, and medium—every size one could imagine. These creatures, animals, were majestic in every way.

"What are they called?" asked the Spirit of God.

"I have not given any of them specific names yet," said the Son. "I do not know why I feel this way, but it seems as though I Am missing something very important."

"Son," broke in Almighty God. "I believe I know what it is You are missing. You see, up until this point, all of the beings You have created have not been as We are. They do not have minds as We do. They are animals. They are living beings and have minds but they do not have souls. They do not have that certain something inside that will cause them to think as We do," explained Almighty God.

"Father, what shall I do?" asked the Son.

"Let Us think on these things for a moment," suggested God the Father.

The Three separated, walking away from the Others to contemplate Their dilemma. The Spirit of God descended to the Earth where the huge animals resided. As He moved among them, talking to and touching them, they responded to His voice and did as He commanded. A thought came to His mind right before He excitedly ascended.

The Son, observing the Spirit interacting with the animal beings on the Earth, had an idea as well. Observing both the Son and the Spirit, God the Father knew both Their thoughts.

"I know," exclaimed the Father. "This is what We will do. We will create another type of being called 'Man.' Man will be a human being created in Our image after Our likeness. We will give Man authority over all We have created—the fish of the sea, the fowl of the air, the cattle and the entire Earth, and everything that creeps upon it."

They applauded each other for Their success. The angels hovered around the Majesty of the Heavens, wondering what this new creature, Man, would be like. Lucifer silently observed the happiness and excitement of the other created beings in Heaven.

"Silly twits," he scoffed. "They just don't understand what's going on. God is going to replace us with this new creature called Man. Look at how much pleasure He derives from what He has created so far. Look at the attention He gives to those dumb ones on His Earth!"

Growing angrier and angrier, Lucifer considered what transpired around him. But he needed an ally, someone who would side with him.

He looked around at the other angels and keyed in on one of the cherubims floating by himself in a corner of Heaven. He had observed the little guy before, always alone, always by himself. What was his name again? *Bright*? No. *Fright*? No. *Night*? No. What was his name?

Lucifer pondered.

Sauntering slyly over to the little angel, his name suddenly popped into Lucifer's mind—*Right*! That's it: *Right*. But Lucifer knew very well the power of persuasion.

"Hello, *Fright*," Lucifer said sonorously as he approached his victim. "Interesting activity going on below, isn't it, *Fright*?" he carefully reiterated the false name, planting the seed of confusion into the mind of the angel.

"What did you call me, Archangel Lucifer?" the little angel asked respectfully, a puzzled look on his face. "I thought my name was *Right*, Archangel, Sir," said the timid little angel.

"*Fright*, angel, your name is *Fright*. I distinctly remember the Master calling you *Fright* when He created you. That *is* your name, isn't it? After all, who would know better than an Archangel such as *I*? *I* was there before you were even created. *I* was on the planning committee with God Himself," Lucifer retorted haughtily to the confused angel.

"But, Sir, I truly thought my name was *Right*," repeated the angel.

The shy little angel had never exercised any of the power God had given him through his name. He did not know the power of his name. As a result, he recognized what he thought to be truth behind Lucifer's statement of authority. *Right* considered the beautiful Archangel standing before him.

Lucifer cast a magnificent presence wherever he went. All the colors of Heaven were in him. He shone brilliantly as the Archangel of the Heavenly Host. As a cherub or cherubim, *Right* was in the lowest rank of angels. It was his job to follow the orders of the Seraphs (next highest) and the Archangels (the chief angels) placed over him under God. So of course Archangel Lucifer would know his name better than he knew it himself.

"I apologize, Sir. Of course you are correct and I am mistaken," acquiesced *Right*, now *Fright*. "Please accept my humble apologies, Archangel Lucifer."

"Of course I accept your apologies, Angel *Fright*. No worries," Lucifer said calmly, pulling the little angel into his web of deceit. "Everyone makes a mistake every once in a while," he said with a deceitfully friendly tone.

Lucifer looked around to make sure no one was near them. As he confided in the little angel, *Fright's* countenance changed to match his new name. *Fright* grew even smaller and took on the appearance of one who was scared out of his wits. His eyes bulged from his scrawny, diaphanous, and scary form. Where he had had glistening gold wings, he now had ugly curved talons dripping with demonic drool.

Lucifer had found his first ally. Lucifer coerced *Fright* into following him down to this new place, Earth, to select a hiding place.

"Score one for me," Lucifer congratulated himself.

Observing the exchange between Lucifer and the little angel *Right*, now *Fright*, God sadly shook His head. Even though he showed little regard for God's way, God had always loved Lucifer. Lucifer was one who had to be the best at everything he did. God now understood—He had been too lenient with Lucifer.

Two

S o, *God created man in His own image, in the image of God created He him; male and female created He them.*

"Now," said God the Father. "We will create two sexes of *Man*—a male and a female—just like the other creatures You created to fill Earth, Son. We must have a male and a female in every species so they can procreate and multiply. We will begin with the male of the species," Almighty God decided.

"Yes, Father, I understand. And what type beings will they be?" asked the Son, curious as to what would make the male and the female tick.

"They shall have Our character," said Almighty God. "They shall be able to think like We do. Unlike the animals You created on Earth and in the sea, they shall also have emotions similar to Ours. This creature Man will be most like Us out of all creation," explained God the Father, excitement and anticipation in His voice.

"So, Father," interjected the Spirit of God. "Will the male Man look like this?" He asked, pulling a handful of atmosphere out of the Heavens, molding and shaping it. Then He handed the brightly shining mass to the Son.

"And when We place this small piece of gray matter here at the top, it will be the operating system or brain of the creature. We will take a piece of this red material and make a heart and place it right here in his chest. Finally, Father, We will place a piece of You, Your Spirit, into Man. Let's see what We have," said the Son.

The Divine Trio worked on Their latest creation to make it into their image. They added wisdom, knowledge, understanding, compassion, emotions, and choice.

"It is very important We give Man choice so he can use the brain We have given him. Now, let Us create more," said Almighty God.

Jeremiah 1:5: *Before I formed thee in the belly I knew thee; and before thou camest forth out of the womb I sanctified thee, and I ordained thee a prophet unto the nations.*

God the Father, the Son, and the Spirit continued to work, creating male and female Man. Soon, Heaven was filled to the brim with the spirits of Man destined to fill Earth.

And God blessed them and said unto them, "Be fruitful and multiply, and replenish the Earth, and subdue it: and have dominion over the fish of the sea, and over the fowl of the air, and over every living thing that moveth upon the Earth."

"Father, just a moment. The atmosphere of Earth," explained the Son, "is different from what We have here in Heaven. Man must be comprised of something that will allow them to survive the elements of Earth. Man is a Spirit being as We are. His spirit should be enclosed in a vessel for protection," the Son finished.

"Let Us go down to the Earth to see what We can see," suggested the Father.

So the Three descended to Earth to see what could be done about Their new challenge. Walking among the animals moving about Earth, They considered the outer shell protecting the animals' insides. Touching the outer shell of one of the four-legged creatures, God the Father asked the Son, "How did You do this again?"

"Well, Father, remember You mentioned that Earth would have different seasons and these creatures would live in different areas of the Earth?" the Son asked. "I decided to create four seasons: autumn, winter, spring, and summer. These seasons will occur at different times on the Earth, beginning with spring, when the Earth is cold but the rays of the sun begin to heat the Earth. It is a time of seed sowing. During the summer, the sun is at its zenith and completely thaws out the Earth from the season of cold before the spring. Autumn is the time of harvesting when all the sown seeds come to their full fruit and can now be eaten. And winter is when the Earth goes back to sleep and rests until the cycle starts all over again," the Son concluded.

The Father nodded His head in understanding.

"What about the coverings on these animals?" He asked, curious as to how They would fashion similar coverings for Man.

"Well, Father, although here in Eden the atmosphere is perfect and the seasons will remain the same, certain parts of the Earth will experience the changing of seasons on a regular basis. Some of the areas will be colder, some warmer than others. Other places on the Earth will experience extreme hot or extreme cold. I designed coverings, skins, to place on the animals according to the area of the Earth they will live in," explained the Son.

"See that creature over there?" He said, pointing to a huge four-legged creature with a white coating. "Eventually, he will live where it is very cold most of the time. His skin will protect him from freezing in the cold temperatures," He continued. "His skin is extremely thick and perfect for protecting Him from the elements."

"Now look at that creature in the water," He explained, pointing to a humongous gray creature swimming in a very large body of water. "The skin on that creature protects it from extremely cold temperatures in the water."

"As for Man, they will have one type of skin to protect them from the atmosphere. His skin will not be as thick as the animals' skin," the Son continued. "This is what I have in mind."

The Son squatted down on the Earth and drew a figure in the sand. Instead of one dimension, though, He molded the figure in three dimensions allowing the Trio to see how this creature would appear.

The Son pulled one of the male Man spirits from the Heavens and instructed him, "Adam, lay down here on the Earth." The Spirit Man obeyed without hesitation.

Looking at His drawing, the Son took some of the Earth and molded it over the Man's top section. As He molded it, He created eyes to see, ears to hear, a nose to smell, a mouth to taste and communicate, and hair to protect the scalp of the head. He added a chin to give the face character. The Son carefully, lovingly molded the dust of the Earth around the male Man.

"Now, for the body," He continued. "The male Man must have strong shoulders enabling him to bear burdens for others. Two strong arms with equally strong hands attached to create, to hold, and to work with. A strong chest to hold the heart inside the ribs which is the foundation of his strength; the ribs will hold all the organs essential for him to live on the Earth."

The Son continued to fashion the human body with the approval of the Father and the Spirit. "A waist meant for bowing, knees meant for bending, feet made for walking." By the time He finished, the Son had covered the entire spirit Man with a shell that would protect his inner-man from the elements.

"Are We missing anything, Father? Spirit?" He asked the Two watching His every move. They wanted to make the Man perfect in every way.

"Spirit," commanded the Father, "breathe life into his nostrils." When the Spirit complied, Man became a living soul.

"Hello, Father," said the newly-created Man, sitting up to observe his surroundings. "Where am I?" he inquired.

"You are on the Earth, My child. The Son, the Spirit, and I decided that in order for you to go forth and multiply and be fruitful on the Earth, We had to give you some extra things you would need to be able to function on the Earth," God the Father explained.

"I feel different," said the Man, looking down at his body.

"Come over here," instructed the Son, "and let Me show you something." He led the Man to a pool of water. "Look down there."

Adam bent over at the waist to examine the water. He jerked his body upright.

"What is that?" he asked anxiously. Peeping cautiously into the water, the face peered up at him again.

"That is you, Child," explained the Son. "Your reflection. That is how you will appear to others like you."

"But You do not look like that, Father. You are clear. Even though I can see your shape, I can also see straight through You," he intoned, worried because he didn't see the image of the Father in the water.

"Don't worry, Adam. You are the image of Me where it counts the most—inside. We had to design a vessel of flesh to carry the real you around. Others coming after you will have the same or similar appearance."

Satisfied with the explanation, Adam turned his attention to his surroundings. This place was similar to but completely different from Heaven, his original home.

"What is this place?" he asked, walking around, touching everything in wonder.

"You are in the Garden of Eden. I have made this place for you to enjoy and to maintain for Me on Earth," said the Voice of Almighty God Whom the Man had always known and loved.

Adam turned toward a creature with four legs that seemed to follow him everywhere he went. "Hello, little fellow. What are you?" he asked, hoping to get to know the creature a little better.

"Adam." He heard his name for the first time in his Earth-suit. He immediately turned to face the voice of His Father and Creator.

"Oh!" Adam exclaimed. "I had almost forgotten my name." He smiled. "Yes, Father," he answered, growing accustomed to the voice coming from his face.

"Adam," continued God. "You must give every living creature a name. You have dominion over all the Earth, over all creation on the Earth and in the sea. Whatever you name something, that will be the name of it," said God the Father.

"Name every creature?" Adam repeated to himself. "Father, that's a big job. Are You certain I am capable of accomplishing this task?" he asked as he stood and talked with the Lord God.

"Yes, Adam, you are more than capable. I have equipped you with wisdom and knowledge concerning everything on the Earth," explained God. "You are called Adam because I have made you the Father of all living," He concluded.

Adam took all this in as he walked through this place where his life on Earth began. Eden was what God had named this place. *Eden,* Adam thought, *what a pleasant name.*

Adam looked at the little creature standing beside him. He pondered what he would call this species of animal. A thought formed in his mind. Hmmm, this creature was an Earth creature and did not live in the water. He had a long face and pointed ears. Fur covered its entire body. It would breed from its own kind to make more of its kind.

And it will be a friend to Man just as God was also a friend to Man in a different way, Adam decided.

"You are a dog, Man's best friend. You will be called Erasmus," he said to the animal, bending down to pat the animal on its head.

"Thank you, sir," the little dog said back to him.

Adam continued throughout Eden, giving names to all the living creatures. He was awed by the beauty on the Earth, the beauty his Creator had created to be enjoyed. As he walked among the animals and the plant life, having conversations with the animals, God the Father, the Son, and the Spirit observed Adam's actions.

Three

I t is not good that Adam should live alone," God the Father said to Himself. "Look at the animals and other living creatures We have created. We created each to have a companion, a mate—not to be alone. We created these creatures to multiply, to make others like themselves. They won't be able to do this if they are one-of-a-kind," reasoned the Lord God. "And neither can Man. We must find a helper, a mate for Man," the Father insisted.

The Divine Trio looked among the cattle and other animals on the Earth but could not find any among those creatures suitable or qualified to be Adam's helper. The Trio walked to and fro over the entire Earth to find that special mate for Their Man, Adam. There was none.

"There has to be someone or something," They mused collectively.

"Father," the Son began, "shouldn't the Man's helper be another Man of his own kind, only a female?" He asked God the Father. "You said Yourself that if they are to reproduce, they must be similar in species but different in physical makeup," He explained to God the Father and His Spirit.

"This creature should be someone who will stand alongside the Man and help him in all he has been assigned to do. This new creature should be called 'Man with a Womb' or 'Woman.' She should be created using a part of the Man's physical body so she will always be a part of him. Then Adam will take her as his mate, his wife, for life. Together, they will be fruitful and multiply and replenish the Earth and subdue it as You desire, Father," explained the Son.

The Son ascended to Heaven considering all the spirits They had created. These beings were the pre-born spirits of the people destined to eventually inhabit the Earth.

Eventually? He thought to Himself. *Well, They already had one on the Earth. Why not . . .*

The Son had an idea.

God the Father considered His Son's explanation. Looking forward into the world They were creating, Almighty God observed that throughout future history, men and women would come together in relationships and bring forth children and populate the Earth. That was His plan from the beginning. He had initiated the process by creating spirit beings that would eventually become a race of people who would give Him pleasure as they inhabited the Earth.

"You're right, My Son. We will have to create a helper for Adam that is as he is. And she must become a part of him that he will love, honor, and cherish. I have an idea. Let's go down to the Earth."

The Holy Trio again descended to the Earth to discuss this new creature, the female Man.

And the Lord God caused a deep sleep to fall upon Adam, and he slept: and He took one of his ribs, and closed up the flesh instead thereof. And the rib, which the Lord God had taken from man, made He a woman, and brought her unto the man.

"Let's see," said the Son. "Which one of the spirits shall We use for the woman?" He considered.

He looked up into the Heavens as the spirits surrounded the gate to see what their Creators were doing. They were excited! Each of them knew they would eventually be chosen for an Earth assignment as well.

As the Son considered the spirits, the Spirit of God pointed to one of the brightly shining spirit bodies.

"Son of God, have you considered Eve? She is a very brilliant spirit. I believe she would be a wonderful help meet for Adam," suggested the Spirit of God.

"Yes, Spirit," God the Father agreed. "You are correct. She will be excellent for the position."

"Well, then," agreed the Son. "Eve it shall be. Pre-born Eve, come down here," the Son commanded and beckoned to Pre-born Spirit Eve. She immediately obeyed her Creator, shining brightly in anticipation.

"Yes, My Lord, what will You have me do?" she asked, quivering excitedly.

All the pre-born spirits were excited about this new place, Earth. While the Father, Son, and Holy Spirit planned out the new place, the pre-borns caught glimpses of the blue-prints. They knew they were all destined to live on this faraway place at some time or other during their existence. Adam had already taken up his position as a human Down There. Now God was choosing another of their ranks to go and join him.

Descending to this new, exciting habitation called Earth, Pre-born Spirit Eve looked around her spirit body. Drawing closer to Earth, vibrant colors shocked her senses! Although this new place looked like the Heaven she came from, there was a distinct difference in all she surveyed. The atmosphere was different.

There were noises she was not yet accustomed to, pleasant noises. She looked forward to discovering what or who made the noises assaulting her hearing senses. *Yes*, she decided, Earth looked like a nice place. Pre-born Spirit Eve was excited to be one of the first of her kind along with Adam to inhabit it.

"Eve," said the Father as the spirit drew closer to Him. "You will be a female, a woman. You will be a helper for Adam. You will be fruitful and help him multiply by bearing children. You will replenish the Earth with mankind. You will also help him control everything going on in the Earth. Your name is Eve which means mother of all living," explained the Father.

Eve couldn't believe her good fortune! Her first assignment was to be the mother of all living? *Wait . . . what exactly did that mean?*

What an honor and privilege God had bestowed upon her! And she would be a wife to Adam and a mother to the first children born on the Earth!? *Were there going to be more created just like Adam and her?* It was all rather overwhelming, she thought, continuing to listen to the instructions being given.

"Eve," continued the Son. "You will be similar in body to Adam with a few physical differences. You will be able to bear children and feed them through your own body. We will equip you with appendages called breasts through which will flow a substance called milk designed to nourish your children. Although your body will not appear to be as physically strong as Adam's body, it will contain an inner strength for bearing children. You will also have uncommon compassion and love for others," the Son continued.

"You will be a highly intelligent and complex creature. You will understand how to do things the male of your species will not immediately know how to do. You will be very wise. In the future, other women will look to you for guidance," the Son instructed this soon-to-be woman, the mother of all living.

"You will discover it is a strong and hard job being a woman. We have equipped you with everything you need to be successful," He concluded.

Eve pondered what she was told. Not completely afraid but more apprehensive, she looked at her Creator and said, "Lord, I am willing to do what You have created me to do."

Beaming with pride at this of Their creation, the Holy Trio set to work creating *Woman*. God the Father placed the rib He had taken from Adam's side onto the ground.

"Son," He instructed, "build the woman around this rib so she will always be a part of the man. In this way, as his other ribs protect the vital organs in his body, he will also feel the need to protect this woman."

The Son set to work following the instructions of the Master Creator. He gathered a mound of dust from the Earth and shaped the outer shell in which He placed the woman's internal organs.

"Hmmm, let Me see," He spoke as much to Himself as to Himself. "She will need reproductive organs such as ovaries and a uterus in which a child can develop, fallopian tubes through which the eggs will flow to the uterus . . ."

As He created this complex, beautiful creature called *Woman,* the Son became lost in thought.

Studying her design, He considered the millions of other males and females who would come from this first pattern. Although Adam and Eve would have no parents, they would parent the human race as each individual came into existence.

He then fashioned the female breasts, which would be used to feed infant children. He filled them with milk-producing ducts and glands that would supply a life-sustaining fluid to her babies. The fluid, milk, would be nourished through her body from the sustenance she took in before, during, and after the birth of the child. The Son desired that a bond take place between the woman and child as the child nursed from the woman's body, creating an unbreakable bond for all time.

Of all the creatures the Son created, this model would be the most complex. It would also be the most copied as He created all animal life to emulate what He created this human specimen to do.

He gave her hips for bearing children—they would also keep the interest of her husband. He placed other organs within the shell she would need to survive in the Earth's atmosphere and finished by adding a mother's heart.

The Son called Eve forward to place her essence within the shell He created to house her.

"All right, Eve, lay down in your shell, your body. I will add the finishing touches," He instructed.

Eve did as she was told. It felt strange and wonderful, this body. She couldn't wait to see what it would be like to be a, what was it He called her? A woman. Woman! How interesting!

The Son finished by adding the brain, eyes, nose, mouth, and ears to the head. He added long, thick hair to the scalp so she would have longer hair than the man. Strong shoulders for her children to rest their head and cry upon. The Son added strong, firm, yet gentle hands to either calm a crying baby or to reprimand as needed. He also gave her a healthy back to bear the burden of childbirth and strong feet to walk beside her mate.

The Divine Trio considered Their creation. Looking at the woman, They saw that she was good.

"Ah," said Almighty God. "This is good. She is a wondrous creature, perfect for the man."

Lucifer stood in the shadows of the Garden. He observed the so-called Holy Trio as They spent much time on the creation of the woman. Something he hadn't experienced before bubbled inside of his being. He didn't know what this new thing was attempting to come out of him.

"Hmmm," he thought, pacing angrily in the shadows. "I have experienced anger at the Almighty for not allowing me to do what I wanted to do. I have coveted because I desire to sit on the throne He occupies high above the rest of us. I have felt outrage at His creating the Man, Adam. But what is this new thing?"

His face twisted as all three emotions overtook him. As he paced, the corresponding demons—Anger, Covetousness, and Outrage—materialized around their master's head. They beat the atmosphere with their crooked, menacing, dirty wings. When Lucifer lured these fallen angels from their destined purposes of Calm, Generosity, and Peace, they shifted their personalities to something completely opposite what God had purposed for them.

A Voice came to him, One he had always known and loved but now despised— the voice of Almighty God.

"It is called *Hatred*, Lucifer," said the gentle, yet authoritative Voice. "You feel hatred toward the humans I have created. This is a very intense emotion that can cause you to do things you otherwise would not do," said God. "Be careful with this emotion, Lucifer. Do not allow it to take you to a place you would not otherwise go," advised Almighty God.

Lucifer glared at God, derision and haughtiness in his demeanor.

"You always think You know what is best, don't You? You created me to be Your little minion. I am no one's minion! I am better than You and I will show You, God," Lucifer spat disrespectfully, shaking his gnarled talons at his Creator.

Almighty God considered Lucifer sadly. He had been one of God's most favored Archangels, shining brighter than all the other angels together. Now he allowed Pride to come and dwell in his heart. Lucifer's entire demeanor drastically changed the moment he rebelled against the Living God.

No longer beautiful and pleasing to the eye, he developed a scaly exterior with dark, fiery coals for eyes. His slender body became gnarled and humped as he stomped away from God, returning to the shadows.

God noticed that Lucifer now traveled with an entourage of angels he had converted to his camp. Very loyal, none of them considered the consequences of converting to the dark side.

"Lucifer, I Am God Almighty! I will not fight with you nor debate with you of My greatness. I created you and I can also destroy you. But, I will not," thundered the voice of Almighty God.

Lucifer looked at Him warily. He realized he had finally gotten to Him. Why wasn't He going to destroy him, he wondered. He had seen other angels destroyed for creating less division in the universe than what he was doing now. What was God's plan?

"Why? Hmmm!" questioned Lucifer sarcastically. "Do You think You can continue to control me with Your so-called greatness?" Lucifer asked belligerently.

Lucifer was finding it more and more difficult to manage the rage he experienced whenever he thought of God attempting to control him again and again.

"I won't stand for it! I will not bow to You anymore!" Lucifer shouted boldly.

The Heavens stood still as Lucifer raged, lashing out at God.

Almighty God's countenance suddenly changed. Long-suffering, full of grace and mercy, He was not quick to anger nor did He hold a grudge. Lucifer, however, had just crossed the line. But still, His grace and mercy prevailed. More importantly, His plan . . .

"Lucifer," He began, loving this Archangel who was so angry with Him. "Have I not been good to you? Have I not been merciful to you? And yet, it is not enough, is it?" God asked sadly, knowing this was the final crossroads in their relationship.

"Lucifer, do what you feel you must do. As My creation, I will always love you. But I will hate your sin," God said with a finality heard throughout the Heavens.

Lucifer glared at God, horrible scorn on his face.

"You are pathetic! And You call Yourself God?" he spat toward Almighty God. "If You were so powerful, You could obliterate me from before Your eyes. And yet You pass it off as Your grace and mercy!" Lucifer taunted in the direction of Almighty God, turning away for the final time.

"This isn't over, Weak One! You will hear more from me. I will outshine Your so-called glory," Lucifer scoffed, descending to the Earth.

He determined to wreak havoc with the man and woman, all men and all women created by God. He wanted to see how sturdy they were. He was sure he could bring them, all of them, over to his camp.

Lucifer gathered his minions, small and large. He created a strategy for the havoc he would bring on the Earth. He would cloud the minds of men . . . but that was another story.

Four

Standing at a distance from the encounter, the Son saw everything. He was appalled, horrified at Lucifer's actions. He had known Lucifer was up to something and had known it was coming.

As eternity progressed, the Son of God had perceived minute changes in Lucifer, none of them good. Lucifer had become prideful. He had been caught several times coercing and proselytizing other angels to come over to darkness.

Now he had finally done it—he had openly rebelled. Heaven stood still as the backlash of the confrontation subsided and Lucifer slunk to the shadows of Earth. Sauntering from the glow of the Holy One to the familiar darkness he allowed to cloud his mind and black heart, Lucifer hissed. He withdrew deeper and deeper into the abyss of the Hell he had created for himself and the other dark angels—the Hell of ignorance, rebellion, and disobedience.

The Heavenly Host scarcely breathed. None of them wanted to believe the scene playing out before them. How could Lucifer rebel like this?

Michael and Gabriel observed the chasm suddenly appearing out of nowhere between them and their former associate. A breach appeared in the center of the new Earth. It smelled of sulfur and tar and spewed out flames they had never observed before. As the Heavenly Host collectively turned away from the breach as it closed upon itself, they caught a brief glimpse of a lake of fire burning with brimstone.

The Son looked sadly at His created beings as they turned away from the horrible picture. He knew the fate of those who chose to rebel against God the Father—never-ending turmoil and suffering. They would never return to Heaven to stay as they had before their act of treason. Their destiny changed from one of glory to one of doom.

Other than a short season when God the Father would allow these demonic fellows to wreak havoc on the Earth against the humans as they pursued God's will on the Earth, all these fallen angels were doomed to the fiery pit for all eternity. During this time, the demons under the mastery of Lucifer/satan were free to roam throughout the Earth seeking whomever they could devour.

"Father, are You all right?" asked the Son, concern heavy in His voice as He turned His attention to the beloved Father. "Is there anything I can do for You, Almighty? I Am at Your service," He assured Him.

Almighty God glanced at His Son, contemplating the decision He had to make. He had already put the decision off for far too long. For now, though, it could wait. Now was a time for rejoicing as they populated the Earth They had carefully planned and created.

"Let Us go down to Earth and see how Adam and Eve fare," He said out loud. He wanted to participate in the joy of His creation and not the sadness, not right now. "In fact, let Us take all the pre-borns with Us to observe what they will experience in their seasons."

"That's a splendid idea, Almighty!" the Son exclaimed. "Sort of like taking them on a field trip, isn't it?" the Son suggested jovially. He was glad Almighty God was not going to allow one bad angel to spoil everything for everyone else.

They corralled thousands upon thousands of pre-born spirits with the help of the Heavenly Host to prepare them for their first field trip.

"This should prove to be interesting," the Son said happily.

Garden of Eden

'Oohs' and 'ahhs' poured from the pre-born spirits descending to the Earth. They had watched Almighty God, the Son, and the Spirit as They created the Earth. Now, though, they were able to see everything up close and personal. They were even allowed to get closer to the Earth animals and beasts.

The pre-born spirits frolicked on the Earth, enjoying the new atmosphere. Heaven was beautiful to them and they enjoyed their home. However, many of them excitedly looked forward to their assignment in the Earth-realm.

They smelled the Earth air for the first time—it was wonderful! Many of them couldn't wait until their turn to make the journey to Earth to live as humans. How exciting! They were all destined to become living souls at some point in time or the other.

Some were skeptical, though, about their upcoming assignments. They really didn't want to leave Heaven. Although everything appeared interesting on the Earth, they knew the things in Heaven were *more* interesting. That's where they wanted to remain!

Seeing the plant and animal life up close for the first time, the pre-born spirits were amazed. Many of the things they saw, touched, and smelled reminded them of Heaven, though Heaven's actual articles were more magnificent! Even the food God created for the inhabitants of Earth was strange and came in so many wonderful colors!

Then the pre-born spirits saw Adam and Eve. They were beautiful creatures, brand spanking new from the creative heart of God. Although their memories of pre-born Adam and Eve were good memories, these creatures in their human shells were exemplary!

The pre-born spirits gathered around God Almighty and Adam and Eve as He gave them final instructions.

"*Of every tree of the garden, thou mayest freely eat: but of the tree of the knowledge of good and evil, thou shalt not eat it: for in the day that thou eatest thereof thou shalt surely die,*" God commanded Adam.

"Die?" twittered the pre-born spirits among themselves. "What does that mean?" they wondered. The Son instantly stood before them to answer their questions.

"To die means your spirit will leave your earthly body to return home to be with Jehovah God. It means you will no longer exist on the Earth except as a memory."

Pre-born Spirit Miriam, piped up. "Does that mean we will be available for another assignment on the Earth, Holy Son?" she asked.

"No," He answered. "It means you will come back home to Heaven after you have accomplished your mission on the Earth," He explained. "And you will stay in Heaven if you have accepted Me as Your Savior," the Son emphasized.

"But Son, what if we don't receive You as our Savior?" asked Pre-born Spirit Kelly, wanting to know, yet fearing the answer.

"My child, you will go to the other place if you do not accept Me," the Son sadly answered. "The place of darkness away from God," He added.

"Oh," murmured the other spirits in hushed understanding.

"We will only live one time on Earth but twice in Heaven?" asked Pre-born Spirit Tiffany, one of the more inquisitive pre-borns. "That sounds good," she said, jittery with excitement. "So, Holy Son, how long will we live on Earth?"

"That is a question you will have to ask Almighty. He holds the balance of each of your lives in the palms of His hands. He alone will determine how long you will do anything in your Earth-life. Be patient and He will answer all your questions," answered the Son, smiling at the eager pre-born spirits ready to get on with their new lives.

Lucifer/satan observed the goings-on between God and the pre-born spirits from his hiding place. He knew he had made the right decision by rebelling against that phony God he had served from the beginning of his existence. But no more! He was tired of being seen and treated as a lesser being! It was time to exercise the power he had been given from the moment of creation.

His deceitful beauty would take him into places that God and His simpering twits could not go. He would deceive his way to the top! He would show God! He already had a seed of an idea for his first spate of treachery with the humans. He was sure the fruit would be very sweet . . . at least to him.

The Pre-Born Baby Blues

Five

Eternity before the foundation of the world . . .

have an assignment for each of you," thundered the voice of Almighty God. "You will leave Heaven to go into the assignments I have for you on Earth. While you are Here, you will be filled with all the gifts and talents you will need to do what I have called you to do while on Earth . . ."

"Abba, Abba," shouted little Pre-born Spirit Joyce, her tiny voice piping up so she could be heard. "Why can't we stay here with You?" She whined the whine of a child who loved being with her Father.

Almighty God looked at the twinkling lights surrounding Him. These were the pre-born spirits who would become children sent to populate the Earth. There were billions upon billions around Him. He had created these beings for His pleasure to do His will on the Earth. He had to help them understand why they were created for His purposes.

"Come to Me, children," He beckoned. The pre-borns gathered around their beloved Creator as the angels gently guided them closer to Father God.

As God gathered these much-loved, created-to-be-human children before His throne, another soft and gentle but ever-present voice spoke, "Father, may I speak?"

"Of course, My Son."

"For God so loved the world that He gave His only begotten Son that whosoever believed in Him should not perish but have eternal life. God sent His Son to the world not to condemn the world but to set men free. I am the Son of the Living God. At creation, I created each of you to be a testimony of My presence in the world. You were created to go forth into the entire world to preach about Me and the authority and ability I have to save. As you are sent into the Earth, I will be with you even unto the end of time. I will always be with you. When it is your season, the Holy Spirit of God will fill you and you will do great exploits. The Kingdom of God will be in your hearts and you will be ministers of God. Some of you will fall away for a season. Others of you will fall away forever. But I shall raise a remnant that will joyfully and lovingly do the work of the Kingdom of God. Do not despise your assignments. *All things work together for them who love God and for them who are called according to His purposes.* You will all be used mightily in carrying out My commandments on the Earth. Do you understand?"

"Yes, Son of God," the pre-borns shouted in awed unison.

"Do you love the Father, the Son, and the Holy Spirit Who will fill you when the season comes?" asked Jesus.

"Yes, Son of God, we do. We love you!" they shouted eagerly.

"Then attend to the things the Father has for you so you will be prepared when you reach your temporary destination," urged Jesus Christ, the Son of the Living God. *"And lo, I am with you always,"* He assured them as His voice faded.

The pre-borns were ecstatic! They knew the story of Jesus. They had known Him from the foundation of the world. They had played with Him before He went to Earth the first time. Since His return, much of His time was spent interceding for the inhabitants of the Earth. Now though, He had taken special time to speak to them about their upcoming assignments.

The angels fluttered back and forth overhead. They were as excited as the pre-borns to see Jesus, their brother and Creator. He was as a brother to them all in spite of the fact He shared in the role as their Master and Creator as well.

And now, God the Father spoke to the pre-borns.

"I will divide you into many categories and groups as you prepare to enter the Earth-realm," His voice thundered. Heaven shook as God spoke to His creation.

"You all have different missions. Therefore, each of you will have different gifts. Some of you will be healers, some lawyers, some teachers, and many other different occupations needed on Earth."

Windows flashed in the Heavens around God and the pre-borns as God spoke. In each of the many windows, humans were doing the things they would soon be doing. Each window represented a different era of time in which the pre-borns would be released into the world beneath them.

The pre-borns excitedly gathered around the windows to see if they could discover what they would be in their life to come on Earth. They observed in awe as they viewed thousands of human beings performing the tasks God had designated for them before the foundation of the Earth was formed.

"When you go to Earth, you will be as Jesus was—an infant. I will assign angels to each of you to keep you until you return to Me," God continued as He showed them the many areas and fields they would go into.

"As Jesus said, many of you will turn away from serving Me for a time. Many will turn away forever. *But I will have a remnant. I am God. I lie not,*" God concluded.

As quickly as He had manifested to be with the pre-borns is as quickly as He turned the training over to the many angels He had assigned for just this purpose.

SIX

N ow, concerning your gifts and talents which will enable you to do the things for which you are being sent to Earth, they are all diverse. The Spirit of the Most High God will equip you with these gifts. Although many of you will be given some of the same gifts and talents, you will also find there are many different uses for these things. However, they all come from God Almighty," instructed Angel Talifa, the Gifts and Talents Supervisory Angel.

"Finally, pre-born spirits, although there are different methods of operation of these gifts and talents, God will operate all these gifts through you. The manifestation of gifts and talents is given to every person Almighty God has created so they may profit in everything they do from these gifts. The Spirit issues these gifts to each of you as He wills in accordance with the purposes of the Father's heart," the angel continued the explanation in preparation for one of the most important sessions of the pre-born spirits' existence.

The pre-born spirits were a-twitter with excitement as they prepared to move forward to their destinies. This was one of the final steps they would take before moving to the Earth-realm to live as humans for a season.

Agnion, the Assistant Angel of Gifts and Talents, spoke to the assembly.

"Pre-borns: pay attention! Time is of the essence! What you see before you are the Chambers of Gifts and Talents. Each chamber is filled with everything you will need to accomplish your missions on the Earth. What God has purposed for you will be performed. God's plans for you will not be frustrated. Do I have a volunteer, please?" Agnion inquired, looking into the vast sea of pre-born spirits. One light flashed into Agnion's periphery before any other could respond.

"I'll volunteer, Angel Agnion," said Pre-born Tiffany. "I can do anything!" the little spirit voice responded to the request, excited because of the new adventure.

"Splendid, Pre-born Tiffany! You will do just fine," Angel Agnion replied. "Now this is what will happen. Tiffany will enter the Chamber of Gifts and Talents through this portal," the angel explained, pointing to what appeared to be a door leading to a tube-like structure.

"We will observe everything through the transparent walls and doors as it happens. The same things you observe happening to Tiffany are the same things that will happen to you while you are in the chamber," assured Angel Agnion.

Apprehensively, Pre-born Spirit Tiffany entered the chamber. Her spiritual light glowed brightly as gifts and talents poured into her as water into a vessel. Future scenes flashed through her cognitive senses as she saw herself as a human female from infancy through adulthood. She observed many people surrounding her at her Earth-birth, as she grew, and as she fulfilled the roles God had destined for her.

As her essence filled with each gift and talent, her light beam glowed brighter and brighter. The intensity was such that the other pre-borns had never seen before except when coming into the presence of Almighty God.

As Pre-born Tiffany proceeded through the chamber, her spiritual light became larger as well. Each gift and talent caused her to become heavier. She became endowed with the skills and abilities she needed to become a musician in her early years and a children's doctor, a pediatrician, in her later years on the Earth. Her essence filled with mathematical and science skills that would cause her to excel in the medical field.

"Oh my," exclaimed Pre-born Tiffany, continuing through the chamber. "Am I going to do all these things? Is that really me, the Earth-me?" she asked as she continued to fill, excitement and apprehension overpowering her as she proceeded through the chamber.

"Yes, Tiffany, that is the Earth-you you have seen through the chamber," Angel Agnion assured as he turned back to the other pre-borns surrounding the chamber.

"Pre-borns," Agnion continued, "notice that the further Tiffany goes through the chamber, not only does she become brighter, she also becomes rounder and heavier. She has received a glimpse of everything she will ever do in the life she is about to enter," he informed the pre-born spirits.

"Everything you will ever need to fulfill the destiny God has for you is poured into your spirit in the chamber. While you receive your gifts and talents, you are being prepared to enter Earth as an infant child. This is your final phase of preparation before entering the Earth-realm," Angel Agnion concluded.

Angel Talifa, the Supervisory Angel of Gifts and Talents, appeared in front of the assembly with a group of angels the pre-borns had not seen before.

"Pre-borns," he said to the spirits, "as you exit the chamber, these angels will take you to your talent classes. Each of you has been filled with particular gifts and talents God has given to you from the moment He created you. Before the Father and the Son created you, They already knew who you would be and what you would do during your assignment on the Earth. While here in the Heavenly-realm," he continued, "you will attend workshops in those specific areas. These gifts and talents will be in you when you transfer to the Earth-realm. They are called your 'innate abilities.' You will be born into the Earth with these abilities."

"During the course of your life on the Earth," Talifa explained, "you will grow more and more in these abilities. Some of you will grasp these abilities and use them and prosper. Some of you will take these abilities for granted and misuse them. Still others of you will wish for other abilities and learn late in life that these are the abilities you were gifted with and that you should use," he continued.

"Those with medical callings, please follow Angel Curé. In the medical workshops, you will observe every aspect of the practice of medicine on people and on animals. Some of you will be doctors, some nurses, some dentists, some veterinarians. Then there are heart surgeons, brain surgeons, cancer specialists. Baby doctors, elder doctors, psychiatrists, psychologists . . ."

"Angel, Angel," shouted Pre-born Spirit Sigmund. "Will we get to choose which area we will go into?" he asked excitedly.

"Well, Sigmund," Angel Curé laughed. "You will be exposed to every aspect of medicine. When you go through the seasons of life on the Earth, you will innately know which area is right for you," the medical angel explained.

Hundreds of thousands of pre-Earth spirits surrounded Angel Curé as he led them to the medical workshop area.

"Those created with musical abilities, please follow Angel Harmoné. Those who will be composers, singers, musicians, and every other aspect of music, now, please," Angel Talifa urged.

"Pre-born Spirits Felix and Franz, you must hurry. You have no time to waste," Angel Harmoné reiterated.

Millions of pre-born spirits surrounded Angel Harmoné in awe at having been chosen to provide music to the world. As they entered the hallowed halls of music,

Pre-born Spirits Fantasia and Alicia hung back from the mass of other musical pre-Earth spirits.

"Do you think we're going to enjoy this music stuff?" asked Fantasia. "I love listening to the Heavenly Choir but I don't know if I want to do that on the Earth," the pre-born spirit confided.

"Well, we can try. I think we'll do well," Alicia brightly replied. "What if we get to Earth and really like this music thing?" she asked, pondering the idea.

"Hey, come on, you two," urged the melodic voice of one of their group, Pre-born Spirit Mahalia. "I'm excited about this music thing. I believe we'll all do well," she encouraged the other spirits.

Things quieted down in Almighty's throne room as He observed the pre-born spirits entering the areas of their calling. Each spirit was filled with the instruments of their calling, things they would use to fulfill the missions for which He would send them into the world.

Scientists, musicians, doctors, lawyers, writers, nurses—there were so many callings He had for His creation.

"Oh, no! I'm not ready!" exclaimed pre-born spirit Emmaline. "I don't want to go to Earth. That place scares me!" she reluctantly admitted to the atmosphere.

Her light dimmed considerably in dismay as she learned she was about to leave the one place she had ever known. She did not want to go to a place she had seen only once, then only fleetingly. It wasn't that interesting to her.

Emmaline had seen the family and the place she would live. None of it looked good to her. Neither was she sure she could fulfill the Father's mission for her as a soldier, a preacher, and an administrator, whatever those things were. She didn't want to go. Maybe she could talk with someone about it.

"All right!" shouted Pre-born Spirit Joyce, her light taking on an effervescent glow of excitement. She was an adventurer! She looked forward with apprehensive excitement as Angel Agnion told the pre-borns what was about to happen to each of them.

In the chambers, Joyce received everything she needed to become a soldier, a mother, and a teacher, just like Jesus. She couldn't wait. Barreling through the chambers, she laughed with glee, looking forward to the adventures she would face on Earth. She was going to have so much fun!

"I'm not going," whined Pre-born Spirit Beverley, reluctantly backing toward the exit. She didn't like what she had seen about that place called Earth. She had attended the humanities preview and observed her assigned family. Now she was being given everything she needed to become a soldier, singer, and a scribe or writer in the chambers.

Her imagination buds filled with images she would use as a writer. There were some other things she received but she closed her spiritual eyes when they flashed before her—they frightened her. She wasn't planning on going down there for this Earth assignment. She would just have to tell Abba she wanted to remain in Heaven with Him.

"I'll go, but I won't like it," groused Pre-born Spirit Margarette Ann. A quiet one, she was willing to do as told but readily admitted she wouldn't like anything about it. As a matter of fact, she really didn't like too much anyway.

She had observed all the goings-on of the other pre-borns and all their silliness. She wanted no part of that Earth-thing. She wanted to stay in Heaven with the Father . . . that's what she wanted to do. She would go on this Earth mission, but they couldn't make her like it.

As Margarette Ann went through the Chamber of Gifts and Talents, she received all she would need to become an evangelist—just like Philip—and a soldier, whatever that meant. But she didn't want any of that stuff.

Evangelist Philip loved talking to people. She didn't even like talking to the other pre-borns. She already knew she wouldn't like talking to other people if she became one of them. Why her? She didn't want to accept this assignment. Unfortunately, she knew she probably had no choice in the matter.

As the pre-borns lined up for their turn in the chambers, time lined up—in Eternity to release them into the Earth and in Earth to receive them in their pre-selected birth dates. As they passed through the chambers, their Earth-mother's bodies prepared to receive these precious seeds into their wombs.

Once the pre-borns cleared the chambers, each was assigned an Angel of Earth Entry to accompany them into the wombs of the women destined to become their mothers. At the moment of conception, the spirit light went into the seed planted within the mother by the father. Although the pre-borns could communicate with the angels through their minds, they quickly moved into the next season of their existence as babies on the Earth.

Beverley

SEVEN

As the first wave of contractions hit the womb Pre-born Spirit Beverley occupied, the pre-born balked again. Not wanting to leave the sanctuary of Heaven in the first place, she was miserable. She loathed the idea of her Earthbound assignment.

She didn't want to be born into the Earth! She definitely didn't want to be in this womb thing. Although warm and secure, it was also dark and frightening, water sloshing around. Adding to that, she also experienced many weird noises, scary weird noises seemingly coming from outside the vessel housing her.

As time went on and she prepared for her assignment as a human infant, Beverley grew more and more hostile concerning the transformation overtaking her. Once she was placed in the womb inside that thing called a body, she started growing things, things she didn't want.

She never realized it would be like this! Beverley recalled the visit she had made with the other pre-borns to Adam and Eve when God first assigned them to Earth. They were whole. They didn't have to spend any time in a dark chamber to form before being born on the Earth. She wanted a creation moment like that!

Not to mention the fact that she would forget everything she had known since she was created. It was so unfair that Adam and Eve were allowed to remember everything from creation even after they were created on the Earth as humans!

But she and the other pre-borns would forget everything they had been taught and instructed in because they would be in the body of a . . . baby!

In actuality, she detested those tiny, squirming, nasty little things. She had seen many of those things during the field trip to Earth. So unnatural! And she did not want to become one of them, not in that way. Where was the high adventure? She was determined to talk to God about this!

Pre-born Beverley grew tired of the noises surrounding her in this tank called a womb. The water sloshed; the woman's heart beat like a drum; everything on the outside of this vessel magnified in sound as she grew. And what was that awful swill the woman ingested all the time? Was that the food God had created for humans to eat on the Earth? *Yuck!* She wanted to go back to Heaven and indulge on the delicacies of angels! She didn't like it in this place.

There were other changes going on that Beverley detested. She was accustomed to talking with Almighty God and the angels spirit-to-spirit. In the tomb . . . err, womb, she was cut off from that. Now all conversations were mind-to-mind.

She couldn't see anything since she was inside this body-thing, she lamented. Her physical eyes hadn't completely formed yet. Even if they were formed, she couldn't see anything inside this dark, dank womb. She had discovered in pre-Earth class that, even after she was born, as an infant she wouldn't be able to really see until she was about four months old or so!

Accustomed to hearing whatever she desired in the Heavenly-realm, now her hearing consisted of sensing vibrations inside her soon-to-be Earth-mother's womb. And she didn't like any of what she heard! Pre-born Beverley was thoroughly disgusted!

Never having to experience limitations in the Eternal Heavens, Beverley now found herself limited to being a body confined inside another body without a voice. The rules had changed. Now, the only way she could let her Earth-mother know how she felt was by causing her body-thing to move about, something she learned to do quickly and well. Beverley made sure she did plenty of moving around just so it was known she was not satisfied with her new position. She didn't appreciate any of this experience!

Pre-born Beverley had looked forward to a high adventure. And look where she was! What a cruel joke, this human thing! She wanted out!

As another contraction hit her Earth-mother's body, she rocked inside that hideous place, the womb. (Tomb!) The sloshing water drove her bonkers. She couldn't stand it any longer! She knew it was her time to make an entrance on the Earth but refused to go.

"*Caldor! Get me out of here!*" she mind-screamed indignantly to her Earthbound Angel, "*I am* not *going out there!*"

Pre-born Beverley rebelled in her spirit while trying to grasp the slippery inner walls of the birth chamber with hands she didn't quite know how to use yet.

"*That place out there is in turmoil. You said so yourself! Why? Why do I have to go and live with this woman as one of* them?" Beverley emphasized the word as she mind-shrieked in frustration. She knew her assignment. She just didn't want any part of it.

She and all the other pre-borns had taken class after class about Earth and humanities and other things they needed while on the Earth. When the pre-borns went on Earth-trips, they were given the opportunity to see what humans looked like and how they functioned before it was their turn to do the same.

Beverley wanted no part of any of it. Once she discovered the type of family she was being assigned to, the matter was clenched for her. From the moment of her Earth-trip to see the man and woman who would be her Earth-parents, Beverley stubbornly refused to accept her assignment.

"A poor *Negro* family? *That's* where I'm going? Why? Why me? Why do I have to be born into this family? There are gazillions of other families and you're releasing me to this family? They aren't even married to each other! They're . . . what's the word Jesus used? Adulterers! Does God know about this? I bet Abba didn't tell you to do this to me," ranted Pre-born Beverley during the class season on human insight.

Each of the pre-borns was taken to his or her designated family and human stations and allowed to observe their assigned families. She sulked during the remainder of the class and made it known that she thought it unfair. She made sure everyone knew she was not pleased to do what she was being asked to do.

"I want to speak with Abba about this," she demanded in a tearful voice. "I know a switch can be made. Some other pre-born can go and be this family's baby," she begged sulkily, hoping Caldor would have sympathy for her.

"Beverley, you know that is not possible," Caldor explained, trying to reason with her. "You know the Creator has designated each of you for a particular task. Once the assignment is given, there is no turning back."

Pre-born Spirit Beverley shimmered in the atmosphere as she worked up the tears growing inside her. She didn't want to go on this assignment. Why would Abba want her to be placed with these poor people? Besides, they weren't even married! At least not to each other! She just didn't understand.

"Angel Caldor," she said respectfully, tears flowing down her shimmering cheeks. "May I please have an audience with Almighty God? Please?" she asked emphatically. Beverley hoped she could change His mind and decision concerning her assignment. She had to try. She really didn't want to go on this assignment. She wanted to understand—she needed to understand.

She was in good company. Many pre-borns didn't understand the choices their Creator made for them as He created them. Many of them didn't like the choices but had no choice in the matter. This was their God-given destiny and purpose.

Almighty God had purposed each and every individual pre-born and the things they would go into in His heart. However, the pre-borns had to understand their place in the Lord.

Angel Caldor manifested in the throne room of the Most High to request an audience for the agitated Pre-born Beverley. Before he could utter a word, God answered the question.

"Caldor, send in the little one. It is time for her to be born into the Earth. There is no time to spare," commanded the booming voice of Almighty God.

Caldor humbly retreated from the presence of the Lord. Instantly, Pre-born Spirit Beverley appeared before the Throne of Grace to hear the answers to the questions she had concerning why she was destined to go into the Earth-realm.

Eight

Eternity

Beverley," God thundered, "I know your concerns, My child. Believe it or not, you are prepared for every good work I have for you on the Earth. But you must trust Me," reasoned Almighty God with this very unwilling pre-born spirit.

Beverley cautiously moved toward her beloved Abba, tears freely flowing down her translucent spirit-cheeks. She didn't want to leave Him and all her friends in Heaven. Surely there was some other way to complete her mission without having to join *that* family God had prepared for her on the Earth.

God looked down at the little pre-born spirit before Him—He knew her thoughts. He also knew each and every situation that would arise in the life of this little one, Beverley. He understood her reluctance to leave Heaven to go on this mission to the Earth. He had to help her understand why it was so important for her to do what He asked and complete what He had created her to do.

"But, Abba," whined the pre-born. "Why do I have to leave You? I don't want to go down there and live with those people. Father, I don't understand why . . ."

"Beverley, let me show you something," God said soothingly. He pulled the little spirit toward Him and settled her in the palm of His hand. Directing her attention to the screen before them, He gently spoke to her, "Look at this."

They watched the screen as Beverley was born.

"Wow, is that me?" the little spirit asked. "But that covering, the skin is so light. I look white. But I thought . . ." she sputtered, wondering.

"Yes, My child, that's you. But through the process of time," He explained as the screens changed and Earth-Beverley became older, "this is what you will look like as you grow."

Beverley observed her Earth-self as she grew through the stages of life from newborn to toddler to teen. She liked what she saw!

"Wow, Abba, she's, I mean, I'm pretty," said the pre-born spirit as she observed the transformation. She saw her Earth-self in school, with friends, playing sports, singing in church. "Oh, Abba, look at me. It looks like fun," she said excitedly as the screens flashed before them. Beverley enjoyed seeing the things she would do on the Earth. She even enjoyed the family life she appeared to have.

Suddenly the screens changed and became darker. As Earth-Beverley grew and matured, more scenes appeared on the screen before the two viewers.

"Why did the screen become darker, Father?" she asked as Almighty God observed her observing the screens.

"Beverley, you will go through some very dark times in your life," He explained. "There will come a time in your life in which you will turn away from Heaven . . ."

"Oh no, Abba!" she quickly interjected, distressed at this news. "I don't want to turn away from You! Why?" she questioned, wanting now more than ever to stay in Heaven to avoid the risk of turning away from the One she loved the most.

"You will have many experiences in preparation for what I have for you to do later in your life," God explained. "Look at the next screens, Beverley," He instructed.

Beverley looked on as the screen suddenly changed to a much older Beverley. The scene became lighter than before.

"What are those clothes I'm wearing with the funny shoes and head coverings?" the little spirit asked, amazed at seeing her Earth-self and the things she was doing on the Earth.

"Those clothes are called a uniform. You will wear them when you enter the Army of the World on the Earth. You will be a soldier," God explained.

"A soldier, Lord? I'm going to be a soldier? Like David and Caleb and Jonathan and Jeshua?" she enquired, incredulous. "But, Abba, what about the dark times? Will they still be with me as a soldier?"

"Yes, My child. You will face many dark times as a soldier in the Army of the World. But," He explained as the screen changed, "it is during this time that you will also join the Army of the Lord."

Beverley considered what she saw, what Abba told her. She remembered going through the Chamber of Gifts and Talents. She had felt empowered, courageous, brave, and mighty when the warrior talents were bestowed upon her. But this person she saw on the screen before her was more than that.

This human woman was strong, beautiful, and all the other things Beverley had experienced in the chamber. She saw a young woman walking with boldness. She wanted to be that person!

Pre-born Beverley continued looking at the screen and saw her older self preaching. This self was powerful. She appeared to walk in the holiness of the Lord. When she went through the myriad Life on Earth classes before her Earthbound journey, many of her instructors had shared how they had also walked with that same power.

"That's me, Abba?" asked the little spirit, not believing the woman she saw, not believing she would become a powerful preacher in the Earth.

"My child, you will affect the lives of many people during your sojourn on the Earth. There will be trials and tribulations occurring in your life. I need for these things to happen so you will mature into the woman you last saw," Almighty God explained.

"Do not be afraid to leave Me here in Heaven," God advised. "You will be surrounded by the angels I have assigned to you. They will be with you throughout your life, my little child," God told Spirit Beverley.

"Oh, Abba, I will miss You and Heaven so very much," she said as she thought back to all the instruction she and the other pre-borns had received prior to being swooshed into the vacuums of time.

"I know you will, child. But you will be back," promised God.

God smiled as he observed the birth of Beverley. He knew everything about to happen in her life. He knew all the good; He knew all the bad. He had ordered the path she would follow. He knew.

Nine

P ush, Anna," Nurse Edna Cummins encouraged. "Come on! One more good push and your baby will be here." The nurse was confident that Anna Horton was near the end of her labor and travail.

Steely-gray hair twisted in a severe bun with twinkling hazel eyes, Nurse Edna smiled as she considered the young woman on the table. This was the third birth she had attended with Anna Mae Horton. Edna felt sorry for the young colored woman. For all three births, there had never been a father present, only her younger sister Evelyn. She wanted to talk to the young woman, perhaps give her some counsel. Unfortunately, all she could do was her job in helping her birth this newest baby.

Anna had been in labor since the early morning hours. It was now after nine at night. Finally, after nine months of waiting, she was about to bear the child she knew would cause Leon to marry her—after she got a divorce, that is. Even though her sister Evelyn had warned her about Leon—that he played with her emotions and was not faithful—Anna knew this baby was what she needed to stabilize their relationship.

Anna believed if she married Leon, she wouldn't have the problems she had faced before. Poor, colored, and with two other children already, Anna knew she

48

wasn't in an ideal situation. She knew she was wrong for having children by one man when she was already married to another.

But she wanted the perfect family. The perfect husband, perfect children, and the perfect little family home with a white picket fence.

And Leon was the husband she wanted. She had left her home in Virginia to follow her dream in New York. Even though she had already made the mistake of marrying someone who would never be good for her, she wouldn't make the same mistake twice. Now her dream was about to come true.

"Push," Nurse Cummins urged. "Come on, Anna, we're almost there," she said excitedly.

Nurse Cummins loved seeing new life come into the world. Working in labor and delivery for twenty years, she knew how to help a baby be born. This one was no exception.

Anna strained with all the power she could muster. OB/GYN Dr. Everett Strong reiterated the call to push as he peered under the sheet. Bearing down, Anna clenched her teeth and pressed in. She was eager to see who this person was that had grown inside her body for the past nine months.

Sensing in her heart that it was another girl, Anna nevertheless prayed for a boy. Leon desired a son. She prayed she would be the one to give him a son.

Lord, if You hear me, please let it be a boy. God, I'll do anything . . . Anna silently prayed as she forced herself to push for what seemed like the thousandth time on this day, the longest of her life. And then . . .

"Uumph," Anna grunted and knew she had done it. The baby whooshed out of her body with a loud resounding *thoomp*. Exhausted, Anna lay back, thankful her job was done for the moment.

Both doctor and nurse gasped as they looked at the newborn little girl. The newborn's skin was alabaster!

"Oh my," exclaimed Dr. Strong. "If I didn't know any better, I would say we have the wrong baby for this mother. But I saw her being born with my own eyes," he whispered to Nurse Cummins, his dark gray eyes blinking in surprise. They were both baffled by the spectacle before them.

"Oh, what a pretty little thing," Nurse Cummins cried out. "But how can she be white, Doctor? What happened?" she questioned Dr. Strong, confused. In all her years in labor and delivery, Edna had never seen anything like this.

The baby was the prettiest little thing they had ever seen with the creamiest white skin one could imagine. The thick covering of slick black hair on her delicate scalp stood out in sharp contrast to her lily-white skin. In all their years working together in labor and delivery, neither Nurse Cummins nor Dr. Strong had ever witnessed such a thing.

Dr. Strong continued gazing at the baby, trying to make sense of what he saw. And then . . .

"Just a second, Edna. Look at the tips of her ears," responded Dr. Strong, immediately at ease after this discovery. "No, this baby will be about the same complexion as her mother. This is only her first color. Thank God," he breathed, exhaling a sigh of relief.

As tenuous as times were right now in New York with racial riots and general unpleasantness between the poor and the more well-to-do, Dr. Strong was glad to find an explanation for the color of the baby's skin. He would hate to have a press-fest going on in the hospital right now.

Anna tuned out once she heard the gender of the baby. She had hoped and prayed hard for a boy child. Maybe God couldn't hear her. She was extremely disappointed, with God and with her situation.

After a few minutes, Nurse Cummins handed Anna the small, just-cleaned-up eight-pound bundle. "Anna, here's your baby girl. She is gorgeous! But she gave us quite a scare. Look at how fair she is," explained Nurse Cummins, laughter in her voice.

Anna gasped in surprise and awe. Her daughter appeared to be just like the little china dolls her employer's daughters played with. This little girl, her little girl, was the prettiest little porcelain doll she had ever seen. And she was *her* daughter?

Anna pondered the color of the child's skin. Leon's mother, Mother Scott, though married to a darker-skinned man, preferred her children marry lighter-skinned people. She wanted her grandchildren to have a better chance in the world.

Not considering the baby's ears, Anna was ecstatic. This might be better than the baby being a boy! This little girl would give her exactly what she wanted, Anna thought, tears of happiness rolling down her face. Dreams really could come true!

In the Unseen . . .

"*Ah, yes,*" said Angel Karno. "*You are a beautiful one, Beverley,*" he said to the child he would oversee during her sojourn on the Earth. "*No worries, little one. God is with you and so am I,*" he cooed as he stroked her brow, causing her first infant smile. He laughed to himself as he thought back to her battle to stay in Heaven. This was going to be an interesting assignment.

Joyce

TEN

In the Unseen . . .

Angel Almara, what is this place?" Joyce asked in her most inquisitive thought-voice.

"*You are in the womb of your Earth-mother, Joyce,*" Angel Almara gently explained to the pre-born. "*This is the place where your Earth-body will grow into being an infant.*"

"*Hey, what happened to the rest of my identity?*" she asked, wondering what was going on with herself. She felt different, a strange but good *different* she couldn't explain.

"*Oh, so you noticed did you, little one?*" asked Almara, smiling at the precociousness of the pre-born. "*Once you leave the Heavenly-realm and enter the in-between place, the womb, you have a new identity. Your spirit, the very essence of who you are, enters into the seed of your Earth-mother and Earth-father. In the womb, you begin to acquire your Earth-identity,*" explained the angel.

"*Oh,*" Joyce said tentatively. "*Am I wearing clothes yet?*" she asked, remembering this word from when she observed her (*what were the words again?*) birth family.

They had those skin-coverings over their spirits just as Adam and Eve had when they were first created on the Earth. These coverings were their protection from the elements of the Earth—heat, cold, and other things they would encounter as humans. They also wore clothes over their skin so they wouldn't be naked in front of each other. Joyce already had an eye for nice clothing and couldn't wait until it was her turn to wear these things!

As pre-born spirits, Joyce and the others discovered during their training classes on Earth that they could see straight through a person's exterior to their interior. Many times, what they saw frightened them. They could see either the dark or the light side of a person's spirit. Even while in Heaven awaiting their assignments, they often saw darkness in the spirits of other pre-borns, which was very frightening. Almighty God tended to separate dark spirits from light spirits quickly so no tainting would occur before their Earth assignments.

Because the pre-born spirits were able to see those who had gone on before them, they knew that many of the same ones they played with in Heaven would become their parents, grandparents, and other important people in their lives on the Earth. Many of the same ones they had cavorted with had already returned after their season on the Earth. Oh what great stories the returnees had to tell when they came back to Heaven! They had amazing adventures! That's what Joyce was looking forward to—her own amazing adventures!

Joyce remembered seeing her Earth-mother's spirit. At the time, she thought the woman had a wonderful spirit. She also saw the covering over her spirit, her skin. It was warm, brown, smooth, and very rich-looking. She noticed she also had pretty hair covering the top of her head. Joyce knew she would eventually have the same skin, hair, and coloring. She mostly remembered the beautiful clothing the woman wore. She was a very nice-looking Earth-mother. Joyce knew they would have fun together.

When Joyce observed her Earth-father's spirit by contrast, it was the exact opposite. His spirit was dark, dead-looking. She didn't like what she saw when she looked into his spirit. Although he had a very handsome face, he was not very nice at all inside. Joyce shuddered, hoping she would not have to spend much time with *that* one.

"*No, Joyce, you are not wearing clothes yet,*" Almara explained. "*But skin now covers your essence.*"

Before the angel could explain any further, Joyce exclaimed, "*Angel Almara, what's happening? I feel . . . hey, I can feel things—funny. Yes, that's it. I feel strange, weird, funny.*"

Pre-born Joyce's essence took on more of a definite shape as her body transformed within the womb.

"You've just experienced your first growth spurt, Joyce," Angel Almara explained. Watching in amazement, the angel considered the work of the Creator in this pre-born infant he was in charge of.

Joyce floated in awe in this new place. Since she had never been enclosed in anything as a spirit, she found this feeling of closeness . . . well, kind of comforting. And she liked it. As her body grew and changed, she *felt* more than she had ever experienced before. As she experienced these new feelings and changes, she became more excited, knowing she would start her adventures soon. Then she noticed she had company.

"Angel Almara," Pre-born Joyce mind-whispered. *"What's that? What's in here with me?"* she questioned. She was aware that she was not alone in this place, this womb. She felt the presence of another like her.

"It's not a what but a who, Joyce. Meet Jeffrey, your twin brother," Almara explained.

"Twin? What's a 'twin?'" she asked, words tripping from her mind faster than the angel could answer. *"A twin brother? Am I going to be his brother, too?"*

"No," laughed Almara. *"You are his sister. You are a girl and Jeffrey is a boy. A twin is someone who shares the same womb with you until your birth on Earth. You will have the same birth date and share similar looks, qualities, and characteristics. Joyce, say hello to your brother, Jeffrey,"* Angel Almara instructed.

"Hi, Jeffrey," Joyce greeted joyfully, wondering who this spirit was going to be. But it didn't matter because . . . she had a twin!

"Hi, Joyce. I've heard a lot about you. My angel Kalem has told me all about your adventures. I look forward to growing with you," Jeffrey piped in.

As Jeffrey ended his greeting, something shifted in the womb. Each of the pre-borns felt a change, a transformation happen inside of and around them. Neither knew what it was.

"Another growth spurt," consulted the angels as they observed the shape changes of their two charges. The angels watched in awe as the pre-borns' heads became more head-like and limbs extended from their bodies.

"Unnhh," said Joyce. *"What's going on? Am I stretching?"* she wondered. The changes weren't scary but sure were strange as both Joyce and Jeffrey floated on the wave of change in their enclosed chamber.

"Wow. What's happening to me?" wondered Jeffrey in his mind. *"I feel heavier."*

Almara caught the thoughts from the twins. *"Yes, Joyce, you are stretching and growing. You are becoming more of an infant in your mother's womb. And yes, Jeffrey, you both are heavier because you now have bodies. Your bodies are gaining weight for entry into the Earth,"* the angel explained.

Having been weightless their entire existence, being heavy was not something either of the twins had given much thought to. But here they were, heavy in comparison to their former states. They were starting to become . . . babies! What an adventure!

Although they couldn't see each other yet, the twins could feel each other. Apprehensive and very excited, they touched the other's body in comfort, knowing they were in this Earthbound thing together.

"*Jeffrey, what do you think our parents will be like?*" Joyce asked in a mind-voice that was changing from rich in timber and confidence to little-girlish and slightly frightened. "*I remember seeing this woman, our mother. She was very pretty. She seemed nice and kind. Did you see her?*"

"*Yes, I did,*" said Jeffrey, voice also changing. His mind-voice was changing from the deepness it had carried since creation to a high-pitched, little boy voice. "*And I saw the man, our father as well. I didn't like him as much as I liked our mother. His spirit was dark, not light like hers and ours. He scared me,*" Jeffrey confided to his sister with a shudder.

"*Yes, I remember him, too,*" returned Joyce. "*He was nice-looking enough, but he seemed, I don't know, cruel.*"

"*Joyce, Jeffrey,*" interjected Kalem, "*prepare for another growth spurt right about . . . NOW!*"

At that moment, both twins felt something strange happening to their new bodies. Those things that would be their hands and feet had something interesting growing out of them—fingers and toes. These new appendages automatically wiggled as though they had minds of their own. Now the twins could touch (instead of head-butt) each other with something other than the stumps that had first grown out of their bodies. They didn't understand everything they experienced but knew they were becoming larger in their mother's womb.

"*It's getting crowded in here,*" they both thought at the same time. As they realized what had just occurred, they giggled as only children can. Already speaking and feeling the same things, the twins were very excited about being together.

"*Children,*" said Almara, "*there are a few more things we have to go over before you are ready to leave the Womb-realm and enter the Earth-realm.*"

Giggling and excited, Jeffrey and Joyce tried their best to focus their attention on what the angels were saying. Although they were not having very good success with focusing, they were having fun!

ELEVEN

O nce you leave the womb," began Kalem, "*you will have to learn everything from birth and all throughout your life on the Earth, even as you grow older. You will find in your seasons on the Earth,*" he instructed the soon-to-be-born twins, "*that there will always be something new to learn and experience. Although you will not be able to speak intelligible sentences until you are about twelve months old, you will soon discover that you can make sounds as infants. You will quickly learn which sounds will cause your Earth-parents and others to respond to you and your needs. Nor will you be able to see as everyone else does until you are about four months old. You will have something like a haze over your eyes. When the haze is gone, you will be able to focus on things around you,*" the angel continued.

"*For the first six months of your life,*" Almara interjected, "*your only sustenance or food will consist of breast milk from your mother and soft foods that can be easily digested. You will not have teeth and will not be able to feed or do anything for yourself during this time,*" the angel explained to the twins. "*Also, by the age of six months, you will learn to sit up by yourself and maybe crawl . . .*"

The reality of what was being said hit Joyce like a spiritual sledgehammer!

"*No teeth! Can't feed myself? Can't walk or sit up by myself?*" Joyce gasped. "*What about my adventures? I won't be able to do* anything *during this time? Except be a baby!*" she realized with horror. "*Adam and Eve didn't go through this! So why should we? It's not fair,*" she mind-sputtered as her new heart sank from the disappointment of being a, a . . . baby.

Angel Almara knew how much Joyce liked to talk and explore. He understood that this was a great setback for her.

"*Joyce, remember—you will be an infant. You will have to grow into everything and will have many adventures as you grow. Even though you will not be able to walk until you become a year old or so, you will have plenty of adventures all throughout your life,*" the angel reassured her.

"*Then I don't know if I will like this. Since we are growing so quickly in here, I thought . . .*" Joyce trailed off as she thought of this new development.

She had already observed the adventures of many of the people on the Earth. She'd caught glimpses of her friends Sally and Amelia in their seasons on the Earth. Joyce knew she would have as good, if not better adventures as they. They had all trained together after receiving their warrior gifts and talents. Joyce knew she was destined to have as many adventures as they'd had. She couldn't have those adventures if she was forced to be a, a . . . a baby!

Jeffrey lay back in his space in the womb and listened to the chatter between his twin and the angels. He secretly liked the thought of being born as a baby into the Earth. He had seen many of his friends, even the Son, go through the process of being born as babies into the Earth. He had received good reports from them when *most* of them returned to Heaven. He didn't understand what his twin was fussing about. They would eventually get to the place she wanted to be. Jeffrey was prepared to sit back and enjoy the ride.

But he knew Joyce would not be satisfied with their predicament now that she knew she would not have any immediate adventures. He had seen Joyce during many of their classes in Heaven. She was one of the most adventurous of all the pre-born spirits. He wondered why Almighty God had placed *them* together as twins. They were very different. She was adventurous—he was laid back. Jeffrey didn't understand the choice but wasn't worried about it either. He was excited because he had never guessed he would be part of a matched set on the Earth.

"*I know what you thought, child,*" Angel Almara interjected gently, "*but you will be on human-time when you are born. Things will slow down for you. And while we are on the subject of time, you will also age according to Earth-age as well.*"

"*Earth-age?*" said Jeffrey, snapping out of his reverie. "*What's that, angel?*"

Angel Kalem resumed instruction. "*Remember this: a day is as a thousand years and a thousand years as a day to God. You have lived in eternity since the moment God created you. You have no concept of Earth-time. Even though you have been with God for a very long time according to Earth standards, it is but a moment to God and to you.*"

"*Oh*," said Joyce, slightly understanding this concept of time. "*So we will grow older how, angel?*" she asked.

"*Your lives will age according to the times and seasons of the Earth when you are born. Time is broken down into segments called seconds, minutes, hours, days, weeks, months, and years. A second is the smallest unit of time you will have to deal with for age purposes*," explained angel Kalem. "*A second passes by very quickly—like this . . .*" He illustrated by snapping his angelic fingers. "*Listen . . .*"

The babies hadn't realized they now had something new attached to the sides of their heads . . . ears. They instinctively turned these organs toward the new sound they hadn't heard before.

"*What's that?*" asked Jeffrey as he listened. "*Tick, tick, tick . . .*"

"*That*," explained Angel Almara, "*is the sound of time. Each tick you hear is one second. There are sixty seconds in one minute so a minute will go by more slowly than a second.*"

Understanding dawned on the twins at the same time. "*Ah-ha. Got it!*" they mind-shouted their understanding.

"*From the moment you are conceived in the Earth-realm, time starts for you. According to the way Almighty God has set things up for humans, you are in your mother's womb for approximately nine months before being born into the Earth-realm. From the day you are born, your age is numbered by days. You will learn more about this later in your lives as you enter a place called school*," Almara continued.

"*For right now, though, understand that you are about to enter a realm . . . uh-oh, hold on. Another growth spurt approaches,*" warned Kalem as the atmosphere became charged with activity.

The angels realized they were coming to the end of the pre-born learning phase for the soon-to-be newborns. They spoke quickly.

"*You will not remember your pre-born existence. But know that Almighty God will be with you always*," the angels continued, taking turns in the explanation. "*When you are born into the Earth, you will each have another set of angels different from us. You won't know they are there but they will be with you for your protection. Blessings to you, Jeffrey and Joyce,*" concluded Almara and Kalem as they whooshed back to the Earthbound clinic in eternity for their next assignments.

Jeffrey and Joyce experienced another growth spurt, their last, as their Earth-mother Marie Jones began contractions. But now, they each had an additional concern as well.

"*What's happening?*" Joyce shouted, afraid, not knowing what to do. "*I don't want new angels! Come back, Almara! Come back . . . please,*" she fretted. "*Is there anyone here to help us?*" she cried, trying to grab hold of the walls of the uterus. Her hands slid down the embryonic-fluid slicked walls. She felt herself turning around and attempted to stop the action. *"Jeffrey, help me!"*

"Joyce, I can't help you because I'm falling down!" Jeffrey cried with as much fear as his sister. He, too, was trying to grab hold of the slickened walls to no avail. He moved into the birth canal as their imminent birth approached.

TWELVE

Marie, you're going to have to push," Dr. Cynthia Sinclair urged, encouraging the young colored woman on her table to push out the first baby.

Thirty year-old Cynthia Jane Sinclair had been Marie's OB/GYN doctor since she first discovered she was pregnant. From their professional relationship grew an even closer personal friendship that Cynthia and Marie cherished in spite of the racial prejudice of 1960's New York.

Coming from a good Catholic family in San Francisco, Cynthia Jane was taught to not look at a person's skin color. Instead, she was taught to look at his or her heart. She had always had colored friends while growing up. Marie was one of her best friends in New York. Since both of them were so far away from family and friends back home, they formed an alliance that was tight and true.

During the course of Marie's pregnancy, Cynthia learned a lot about the South where twenty-one-year-old Marie grew up. What she learned she did not like. Cynthia had never seen nor heard of such prejudicial practices in her life! She shared all she gleaned from her new friend with her family back home in California.

Cynthia heard her friend groan in pre-birth agony as she snapped from her reverie to the task at hand. She discovered during one of her final examinations that Marie Jones was not expecting one rather large infant, but two—twins.

If I could get my hands on that Leroy, Cynthia thought as she spoke soothingly to her friend. *How could he leave her in this predicament?* she wondered, coaxing Marie to push a little more.

"Come on, Ree," Cynthia urged softly, calling her friend the pet name she had come to know her by. "You can do it," she encouraged the sweating, panting young woman.

"Come on, sweetie," Nurse Shirley Granderson joined in with the doctor's encouragement in her Jamaican-accented voice. "Push, honey-chile! You can do it, girl!"

Shirley had worked with Dr. Sinclair her entire five years in the United States. She loved this wonderful woman of medicine. Dr. Sinclair had more colored patients than many of the colored doctors who practiced in the city, mainly due to the way she cared for people.

Originally from Barbados, Shirley had come to the US so she could pursue her nursing vocation. She had not been disappointed. Marie Jones was her thousandth delivery or so it seemed. She was excited about this delivery after discovering it would be twins.

Marie Helen Jones grunted. Sweat poured from her brow. She panted as though she were running in a race. She was using all she could to work up the energy to force these babies out of her body.

God, she thought to herself. *What have I done? How could I have allowed myself to get in this dilemma? And I'm having* two *babies?* she scolded herself. *One was enough to embarrass my family. God must really be disappointed with me to allow me to have two babies out of wedlock at the same time. And Leroy, the so-called father of these babies*, she continued the tirade in her mind. *Where is he?*

Leroy Julius Adams had promised Marie the moon. As soon as he discovered she was pregnant, he had obviously *gone* to the moon. She knew she should have never . . .

"Ohhhh, please, give me something for the pain. I feel like I'm going to die," she pleaded as the first baby tried to push its way out of her body.

Such indescribable pain she had never felt before in her life! How in the world had her mother given birth to fifteen children (the majority born at home!) she would never know. Why hadn't someone warned her about the pain?

Then she thought about it as she strained to get these babies out. She couldn't have asked anyone from her family about the pain of childbirth because no one at home in Alabama knew she was pregnant. Her family didn't know what she was going through right now. She hadn't been home to Alabama since before she got pregnant. Plus, she wasn't planning to go home any time soon—*maybe when the kids are grown*, she sarcastically thought. She didn't want to embarrass her parents. They didn't even know she had been seeing anyone, much less having babies today.

What a mess she was in! She didn't have anyone else besides Cynthia and Shirley in this crazy New York town that cared enough about her to be concerned that she was having these babies today by herself. And thank God for them! Marie could only guess how she would have made it had it not been for her two new friends of about nine months. She had pretty much cut herself off from the people who loved her most—her family.

Even though she had made only a few friends before her pregnancy, once she became pregnant, Marie was reluctant to make any more friends. She was ashamed for people to know she was an unwed mother. Frequenting only three places in this crazy town—work, home, and the grocery store—Marie spent the majority of her time alone trying to figure out a way to tell her family about the mess she was in. Since Leroy had treated her so badly, she didn't want her family to know anything about him. She feared her brothers coming to New York and ending up in prison for killing Leroy's worthless behind.

Her only *friend* besides Cynthia and Shirley was Sophia Conti in Apartment 3B. Sophia would take care of her babies while she worked after she got back on her feet.

Marie's parents were salt-of-the-earth Christians. Homer and Ethel Jones had raised seven boys and eight girls to be good, God-fearing people. Now look at what she had done! Marie couldn't imagine going back to Alabama to visit her family with her illegitimate children. She had condemned herself to raising these children alone.

Never mind that no self-respecting man would want anything to do with a woman who had one child out of wedlock, much less two. She was in a fix. But she had to get past bringing these babies into the world before she could deal with anything else.

"Unnhh," she moaned, clenching her teeth and holding onto the straps on the bed.

"Ahh," she screamed as the first baby almost shot from between her legs. The doctor caught him just as he cried a loud wail, the loudest she had ever heard. The clock read 11:26 a.m.

"Welcome to New York, little boy," Dr. Sinclair whispered to the first-born as she determined his sex. She looked at his tiny face as he wailed. He seemed to experience some form of discomfort. She couldn't determine what could be causing this little one's pain.

In the Unseen . . .

Earth-angel Rohan stood at Cynthia's right shoulder peering down into the bright red squalling face of his new charge, Jeffrey Earl Jones. He smiled as he saw that the baby appeared to be all there. Rohan knew why Jeffrey was wailing so loudly. His sister was trying to *not* make an appearance on the Earth!

Labor and Delivery . . .

Dr. Sinclair handed the squalling infant to Nurse Granderson as she turned to prepare for the arrival of the second baby.

"Come on, Marie," the doctor encouraged the young woman. "I know you're tired but you have to give it one last big push. You already have a very handsome young man waiting for his twin to come out."

In spite of her tiredness, Marie perked up slightly as she heard the sex of the first baby. A *boy*! Maybe it would make it easier when she presented him to her daddy. Boy babies seemed to be more favored down South in the farmland, especially in the Jones household. All Marie's brothers worked on either the family farm or on their own farms if they were married. A baby boy would fit in well with the rest of the nephews, boy cousins, and sons-in-law Marie had grown up with.

Marie knew her children would find favor quickly with their grandfather, Homer. Although a stern disciplinarian, Homer loved his children and grandchildren dearly. Marie remembered how he had once beaten her nineteen-year-old brother Johnny when he thought he could back-talk their mama. Homer came out of nowhere, beat Johnny with no mercy, then prayed with him and hugged him. That was Homer's way and his children loved him all the more for it.

Marie found the strength to push again. She felt this second baby moving around as though it were holding on for dear life.

"Unnhh," she grunted, trying to help her second child come out and make an appearance in its new world.

"Ahh," she screamed. "Oh, God, please help me!" she cried out, unbearable pain saturating her lower extremities. She didn't know how much longer she could stand this pain.

"OK, Marie, rest for a few moments," advised Dr. Sinclair as Nurse Granderson wiped Marie's brow.

She couldn't understand why this baby was being so stubborn about coming out. She felt around inside Marie. She found that although the baby's position was correct, something was definitely wrong. Cynthia Sinclair discovered that the umbilical cord had somehow become wrapped around the baby's neck. The baby was holding onto the umbilical cord with its fist as though it wanted to choke itself to death.

Horrified, Cynthia urgently whispered a quick, silent prayer, *God, please give me wisdom and strength!* She had never had this happen before during a birth, but she was not prepared to lose.

THIRTEEN

In Eternity

Earthbound Angel Almara reporting as directed, Almighty God," Almara said reverently to the Being on the Throne of Grace.

It wasn't often that a particular angel was pinpointed. When it happened, there was no doubt that the angel was to immediately appear before Almighty God for whatever reason.

His voice thundering with urgency, God instructed the angel to go back into the womb to assist and answer Dr. Sinclair's urgent plea.

"Almara, Joyce is being stubborn. She is causing grave danger to her Earth-body. I need you to help her to let go," Father God instructed the angel. Time was of the essence. Almara was on the move even before he answered, "Yes, God," and dissipated before the King of Kings. In an instant, he was back in Marie's womb. She was quickly running out of strength to bring forth the second twin.

In the Unseen at Long Island General Hospital

"*Joyce*," Almara said, urgently but gently. He could tell that everything was in distress. As she continued to choke the life out of her fragile body, her face registered anguish as she held onto the umbilical cord.

Although her heart had slowed down considerably, she was still able to mind-gasp, "*I don't want to go out there. I'm afraid. I want to go back to Heaven, Angel Almara. I miss Abba.*"

Almara knew that if he didn't do something quickly, baby Joyce would be born with irreversible brain damage.

"*Joyce,*" he began. "*Do you remember the Chamber of Gifts and Talents? Remember what you received there?*" he asked, attempting to cause her to focus on him and his words to her.

Joyce's rigid infant-body temporarily relaxed as she remembered the things that filled her essence as she went through the chamber—obedience, discipline, perseverance, energy, adventure, and other things. She knew she was destined to go into this thing called the Army and would be a soldier and teacher in life on the Earth.

But she was afraid now because of what she had felt her brother Jeffrey go through as he entered the Earth-realm. When he went through the birth canal, she felt his body quake from the force used to bring him into the world. As he passed through the opening, she felt a rush of cold air as the opening closed, keeping her inside the womb.

Remembering her brother's sudden departure from this place of comfort, Joyce's tiny body stiffened again. She immediately clutched the umbilical cord again. For all she knew, it was the only piece of security she had right now. Because she was afraid, she didn't realize it was closing her airway.

"*Angel Almara, what if I fail?*" she asked, slightly loosening her grip on the umbilical cord again. "*What if I don't make it with these gifts and talents? God will be angry and disappointed with me, won't He?*" she queried, once more loosening her grip.

As she loosened her grip, she was able to get more air into her Earth-body. She felt a little better although she was still frightened of the unknown.

"*Child, God will always love you,*" Angel Almara said soothingly. As he consoled the frightened pre-born child, he was able to remove the cord from around her neck allowing her body to breath. "*Child, Almighty God has not destined you for failure but for His glory. Joyce, everything will be all right. Now, let go, child,*" the angel instructed her.

Joyce's body relaxed. She completely loosened her grip on the umbilical cord. Once this was accomplished, Marie gave a final grunt and Angel Almara returned to eternity.

"*Mission accomplished, Almighty,*" Angel Almara informed Almighty God.

God the Father nodded His head. He looked through the atmosphere to the labor and delivery room of Long Island General just in time to see the birth of the second twin.

Labor and Delivery, Long Island General Hospital

"That's right, Marie," Dr. Sinclair spoke softly.

She was finally able to loosen the cord from around the baby's neck.

"OK, now, one . . . more . . . push," Dr. Sinclair urged the weakening young woman.

A praying woman, Cynthia Sinclair prayed in her heart that God would not only help Marie Jones birth these babies but also take care of them. Her constant prayer since she had known Marie was that God would have mercy on her and send a special man to marry her and help raise these precious babies.

With a final energy-stealing push, Marie Jones bore down. Her only interest was in getting this baby out of her body. Joyce Renee Jones entered the Earth-realm approximately fifteen minutes after her older brother, Jeffrey Earl. She came into the world angry, red-faced, and crying with the most powerful set of lungs Long Island General had ever heard. But, she made it.

In the Unseen . . .

As Joyce finally slid out of the birth canal, Earth-angel Clematis gave a shout to welcome his new charge into the world. He could tell she was a fighter. He welcomed the challenge to keep her headed in the right direction—the Road to Glory.

Margarette Ann

FOURTEEN

Eternity

Margarette Ann glumly floated in the atmosphere surrounding the Chamber of Gifts and Talents. Brooding over the gifts and talents she had just received, she sadly looked around. She tenderly observed the home she loved but was destined to leave for a season for the assignment she had been given.

Margarette Ann had received soldier and leadership skills, evangelism, and other skills she would need for her Earth stay. She was chosen to serve in the Army of the world and as an evangelist and preacher but really didn't want to go. She didn't want to be a soldier. Nor did she want to be an evangelist. Surely, she thought, something could be done so she could stay here in Heaven.

"Margarette Ann, what seems to be the problem? You seem dark for some reason. Is there anything I can help with?" enquired Earthbound Angel Saran, observing the mood of his charge. Always somber, Margarette Ann seemed to be a little more solemn than usual.

This pre-born clearly did not want an Earth assignment. She wanted no part of those humans on that place called Earth. They were selfish, lazy, ugly, and just not her type at all. And she was not afraid to let her feelings be known.

71

When she visited the family she was assigned to, she was not impressed by any of them. This gave her all the more reason for not wanting to go on the assignment the Lord had for her on the Earth. She didn't want to go to Earth to be around people and she didn't want to be stuck with these people for an extended assignment on Earth if she didn't like them.

She didn't know why but she really just didn't like people. After all, she barely wanted anything to do with the other pre-borns in Heaven. All she wanted to do was be with the Father and the Son.

Why couldn't they just let her be?

She wasn't like many of the other pre-borns, who were always ready for another adventure. She had had all the adventure she wanted or needed the few times she had visited Adam and Eve during their assignment in Eden. And that was an education in itself! After observing them and seeing how easy it was to turn away from God, she decided she had seen enough. She didn't want to learn any more about Earth. She was satisfied right where she was.

"Angel," she began in that stoic voice Angel Saran had come to recognize and love. "I don't understand why I must go down to Earth to do something I have no interest in doing," she said matter-of-factly. "God has plenty of pre-borns who would love to go to Earth to be human and do whatever," she explained morosely.

Every so often, one just like Margarette Ann would come along and be extremely reluctant to go into the Earth-realm. The last one had been a pre-born named Oprah who eventually succeeded in making the largest impact on the Earth the world had ever known from a woman, especially a woman of color. But that was another story . . .

Margarette Ann was bright and inquisitive. This little pre-born was always the first to love on the Almighty and His Son. She was extremely averse to leaving Heaven and did not want to be used in the Earth-realm.

"Margarette Ann," said Angel Saran, "you will do much good in the Earth-realm. You will save many lives and have a positive influence on those you meet."

"Angel Saran, I know what you are saying is true, but I really don't want to leave here. Can't I be an angel like you? I think I would make a good angel, don't you?" pleaded Margarette Ann.

To make her point, the pre-born shot through the atmosphere as she had seen the warrior angels do many times during practice. She dove and twisted, pretending to have her angelic sword drawn to fight off fallen angels who continually attempted to battle their way back into Heaven.

She swept across the sky in a series of moves she had watched the warriors perform many times, wishing she could be assigned to their war teams. With expert moves, Margarette Ann thrust, whirled, and slid from position to position as though she had been created for such an assignment. Oh, how she would love to be with the warrior angels as they engaged in conflict after conflict in the Heavens for the Saints of God!

Angel Saran lovingly shook his head at this pre-born. He could tell she had studied the warrior angels. He could also discern that God had poured these abilities into this pre-born spirit for the battles she would face in her assignments on the Earth.

"Can I tell Abba? Can I talk to Him about this?" she asked as she came to a halt before Saran. "Maybe He'll change His mind," she pleaded with her angel. Surely, God wouldn't want her to go to Earth when she was so adamant about not going. Surely . . .

In an instant, Margarette Ann was in the presence of Almighty God and His Son. As she experienced the warmth of His presence and His love, she glowed brighter than she had since before entering the Chamber of Gifts and Talents. She loved her Creator and basked in the warmth of His glory, desiring to be able to do this for all eternity.

"Come to Me, Spirit Child," the Almighty beckoned. "I understand you are experiencing great reluctance in going on the mission I have designed just for you."

"Yes, Abba," she admitted, reverently approaching the One she loved so much. "I have great reluctance and a little apprehension. Can't you send someone else? Someone who likes others? What about Carolyn or Anna?"

"Abba, didn't you see the exhibition I put on for Angel Saran? Don't You think I would make a good warrior angel, Father God?" she asked, ready to make her case again if needed. "Besides," she continued, "I love others but I don't *like* them! Carolyn and Anna at least like everyone. I don't like being around anyone but You, Jesus, and Your Holy Spirit," she explained, shimmering in the brightness of the Light surrounding her.

The Voice of the Ages boomed in laughter. "And that, My beloved one, is why I have chosen to send you on the assignment I have planned just for you. You see, spirit child, I don't like the humans I have placed on the Earth either. They are never satisfied and always want more of what they already have. They don't want to listen to Me yet they want Me to do things for them," Almighty God explained. "But like you, I do love them. I am sending you as a dose of reality. When you come into the knowledge of My Truth as a human, you will be a very strong preacher, much like Evangelist Philip, and spread about the truth of My Word. I am sending you not to like people but to love them," Abba concluded with a thunderous laugh.

Margarette Ann brightened as she understood her assignment.

"I'll try, Father," she promised. "But I'm telling You right now . . . I am *not* going to like it," the pre-born spirit said boldly yet reverently.

FIFTEEN

Youngstown Ohio General Hospital: November 17, 1959

Emma, how many minutes apart are your contractions?" the maternity ward nurse asked Emma Wells. Twenty-two-year-old Emma looked over her shoulder to ask her husband of one year, Albert.

"It's about fifteen minutes, ma'am," Albert answered Nurse Anna Peters. "Her water broke about an hour ago as she cleaned up the lunch dishes. Pert near scared me to death," Albert said with a grin in his slow country drawl.

Today was his and Emma's one-year wedding anniversary. When he met Emma at the community youth sock-hop, he had known immediately she was the one for him. That was four years ago and he had gotten his bride.

"Unnhh," Emma groaned quietly.

This was the first of the six children she and Albert dreamed of having—four boys and two girls. Neither of them came from small families. Albert had eight brothers and sisters; she had ten. They had decided when they first married that they wanted to start right away so they could grow with their children. They both loved children and wanted at least six so not one child of theirs would be lonely. Each child would always have a best friend in the same way their mother and father had in their brothers and sisters.

"That pain was stronger," Emma whispered shyly to her attentive husband.

As she prepared to say something else to him, another pain shook her body. It wasn't quite five minutes after the last one. So far, her labor had been slow and steady, nothing severe. She had prayed for an easy delivery and knew God had heard her plea.

Emma grasped the hand Albert offered. She squeezed with more power than he realized she had. When she finally let go of his hand, he rubbed his fingers to get the feeling back.

Recovering from the pain, Emma saw her obstetrician, Dr. Frank Gaston, striding down the hall toward her. Youngstown was a small town. Dr. Frank was the only OB/GYN around for hundreds of miles. He had attended her birth twenty-two years ago as well as her brothers and sisters and Albert's brothers and sisters. He knew both their families.

"Emma? How we doing, hun?" Dr. Frank inquired with his familiar bedside manner, touching her shoulder. Before Emma could answer, another contraction wracked her body. Dr. Frank checked her pulse while the pain abated.

"The pains are about three minutes apart now, Dr. Frank," Emma gasped her answer, hazel eyes shining brightly at the prospect of meeting her first child.

"Doc, they're coming quicker than before now. She just went from fifteen to five to three minutes apart. Is it time?" Albert enquired, concern etched on his sun-touched face.

Not really worried, Albert had experienced many births his entire life. Growing up on a farm allowed a person to experience life in its rawest form most of the time. And with many sisters and brothers older than he, he had experienced the joy of childbirth many times over in his family. But this was different. This was a first for him—his first child. Excitement filled his heart as he anticipated the child who would be born today.

Dr. Gaston went to the nurses' station and instructed Nurse Peters to go ahead and take Emma to the prep room. Turning back to Albert, he said, "Albert, I'm taking her in. You go on in the waiting room and call your folks. We're gonna have us a baby before too long."

He continued down the corridor to prepare for the birth of this young couple's first child. Albert kissed his bride lovingly on the cheek before the nurse rolled her toward labor and delivery. Dr. Frank prayed for a safe, quick delivery . . . and that it would be a boy. In farming communities such as Youngstown and the surrounding areas, families always prayed for boys first because of all the work to be done on a farm. Albert and Emma Wells were no different.

Albert silently prayed as he went into the maternity ward waiting room. He had dreamed of this moment for what seemed an eternity. Now the time had come for Emma to have their first child. He knew that where they lived called for more sons than daughters to work on the farm, but in his heart, he wanted a little girl that looked just like her mother, his beautiful Emma. More than that, though, he wanted a healthy, happy child who would bring joy into their family.

Albert made the phone calls to both sides of the family. Within the hour, there were more repeat aunts, uncles, and grandparents in the waiting room than the room could hold.

"Any word yet, son?" asked Daddy Cooper, worry in his voice and his hazel-colored eyes. Albert could see much of his wife in her dad's face as Earl Cooper touched him on the arm.

"Not yet, sir. She's only been in there about an hour," Albert answered his father-in-law.

He and Earl Cooper had become close over the years while he dated Emma. Albert always said that if something were to happen to his dad, he already had a substitute on hand with Daddy Earl.

"Well," joined in Jim, Albert's dad, clasping his son's shoulder. "Come on, let's pray this grandbaby out."

The combined family members quickly joined hands. In that instant, that little hospital waiting room transformed into a tabernacle where the presence of the Lord could visit with them. Mama Dorothy Cooper, an associate pastor at the Youngstown Community Church where both families had attended many years, started the prayer.

"Dear Heavenly Father . . ."

In the Unseen . . .

"Shhhh," commanded Jesus, the Son of the Living God. "Angels of Intercession, let us join in with the saints as they pray Margarette Ann into the Earth," He directed.

Maternity Waiting Room . . .

" . . . we thank You for bringing us to this present point. God, we thank You that You are able to bring our Emma and the baby through this delivery safely. Heavenly Father, we commit them both into Your hands. And we thank You, Lord, that You have already answered our prayers. In the name of Jesus," Dorothy finished amid a chorus of "Amen's," and "Thank You, Lord's," tears streaming down her cheeks as she rejoiced in her baby girl safely starting her family.

Katherine Wells, Albert's mom, took over.

"Lord Jesus, we thank You that both of these children are kept by You. Father, we thank You that Your Holy Guardian Angels are in the room with them right now, Lord. Oh, Lord, we ask that Your favor, Your divine favor, flows through each and every room of this hospital right now. God, we thank You for guiding the hands of Dr. Frank and his assistants. Lord God, we thank You that even right now You are bringing forth a healthy baby from the womb of its mother . . ."

All around the room, family members agreed in prayer, some with their heads bowed, some praying along, but all with tears in their eyes.

The presence of Almighty God was heavy in the atmosphere as He listened to the praises of these saints as they ushered in the birth of this new child. The angels of God were all over the hospital, protecting what God had ordained to take place at this particular moment in time.

As the praises continued to flow in that tiny waiting room, Dr. Frank coaxed Emma to push one last time. She obeyed his direction. The result was the appearance of a blonde, downy-covered head from the birth canal.

"You're almost there, Emma, just a little more," urged Dr. Frank as he guided the little body out of its mother.

As the transition completed, he checked out the little one who lay in his arms. A little disappointed, he discovered that *it* was a *she*; a beautiful little girl with a very stern look on her face.

As he turned the baby upside down to get the airflow started in her lungs, the little body twisted to face him. Her hazel-colored eyes popped open, looking directly at him as if to say, "Don't you *dare* spank me!" Then she wailed as if her heart were broken.

In the Unseen . . .

The Heavenly Host gave a shout as little Margarette Ann Wells was born into the Earth at 1:30 p.m. on November 17, 1959. Warrior angels stood guard around the throne of God, observing Almighty God as He took in the scene below them. They were prepared for the moment Almighty God would give them marching orders to protect the life entering the Earth-realm. They didn't wait long.

SIXTEEN

In the Unseen . . .

Earth-Angel Crenado grinned at the expression on Margarette Ann's face when she entered the Earth-realm. It was quite obvious that this baby did not want to be here. Crenado didn't know how, but Margarette Ann let the doctor know she was not pleased with this place already.

Although he knew it was impossible, Angel Crenado thought there was a slight possibility that Margarette Ann remembered something from the Heaven-realm. *But that can't be,* he considered.

Her countenance indicated she remembered the conversation she had had with Almighty God prior to being swooshed into the Earth atmosphere. She had such an expression of disdain on her face. It was almost as though she wanted to spit in the doctor's face instead of look at him. What a journey this was going to be with Margarette Ann!

Maternity Ward Waiting Room

Startled, with a perplexed look on his face, Dr. Frank handed the baby to the nurse to be cleaned up. Taking off his gloves, he shook his head in an attempt to loosen the fog that obviously clouded his mind.

I must be having a spell of hallucination, he thought to himself. Absentmindedly ruffling his salt and pepper crew cut, he admitted to himself that he was probably a little more tired than usual from the activity of delivering eight babies in the past two days.

"What's wrong, Dr. Frank?" asked his young dark-haired assistant, Nurse Florence Watson, concerned.

"Nothing," he said. He thought his eyes were playing tricks on him. If he only knew . . .

Walking toward the waiting room, Dr. Frank smiled as he heard the combined praises of the Wells and Cooper families to God. He knew that this little girl would be brought up in a God-fearing, loving atmosphere. For the young couple's sake, though, he wished that *she* had been a *he*.

Oh, well, he thought, *such is life*.

Quietly and respectfully, Dr. Gaston entered the room with an apprehensive smile on his face. Born and bred Catholic, Frank didn't understand all the praising going on. He and Cathy, his wife of forty-five years, attended Mass and any other special services religiously but never did any of this vigorous praising the people from the Community Church did.

Different strokes for different folks, he mused.

Everything quieted when Frank entered the room. The praises stopped and all faces turned expectantly to him. With a huge grin, he cleared his throat.

"Both mother and baby are fine," he began.

Everyone said a quick "Thank You, Jesus," and waited for him to continue. Frank always looked forward to this part with apprehension.

Some families had actually cried when they found out that the first child of a couple was a girl. Others reluctantly accepted it because there was nothing they could do about it. He just couldn't imagine in which direction this family would swing.

"It's a . . . girl," he finally said, sweat popping out on his brow. Whew, that was over but he didn't expect what happened next.

"A girl . . ." said Albert, not believing his ears. "A girl . . ." he said again. "It's a girl! I have a daughter! Thank You, Lord! Thank You, Lord! I have a daughter!" he shouted, triumph in his voice.

His family glanced strangely at him. Each of them thought he would want a boy since he owned the largest farm of them all.

"You guys, I prayed for a girl," he explained excitedly. "I wanted a little girl who would look just like her mother. God gave me just what I wanted! Rejoice with me. We'll have sons. But I wanted our first child to be a daughter so I can spoil them both."

All the sisters cheered for their brother and brother-in-law and the brothers just slapped their crazy brother on the back. Praise the Lord! Albert had received just what he had asked for.

Dr. Frank shook hands, congratulating the new aunts, uncles, and grandparents all around the room. "You should be able to see them both in about an hour. Please try not to overwhelm the staff," he chuckled good-naturedly.

He knew they would all try to see Emma and the baby at the same time but it was OK. In a small country hospital, it was quite common for large families to show up at the bedside of an ill family member. They all knew how to conduct themselves so no one really enforced the rule of only two visitors per patient.

The hour passed quickly as the families chatted excitedly in the waiting room. Albert's brother Jim Jr. went to the hospital gift shop to buy cigars so they could hand them out to whoever was interested to know that the Wells and Cooper families had a new baby.

Dottie and Katherine hugged as they discussed the new baby girl. Friends for years, they were excited at the prospect of sharing a granddaughter.

"I wonder if she has those hazel eyes of Emma's or Albert's blue eyes," Katherine wondered.

"Praise the Lord! She is finally here!" exclaimed Dottie. "This seemed like the longest pregnancy ever," she told her friend.

"Amen to that, Dottie," Katherine agreed. "I thought my boy was going to have a heart attack last month when Emma went into false labor. Thank God it's over! Oh, I can't wait to see that precious little thing!"

This was the first granddaughter in ten years for either family. Being the youngest, Albert had nieces and nephews almost as old as he; so did Emma. Both families were excited about the new granddaughter and niece who had just arrived. Unfortunately, they were not the only ones anticipating the arrival of this little one.

SEVENTEEN

Eternity

"Angels Candol and Anka, this is a special child I have placed in your care," Almighty God said to the attentive Earth-angels.

Mostly sent out by ones, these angels were part of a special brigade of angels sent out in teams to provide high-security protection to certain subjects as Almighty God deemed necessary. This was one of those times.

"She is destined to preach in all corners of their known world. But she will endure much pain and hurt before I will be able to use her. Stay with her at all times," God instructed.

"Never leave her side no matter what happens to or with her. The forces of evil will attempt to take her away from the Kingdom of God. She will turn for a season. Even during that season, guard Margarette Ann with your very lives. Do you understand?" commanded God sternly.

"Yes, Almighty, we understand," the angels answered in unison as they understood the magnitude of the situation.

This was a rarity in the angelic-realm. Though the vast majority of their missions were one guardian angel per Earthbound pre-born spirit, every so often a pair of angels would be sent to protect one pre-born. As a matter of fact, the last time was for . . . well, that was another story altogether.

They pondered for just a moment on what this little human would endure. They quickly put it out of their minds. Almighty God had spoken.

In the Nursery in the Unseen . . .

"Look, Candol," whispered Anka. "Up in the corner of the room."

Ever alert, Candol followed Anka's gaze to the upper corner of the room. What he saw caused his wings to unfurl—legions of demons filled the upper spaces of the room.

Anka immediately touched his cohort's arm to quiet him. "Let us not reveal our position yet," he advised Candol. "Let's see what Almighty God is going to do in this situation," he concluded as they both drew back into the shadows of their corner.

The Earth-angels prepared themselves for the battle ahead. Considering their position, they observed the demons glaring at the child, hunger in their eyes, venom dripping from their ugly mouths.

Considering the adversary's minions, Candol and Anka caught a glimpse of the atmosphere surrounding the family who had just received the newborn into their midst. Darkness spread around the family in the spiritual realm, darkness such as these protective Earth-angels had not experienced . . . at least not for a very long time.

Candol and Anka conferred in their corner of the nursery. Staying in the shadows, they measured their next moves as they sternly gazed at the demons floating in the atmosphere. They did not want to create a disturbance until they knew more of what was going on in the life of this child and had received instruction from on high. But one thing they knew for certain—it had already begun.

Emmaline

EIGHTEEN

Charlotte, North Carolina: May 27, 1959

She wasn't afraid for herself.

He had beaten her off and on for the past two years. She had grown accustomed to the beatings. No, she was more afraid for the baby that was ready to be born.

Maybelle Johnson was twenty-four years old and frightened for the life of this child. Once a very pretty girl, Maybelle looked well beyond her years as a result of the abuse she suffered from the hands of her husband.

Alton, her once handsome and loving husband of five years, had already caused the miscarriage of three other babies from his brutal beatings. Hiding the pregnancy as much as she could with her slight frame, this was the only one Maybelle had brought to full term. Alton hated life and took it out on Maybelle as much as he possibly could.

"Alton, please," she pleaded. Pain flashed in her light-brown eyes as she attempted to shelter her midsection from his fists. *Oh, how I had loved this man,* Maybelle thought as pain jarred her entire body. At this point, she didn't know whether it was the pain of contractions or the pain of Alton's fists causing her all the discomfort. All she knew was that she was enduring a pain she had never experienced before.

High school sweethearts, Alton and Maybelle attended Fisk University after graduation to follow their dreams together. Everything went well for them on the college campus. They were both popular from the beginning and thrived in the college atmosphere. Until the incident . . .

They met during their junior year of high school. Six foot four, Alton Wayne Johnson was the star everything at Charlotte West Negro High School: football, basketball, baseball, even bowling. Handsome, popular, and a straight-A student, Alton loved and was friends with everyone. All the guys wanted to be like him. All the girls wanted to be with him. But his hazel eyes were set on only one— Maybelle Julia Carter.

Maybelle, the second and youngest daughter of Emmaline and Stanley Carter was beautiful, petite, and very shy. A model student, Maybelle aspired to become a trial attorney. Determined to attain her dreams of being the first college graduate from her family and an attorney, Maybelle began checking her options for colleges during her freshman year. She laid out her course with a set mind. Her family encouraged her and she knew she would make it. She just hadn't counted on falling for Alton Johnson.

After meeting and discovering they liked each other and shared many of the same goals and dreams, Maybelle and Alton were inseparable. Maybelle went to each of Alton's sporting events. He in turn attended her major debates. When their families celebrated birthdays and other special events, they each attended the others'.

As their May 1953 high school graduation approached, Alton and Maybelle aimed their college preferences at colleges and universities they could attend together. Having above-average intelligence for the sciences, Alton stood a very good chance of winning a full academic scholarship to the college of his choice, Fisk University, for medical school. Located in Nashville, Tennessee, Fisk also offered a premier law program for his precious Maybelle. Alton had faith that things would work out for them.

On graduation day, family and friends threw a huge celebration for their star pupils who were both accepted into Fisk. Because of their grades, both students had also been accepted into Harvard, but neither wanted to be that far away from his or her family. Besides, Alton had not heard very good things about their athletics programs.

Members of Greater Faith Tabernacle in Charlotte, Alton and Maybelle served as youth leaders. Their church family supported them as they went off to college, awarding scholarships and arranging for other stipends for them so they wouldn't have to work. Instead, the stipends and scholarships afforded them the opportunity to concentrate on their schoolwork and, for Alton, sports. Their families and friends were setting them up to be homegrown success stories for Charlotte.

Greater Faith's pastor, Alan Turner, arranged for them to become involved with Evangeline Tabernacle of Faith in Nashville. He gave his friend Pastor Anthony Boston such a good report on Alton and Maybelle that, upon meeting and observing them, Pastor Tony immediately promoted Alton and Maybelle to the Youth Elder Board to help him with the youth of his church. Everything was going well for Alton and Maybelle.

The bright young couple's freshman year started without a hitch. Not sharing any classes but seeing each other every break they could manage, Alton and Maybelle thrived in the college atmosphere.

His physical prowess in basketball made a place for Alton with the Fisk basketball team. After attending basketball camp the previous summer, Alton was chosen for the basketball program at Fisk with high praise from the coaching staff. Once he was physically on campus, the coaches immediately placed him on first string as a guard. Alton grew more skillful with each practice.

During their first scrimmage with predominantly white Tennessee State, Nashville's other university, words passed between Alton and a white player, Fletcher Conroy. When the coaches broke up the scuffle, Fletcher angrily made it his business to warn Alton that it wasn't over.

Observing the interchange between her boyfriend and the other boy, Maybelle felt something discomfiting go through her spirit. It only happened for a second and she forgot about it almost instantly. Alton completely forgot about it since stuff like that was bound to happen between players on opposing teams in basketball or any other sport for that matter. But this was different.

The Fisk Bulldogs basketball team played and won their first twelve games. Well on their way to the playoffs, Fisk had the most magnificent players the school had ever seen. Alton was the leader of the pack. Although only a freshman, Alton exhibited skill and wisdom on the court his coaches had rarely seen coming through their basketball roles before, especially from such a young player.

Alton led Fisk to the NCAA championships in 1954. Major professional basketball scouts watched him. Assigned as a shooting guard, Alton averaged twenty-five to thirty points per game and gave an outstanding defensive performance as well.

Doing well in school and keeping their grades up, Alton and Maybelle were more in love than ever. Alton Johnson was on top of the world. Unfortunately, there were forces that wanted to bring Alton to the bottom.

NINETEEN

Eternity

Almighty," inquired the deceptively respectful voice of the Accuser of the Brethren. "Will this human continue to serve You if You allow certain things to happen in his life?"

Almighty God considered Lucifer's request. God knew the Enemy wanted to throw a wrench into the plans He had for Alton Johnson and Maybelle Carter, for all those called by His name. Lucifer, now satan, had plotted from the beginning to turn humanity away from God and to the Dark Kingdom. He hadn't changed and never would.

God had great plans for Alton and Maybelle. But His perfect plan for humanity called for testing and maturity through all manner of trials and tribulations during their assignments on Earth.

"What do you have in mind, devil?" God thundered, already knowing what the Enemy determined to do.

Having played everything forward in the continuum of time, God already knew the result of everything satan would attempt on the Earth.

"I was thinking, Majesty," satan said invitingly. "What if You allowed something to happen to the man so he could not play basketball anymore? Something to test his faith, Almighty? Will the human still serve you?"

God listened to what the Adversary proposed. It wasn't a bad idea, but . . .

"I have created all things for My purpose, even evil for the evil day. Whatever is in your mind to do, devil, perform it. However, you cannot take his life," God commanded, thundering his response as He dismissed the wicked one from His presence.

Satan departed from the throne room of God. Laughing maniacally to himself, he contemplated what he would do to the man Alton Johnson. He wouldn't kill him . . . just make him *wish* he were dead.

In the Unseen, Nashville

Slayer roamed the streets of Nashville waiting for the command from his master the Prince of Darkness. Racism, Hatred, Jealousy, and Anger roamed the streets behind him, causing minor skirmishes to while away the time until they found out if everything was a go concerning Alton Johnson.

"Oh, mighty Prince Slayer," complained Racism to his boss. "What is taking so long? It seems as though we have waited eons to hear from the Throne of Darkness on this matter, Master," Racism exaggerated.

Slayer processed the information Racism brought to his attention. He deliberated whether or not to send one of his assigned minions to see if there was an answer from satan as yet. He didn't want to disturb the Master of Darkness. He knew how volatile he could be at times.

"Be patient, lackey," Slayer said. He decided to wait until the Master sent someone to him with word. *No need in stirring the old dog up if I don't need to,* he contemptuously thought to himself.

"*Dog* am I, Slayer?" inquired the slippery, slimy, wicked voice out of the atmosphere.

As the leader of the Dominions of Darkness, it was quite common for satan to explore other demons' thoughts. Slayer's black heart quivered as he considered the havoc satan could wreak upon him without much effort.

"Master, please forgive me. I meant 'dog' in the kindest sense, your Highness," Slayer explained, groveling to deflect the wrath of the Fallen One.

But there was no need. From the appearance of his countenance, satan was . . . happy.

"No need for all that, slave," satan said to Slayer, reminding him that he was, after all, only a servant. "We have permission to do as we will with this human. The only thing we can't do is kill him. But we can certainly make him desire death," satan said, a sneer on his face and a scoffing laugh emanating from his raspy throat.

Slayer rubbed his hands together at the prospect of causing pain in the life of one of those calling himself by the name of the Most High God.

He refocused on Alton. Slayer had watched this human for quite some time. Now he would see if Alton Johnson was truly a servant of God or if he would fall from grace. Slayer had looked forward to this moment. He desired to shine in the face of Darkness.

Slayer called his minions to gather around him. "Hmm, let's see—Anger, Racism, Hatred, and Jealousy. Yes, you all will do just fine. But there are two more I want to use for this assault party—Callousness and Revenge," he added gleefully.

Revenge would be the impetus for this siege. Callousness would lead the charge. Slayer knew once Revenge took hold of the young men as they assaulted Alton Johnson, Cruelty would step in and endue the attackers with dark power to bring forth a beating that would make Alton want to die.

Nashville, Tennessee: September 1954

Alton escorted Maybelle safely to her dorm after the Sunday night service at church. Afterward, he and a couple of his teammates went to one of the burger places for a late-night snack before returning to their dorm. He, Maurice, and Sam enjoyed the burgers and fries served at Mabel's Diner, one of the few colored-owned establishments in town. Because they were basketball players, they received healthier portions of whatever they ordered. And they enjoyed the attention.

As Alton and his friends came out of the diner at about 10:30, a voice called to him belligerently, "Hey, boy. Aren't you that Alton Johnson boy from Fisk?"

Always respectful, Alton turned toward the voice to answer, "Yes, sir . . ."

When he saw the asker, Alton changed his tact. It was Fletcher Conroy, the same guy he'd had words with during the scrimmage in the fall of last year.

"Hey, Fletcher, man, let's not get started on that. It's over," Alton offered, looking at this guy and his friends. Alton felt that something was about to happen.

Blonde-haired, blue-eyed Fletcher rode on the back of the seat with the top down on the almost new sky-blue Dodge Cornette convertible. Lights shining brightly, the car rolled slowly down the street toward Alton and his friends as though the occupants had been waiting for them to make an appearance.

Looking closer, Alton could tell the boys in the car were drunk. Fletcher and his five friends brandished sticks, sledge hammers, and chains. It didn't take much for Alton to realize that he and his friends were outnumbered.

"Boy," Fletcher slurred, "I been looking for you for a long time. I come to get muh respect, darkie."

Alton whispered a quick, "Lord, please help us," before he said to Fletcher, "There's no need for name-calling, man. Look, I'm sorry we got into it that day. I apologize for disrespecting you. Please forgive me."

Alton looked for an escape route so he and his friends could avoid the impending altercation. Unfortunately, there was no place to go except back to the diner. Six against three, the odds didn't look good for Alton or his friends to make it back to the diner without being hit with one of the objects in the hands of their aggressors.

In 1954 in the Deep South, colored men were still being lynched. He didn't want anything to happen to his friends or to himself because of pride or arrogance. There had to be a way they could get out of this situation without too much harm coming to any of them.

"Please let my friends go. They had nothing to do with this," Alton pleaded as the driver stopped the car and Fletcher and his friends got out.

If they couldn't find a way to escape, the menacing items held in the hands of the other young men were set to inflict much damage to Alton, Maurice, and Sam.

Keeping his eyes on their aggressors, Alton whispered urgently, "Maurice, Sam, when I tell you, run across the street and back up to the diner! They only want me. You can get to the diner and call the police. Get ready! Now!"

Hoping this was a good plan, Maurice and Sam didn't hesitate. They quickly split up and darted away from the threat. Maurice quickly sprinted across the street then back toward the diner they had just left. Sam ran past the almost empty car then sprinted across the street in a zigzag course behind Maurice.

Maurice burst through the diner door and quickly asked the waitress to phone the police. Sam entered right behind him. Both panting from the sprint, they attempted to explain to the waitress what was going on.

It didn't take Ellie long to understand what was happening. She immediately alerted the police.

In the Unseen . . .

Slayer sat on the hood of a chromed black 1950 Studebaker parked in front of the diner. He watched as the situation amplified to where he wanted it to be.

Anger, Racism, Hatred, and Jealousy surrounded Fletcher and his cronies. They knew all the buttons to push and made good use of those buttons.

Slayer called Anger to his side. "Look, this is what I want you and the others to do," he said aggressively. "Surround the human Fletcher and his friends and cloud their minds to commonsense. Help them remember that Alton is a better *everything* than they are. Then, let Jealousy have his way with them," Slayer instructed. Anger understood.

Slayer failed to see the figures sitting on top of the building across the street from the diner. He allowed his zeal to carry him well beyond the parameters satan had set for this assault. He would not be denied.

Holy Guardian Angels Hazmar, Kangor, and Eliasa considered the happenings beneath them on the street. Knowing what was about to transpire, they discreetly followed Alton and his friends from the diner. They saw the forces of evil gathering around the six boys in the car. Recognizing Anger, Racism, Hatred, and Jealousy, they also observed Slayer sitting on his temporary throne, instructing his minions in their mission.

Hazmar instinctively knew these were not the only demons present. The others had just not made themselves known as of yet.

"Be on the lookout, Protectors," Hazmar warned. "I fear there are more demons than what we see at this moment."

He spoke not a moment too soon. Like a flash, Callousness and Revenge flew toward Fletcher and his friends, Andy, Bobby, Carl, Stan, and Steve. As Callousness and Revenge touched down in their midst, the boys staggered as the demonic power engulfed them, seemingly taking control. There was no turning back.

Fisk University: Women's Dormitory, Room 211

Maybelle suddenly felt an overwhelming urge to pray. She heard the still quiet voice say, *Quickly! Pray for Alton.*

She had already turned off the lamp and lay down in her bed to go to sleep. She immediately rolled out of bed and onto her knees.

As she murmured, "Father God . . ." Alton received the first blow to his knees.

Eternity

The Intercessor heard the plea from the dormitory room.

Father God in the name of Jesus, I don't know what's going on with Alton. I don't know if he's in his dorm room or out somewhere getting a bite to eat. But Lord, please protect him and anyone he might be with right now. In Jesus's precious name.

The voice of the young woman continued in prayer, supplication, and thanksgiving because she knew her prayer was being heard in the Heavens.

"Come, Angels of Intercession. Let us assist this woman in praying for the situation on the Earth. We will pray that the Grace and Mercy of God will prevail in this situation," directed the Intercessor to His staff of interceding angels surrounding

Him. "Spirit of God, endue the woman with power from on high to pray for what she knows not."

He knew of the conversation between the Father and the Accuser of the Brethren. He knew that Alton Johnson would be physically injured. However, it was up to Alton whether he allowed himself to become spiritually injured as well.

TWENTY

Charlotte, North Carolina: May 27, 1959

Woman, I told you before: we are not bringing any children into this horrible world," Alton shouted. "And if I have to beat every one of them out of you, I will," he threatened angrily.

Alton refused to bring a child into this cruel world to endure what he had barely survived. After his beating that night at the hands of those white boys in Nashville, all his dreams were dashed away—medical school, a pro-basketball career, being prosperous in this world—everything was gone as a result of the beating he received on that fateful night.

And every time he struck Maybelle on this day, in his mind he hit Fletcher or one of his buddies in a way he wished he could have struck out that night nearly five years ago. Alton had never felt as helpless as he had felt that night . . .

Fletcher Conroy and his friends beat Alton mercilessly. His knees were their main concern. The young thugs reasoned that if his knees were destroyed, he could not play basketball or any other sport ever again. Fletcher exacted revenge against Alton because Alton was better than he was at every sport—basketball, baseball, football, everything.

Fletcher hated Alton with pure hatred. He poured out that hatred on Alton as he and his friends beat him. Fletcher derived great pleasure in hearing Alton's knees give way. As Fletcher swung the sledgehammer for the first blow, Alton screamed like a little girl. That scream inspired Fletcher to bury all his frustration and anger in his victim.

The beating the six young men meted out to Alton prior to the arrival of the police kept Alton in Intensive Care for six months. The staff and students of Fisk University were in an uproar—how could this have happened?

Nashville had long accepted the colored students of Fisk. The Nashville residents looked on them as success stories of the time. The lingering racial tension was all kept at bay because of the townspeople and the schools. What happened to Alton Johnson set race relations back at least a hundred years as everyone tried to understand how this could have transpired and escalated in such a fashion.

When he finally regained consciousness, Alton was moved from Fisk Medical Center to Charlotte General Hospital so his parents and family could care for him. Friends, family, and church family rallied around Alton's family to help out as much as possible. Prayer was continually lifted up as their community came together to bring this outstanding young man back to his feet.

Unfortunately, Fletcher's father was a top attorney in Chattanooga. He very carefully constructed Fletcher and his cohorts' defenses so they were able to serve no time other than the time they spent in the county lockup—forty-five days. They were able to go on with their lives as basketball players for TSU. They had gotten the revenge they sought with Alton.

Because the trials were held in Nashville, Mr. Conroy was able to equip the jury with his own people so the boys he represented would be favored. Alton's attorneys were impotent against the cadre of lawyers representing his opponents. Not only did Alton consider himself defeated by the boys who had beaten him but also by life itself.

Unable to walk, much less play basketball, Alton sat bitterly in his wheelchair for over a year before he could make himself get up and start the rehabilitative process. Alton despised the fact that Maybelle was able to go on with school while he sat at home, unable to do anything but grow more and more hateful to those around him.

Maybelle went home every chance she could to see him. She was more in love with him than ever, assuring him that she didn't want anyone else in her life. He was the only one for her. He didn't believe her—didn't, couldn't, and wouldn't. He was miserable.

Although Alton could no longer play basketball as a result of the beating, he had other options. Because of his grades, Fisk counselors advised him to switch to an academic scholarship. Alton didn't see any reason to do that. Stuck in a wheelchair and not wanting anyone's sympathy, Alton allowed himself to wallow in self-pity, disappointing everyone around him . . .

Slap!

Alton hit Maybelle on the face again. He attempted to get to her stomach. Maybelle fiercely guarded the baby who should have been conceived in love. Instead, this child was conceived because her husband had brutally violated her body when she was at her most vulnerable.

After Alton's unpleasant incident, Maybelle completed two years of college and was awarded an Associate's degree in English with a 4.0 grade point average. By the end of her second year, with Alton working on her love and sympathy for him, Maybelle quit school and came home to help care for him. Before that, he cried when she came home for the weekend and sobbed when it was time for her to return to Fisk.

"Don't you love me, Maybelle?" he pleaded. "Please stay with me. I need you," he begged.

Maybelle finally relented amid protests from her family. She told her parents she would return to school later and finish what she had started. Just right now, though, she felt that the Lord was calling her back home for a while to help Alton get back on his feet.

Within a year of dropping out of Fisk, Alton convinced Maybelle to marry him. Emmaline and Stanley Carter were reluctant and uneasy about allowing their daughter to marry Alton. It wasn't because he was crippled, though. Since his accident, many changes had come over him. Everyone had faith that Alton would eventually recover the ability to walk. But something inside him had changed. He now acted very strangely toward everyone.

Once a very loving boy, Alton now acted as though he hated people and hated being around anyone. When Emmaline and Stanley spoke with Alton's parents, Henry and Annie, they were told how sad it was to see their boy change so much.

The oldest of six strapping boys, Alton was the hope of his family. Always an encouragement to his younger brothers, in the past, Alton had tried to keep them on the straight path so they could accomplish something with their lives.

"He's always been the first to speak positively over any situation," said his mom, Annie. "Now," she told the Carters, "he's completely opposite."

The two sets of parents came together often to pray for Alton and Maybelle. They wanted to see their children married to each other. But they also wanted them to wait until Alton was not only on his feet again but also moving out of the slump the tragic incident had placed him in. That didn't happen.

Alton and Maybelle married on Tuesday, February 14, 1956 to the chagrin and dismay of their parents. Finally walking after almost two years in the wheelchair, Alton looked very handsome as he stood with a white walking cane to match his white tuxedo at the front of their church. The doctors had diagnosed that he would never be able to walk again. Sheer determination and bitterness caused Alton to come out of the wheelchair.

Maybelle was very proud of him and happily married him. After their brief honeymoon, she started up a campaign to get him to return to school. Maybelle was ready to return to school and had been accepted with a full scholarship to Johnson C. Smith University nearby in Charlotte. Changing her major from law to education, Maybelle decided to become a school teacher so she could make a difference in the lives of the children in her community.

Fisk University extended an invitation to Alton to return under an academic scholarship. He decided he wanted no part of Nashville. After his parents spoke with the counselors at Fisk, they took it upon themselves to work with Alton because of his special circumstances.

The Fisk Dean of Admissions was able to open the door for him to attend Winston-Salem State University. He was also able to transfer his scholarship and arrange for other scholarships and stipends as well.

In spite of all the assistance being given, Alton wanted no part of college. He bitterly maintained that college was only a pipedream and not meant for him. His dreams of becoming a doctor were over. He was equally determined not to allow Maybelle to achieve her dreams either. His bitterness caused him to strike out at those around him who loved him and wanted better for him.

As Alton raised his hand to hit Maybelle again, a sharp contraction hit her. She yelped with the pain. It was worse than any pain Alton could inflict upon her.

Maybelle began praying inwardly, *The Lord is my Shepherd, I shall not want . . .*
Slap!

Alton's hand made contact with the back of her head. The sound reverberated through the room and through Maybelle's head.

"I will kill you and your child, woman!" Alton's voice took on an otherworldly quality.

Right before he hit her shoulder with the largest encyclopedia he could lay his hands on, Maybelle looked up just in time to observe a monstrous look on Alton's face. Almost unconscious, Maybelle continued with her prayer.

Lord, if it be Thy will, please let this cup pass from me, she pleaded in her mind. *God, please let Jimmy and Florina get here before it's too late.*

Bent over double to protect her baby, Maybelle's body ached from the brutal beating her husband was administering to her.

"God, please help me," she murmured faintly, fighting to remain conscious.

In the Unseen . . .

The call came for angels Hazmar, Kangor, and Eliasa to quickly attend to the pregnant young woman. The three of them deflected as many of the blows as they could so that pre-born Emmaline would not be harmed during the assault.

These same three had helped the pre-born's Earth-father when he was assaulted by the six men in Nashville. They knew that Almighty God had heard the woman's cry. He had released them to come now. It was a matter of urgency as three other pre-borns had not made it to Earth-life from the brutality the man meted out to the woman during her previous pregnancies.

Charlotte, North Carolina

Unable to hold onto consciousness any longer, Maybelle slid to the floor just as the front door of their little house flung open. Fearing the worst, her brother Jimmy broke through the frame. Outraged to see what was going on, he tackled Alton. Jimmy threw Alton against the wall away from his sister just as Alton's foot swung to kick Maybelle's still body yet again.

"Man, what's wrong with you?" Jimmy shouted questioningly at his brother-in-law.

As he held Alton down, Florina ran to her sister-in-law to see if she was alive.

"My God, Jimmy. My God," she uttered, horrified at the appearance of her sister-in-law.

Maybelle looked as though she had been beaten by Joe Louis. She couldn't believe what she saw. Florina couldn't comprehend that Alton had beaten his wife, the woman he supposedly loved so much, as badly as he had beaten Maybelle.

Even in an unconscious state, Maybelle had her arms wrapped around her torso in an attempt to protect her precious cargo as best she could.

Florina checked her pulse. Weak and thready, she was thankful Maybelle still had a pulse. She and Jimmy had made two calls before they left their home two miles away—for the police and an ambulance. Thank God they heard both pulling into the driveway right behind them. And not a moment too soon. An LPN, Florina knew they would have to hurry if they were to save both these battered victims.

As the policemen ran through the front door, guns drawn, Florina quickly let them know who was who.

"Officers, please. That's my husband, this woman's brother, holding her husband down on the floor. He's the one who beat this woman, my sister-in-law," she quickly explained, tearfully.

Upon hearing that, the policemen quickly took over and handcuffed a struggling Alton then took him to their waiting squad car. As they took Alton out, the paramedics came in to assess the situation. Recognizing Florina from the hospital, they quickly asked what was going on.

She urged them to hurry. Not only was Maybelle brutally beaten, the baby was severely traumatized from being knocked around inside the mother. They quickly moved Maybelle to the gurney after beginning an IV in her arm. She moaned as they moved her. Florina noticed that the baby had not moved since she had arrived.

"Please hurry! Don't let her lose the baby! Please!" Florina begged the ambulance driver. They moved quickly because of her tone of voice. Nurse Carter was one of the best at Charlotte General. If she was moving them urgently out the door, there was good reason.

"Jimmy, I'll ride with Maybelle. Call your and Alton's parents. Have them meet us at the hospital," she said as they closed the doors of the ambulance.

Jimmy went back into the house. Taking in the mess around him for the first time, he couldn't believe his eyes! It looked as though a barroom brawl had broken out in his sister's home. Why hadn't she let her family know it had gotten this bad with Alton? Couldn't she see how much they all loved her and would not allow this jerk to mistreat her?

Jimmy called his parents first. Even though he tried to be strong, he choked when his mother answered the phone.

"Mom, Maybelle's on the way to the hospital. Mama," he said in a little boy voice of long ago. "Mama, he beat her, Mama," he cried.

"Jimmy? Jimmy-Dee, is that you?" Emmaline Carter shouted, fear causing her to quake in her innermost being. "Jimmy-Dee (she hadn't called him that since he was a toddler), calm down, son. Tell Mama what happened." She signaled to her husband Stanley to pick up the extension.

"Mama," Jimmy got out through his sobs. "Maybelle called Florina and me to take her to the hospital to have the baby. By the time we got here, Alton had beaten her so bad, Mama." He sobbed again as he thought of the spectacle he had just witnessed as he broke through the front door.

"Mama, Daddy, just go to the hospital. Florina is with her. Hurry," Jimmy pleaded with his parents as he hung up the phone. He hung his head down in his hands. Oh, how he loved his little sister! Didn't she know her family would have never allowed this to happen if only she had called?

"Oh, God, please help my baby sister. Please don't let her die! Don't let her lose the baby. Please, Lord," Jimmy whispered in his anguish, praying God would hear his cry.

TWENTY-ONE

Eternity

The Lord is My Shepherd, whispered the faint prayer from the Earth-realm. The moment it hit the foot of His throne, Almighty God shushed the activity all around Him in Heaven's atmosphere. *I shall not want . . .*

His beloved daughter Maybelle uttered these words with fading breath. After observing the devastating incident, Almighty God dispatched warrior angels to be around this vessel—Hazmar, Kangor, and Eliasa. He also dispatched Axel and Virdon to surround pre-born Emmaline. The warrior angels were able to deflect many of the blows of this woman's bitter husband, Alton.

God had sadly watched the developments in this house. He had trained pre-born spirit Emmaline to be ready to endure many trials and tribulations during her Earth sojourn. He would use her in a mighty way to minister to battered women and children.

He had allowed much to happen to her even before her birth in the Earth-realm. But He would allow neither her Earth-mother nor her to die from the beating inflicted upon them.

Lord, called out that tiny voice again, almost gone but still there, *if it be Thy will, please let this cup pass from me,* the tiny voice pleaded with the Ancient of Days.

Tears flowed down His face as the Father observed the distress of this young woman. She had already been through so much. He knew this could very well put her over the edge. But He knew the ending, He knew she would triumph.

"Now, Hazmar! Now, Kangor! Now, Eliasa!" He thundered, commanding His warrior angels as He endowed them with strength to help the young woman's brother break down the solid wooden door. Jimmy displayed super-human power as he went through the door, treating it as though it were made of flimsy plywood.

As Jimmy tackled Alton, another angel joined Axel and Virdon by the young woman lying on the floor. Angel Echol reached in his hand to see how the baby was faring throughout the brutality.

"*I'm all right, Angel*," said the high-pitched mind-voice in the womb, winded but strong. "*Please take care of the woman, my Earth-mother.*"

God smiled through His tears as he listened to Emmaline. This was one of His Earth-warriors. She would endure in prayer and be strong and courageous. He had equipped her with a strong will to survive through much. He had confidence she would make it.

"Father," said His Son, standing by His right hand. "It was touch and go for a season but this child is strong. Both the mother and child have gone through so much. But they will make it."

A chorus of shouts arose in the Heavens as they watched the spectacle on Earth. Hazmar, Kangor, Eliasa, Axel, and Virdon flew above the speeding ambulance as Echol sat beside the mother, child, and woman in the ambulance.

Charlotte, North Carolina

As the ambulance flew along the surface streets toward the hospital, Maybelle revived when a sharp contraction hit her frail body. She was alive! She had made it through. But what about the baby?

"Ohhh," she groaned as she bore down. She looked over at her sister-in-law and murmured quietly, "Please help me. Help my baby, sis."

Realizing that Maybelle was going to be all right, Florina cried tears of joy. The hospital was another five miles away. Florina had to make a quick decision right now. She knew the baby needed to be born and that the birth was happening quickly.

Florina made a decision. Moving quickly before she gave herself a chance to think about it, she retrieved a pair of scissors out of one of the drawers in front of her. She cut off her sister-in-law's soaked panties. Maybelle's water had broken long ago while Alton was battering her.

Florina alerted the driver and his partner as to what she was doing. It wasn't as though she hadn't done this before. A nurse for almost twenty years, she had delivered many babies. She knew this delivery would be quick because of the trauma. It would also be almost painless considering the pain Maybelle had already endured.

"OK, honey," she said to Maybelle. "On the count of three, I want you to push as hard as you can," she instructed. She didn't expect Maybelle would be able to push much. However, Maybelle surprised them both.

"In . . . the . . . name . . . of . . . Jesus," Maybelle grunted purposely, punctuating each word with a strength she didn't realize she had. She gave a shout of triumph at the fact that she and the baby had made it through.

When she said, "Jesus," the baby's head quickly popped out from between her legs. Florina caught the baby and helped Maybelle by gently tugging the baby as it came out completely. Without looking below the waist of the baby, Florina quickly anchored the newborn in the crook of her left arm. Able to use both hands now, she firmly grasped the umbilical cord and cut it.

Now that the task of bringing a child into the world was completed, Florina found a thermal blanket to wrap the newborn in after she spanked the baby to help it cry. Quickly finding another thermal blanket to place over the mother, Florina then looked to see what everyone else would want to know. Glory Hallelujah! It was a *she*!

"Maybelle," she said to the exhausted new mother. "You have a beautiful baby girl, none the worse for wear."

Florina wrapped the baby in the blanket. She handed her to her battered and eager mother. Florina let the guys up front in the ambulance know they had a baby who was in fine condition and that they could slow the vehicle down.

The ambulance arrived at the ER door within a few moments. Florina saw Emmaline and Stanley frantically waiting for them. No sooner had the ambulance pulled up to the door than Stanley flung open the doors to see if his daughter was alright.

Maybelle smiled weakly at her dad. She was still in pain but ecstatic that she had made it through. She decided then and there that this would be the last time Alton would have the opportunity to abuse her. And he definitely would not abuse her baby. She had not been raised like this! She would not allow her daughter to be brought up in an atmosphere of anger and abuse.

Maybelle decided to bring charges against Alton to keep him away from them for a while. Even though she knew she would always love Alton, she now realized she had to think about her baby as well as herself.

"Daddy," she spoke quietly. "Here's little Emmaline. You should have heard her cry when Florina spanked her," Maybelle continued with a weak smile. "She sounded like Mom does when she's upset."

Stanley Carter glanced at this amazing young woman God had allowed him to father. At twenty-four, his daughter had endured some things he wished could have been avoided. Thank God she had made it through! He vowed to God and to himself that these things would not happen again if he had anything to do with it.

He and his wife peered at the little face in the blanket. Little Emmaline Ruth Johnson, their newest granddaughter, was born into brutality . . . but born nonetheless. They wondered who this child would eventually become.

Tears flowed as Maybelle and her family went into the emergency room. Weak and still in pain, Maybelle told her parents all that had occurred and what her plans were. Her mother wept softly as she listened to the pain and agony in Maybelle's voice as she admitted the three previous miscarriages had been caused by Alton. The main reason Maybelle hadn't said much about his abuse was because she hoped they could work through his problems and bitterness.

Stanley and Emmaline glanced at each other, tears flowing freely from them both. They assured Maybelle that none of this was her fault. They also assured her they would stand with her no matter what decision she made concerning Alton. Knowing it would be a long, hard road, they prayed that God would keep them on the path He had made for them and that they would do it for His glory.

Eternity

"Angel Ehcol, you will be assigned to Emmaline Ruth Johnson along with angels Axel and Virdon for her entire sojourn on Earth. She will endure much but she has My joy within which will strengthen her for what she will do for the Kingdom of God. Darkness attempted to eliminate her before birth into the Earth-realm. The Light of the Lord has prevailed. Stay with the child. There is much I have for her to do," commanded Jehovah God.

The angels bowed in submission to their beloved Creator. They vanished as they entered the Earth-realm. Each angel looked forward to spending time with this child. Created to serve her, they would serve her well. They knew God had given them all they needed to serve her.

Bringing up a child . . .

History Lessons

TWENTY-TWO

In the Garden . . .

Eve considered the beautiful creature standing before her. It possessed silky skin with many different colors coursing through. If the creature turned a certain way, the color of its skin changed.

Eve looked into the beautiful, soulful eyes of the creature, beautiful dark-brown eyes, which seemed to draw her into its very depths. Attempting to look away, she found herself compelled to look back into those hypnotic eyes.

Standing on his legs, the serpent exulted in the power he had been given to mesmerize this woman who was created to take dominion over him and all the others called animals. After his discussion with Lucifer, the serpent was more than willing to help Lucifer deceive man so they could be in charge of the Earth.

"Sooo," he hissed, his forked sliver of a tongue slipping from his mouth as he coyly, subtly spoke to Eve. "Has God told you to not eat of every tree in the Garden, Eve?" he slyly asked.

"Yes," Eve said sadly. "We can eat of the fruit of all the trees in the Garden except *that* one," she answered, pointing to the tree of the knowledge of good and evil.

"But why?" the serpent asked silkily. He was prompting, tempting her to really think about why she couldn't eat from that *one* tree. "Why can't you eat from *that* tree? Look at it. The fruit on *that* tree seems to be larger and fresher than the fruit on the other trees, doesn't it?" the serpent asked again.

"Yes, I know," answered Eve, torn now because she really wanted to understand. "But God said we can neither eat from it nor touch it. If we do, we will die."

The serpent knew immediately that he had her. He knew what the Creator had said to Adam before Eve was created. The serpent had been there, lurking in the bushes as God walked through the Garden with Adam, pointing out things and giving him instruction.

He was there when God told Adam, "But of the tree of the knowledge of good and evil, thou shalt not eat of it: for in the day that thou eatest thereof thou shalt surely die."

The serpent had heard it all. He had waited for just this moment. He realized that if he could deceive the woman, half his mission would be accomplished.

"Eve, God didn't mean you would physically die when He said that to Adam," he deceitfully explained. "He meant you would be dead to hearing Him because you would become more like Him. You would become a goddess and know as much as He does about all He has created," said the serpent matter-of-factly, his sibilant tongue curling in and out of his mouth.

He knew he had her. Her eyes changed and understanding became clear. He could tell she understood what he filled her mind with.

"What!" she exclaimed indignantly. "We won't die but will become intelligent? Is that why we can't eat from the tree?" she asked, anger growing at the thought.

The serpent watched Eve, observing as she became highly agitated at this new development. She got up from her seat across from the tree of the knowledge of good and evil. Slowly walking toward the tree, Eve looked at it from different angles as she approached it.

"Eve. No." said the Voice.

She stopped about ten feet from the tree and looked around. Seeing no one, she stood there and listened. Nothing.

Taking another tentative step toward the tree and taking care not to touch, Eve very slowly walked around the side of the tree. It was a beautiful tree. The bark on it was new and supple, thick. The leaves were a vibrant green with rosy-colored blossoms all over the top branches. Then, she saw the fruit.

"Eve! No! Stop!" the Voice said urgently this time. "Think about what you are doing."

"Eve," spoke the syrupy sweet voice of the serpent. "Look at *that* fruit," he tantalized. "Mmm," he tempted. "*That* fruit is sooo gorgeous," he hissed. "Look at *that* firm skin. What's *that*? Is *that* juice oozing out of the skin?" he tempted her more than she had ever been tempted before.

"Eve, please," pleaded the Spirit of God.

He followed this unlikely duo as they moved closer to the forbidden tree. He watched for Eve's soul. He knew the commandment of the Lord.

Eve stopped again, indecision etched on her face. She peered closely at the piece of fruit. It looked so pretty and harmless. Surely God didn't mean what He had said about dying. Surely He would want Eve and Adam to partake of this beautiful fruit that would make them even as He was. Surely!

Eve contemplated these "surely's" as she slowly reached toward the piece of fruit on the lowest branch closest to her. As her outstretched hand reached toward it, the serpent coaxed her even more.

"That's right, Eve," he said compellingly, excitement coursing through his very being.

He knew he had her. He didn't want to rush her as he enjoyed the sweetness of this triumph against the Hated One.

"Look at it, Eve," he whispered in her ear as the thought of possessing this one piece of fruit mesmerized her. "What a pretty color!" he coaxed. He knew it was only a matter of time.

"Eve," the Spirit of God gave His final plea. "Don't . . ." he whispered as her hand finally touched the fruit.

Eve pulled the fruit from the stem and tentatively regarded it.

"I didn't die," she audibly whispered, amazed that God hadn't struck her down yet.

She brought the piece of fruit to her nose, brushing it against the tip. Although it felt fuzzy, the skin was smooth. She breathed in its fragrance, closing her eyes to discern the fragrance.

She heard that tiny Voice again.

"It's not too late yet, Eve. Put the fruit down. Walk away," she heard.

She knew the voice of the Spirit of God. She had heard it many times before. Previously, she had always done as the voice directed. This time was different. This time *she* was different.

Eve bit into the fruit. Savoring the pungency that overwhelmed her taste buds, things began to happen to her. Looking at the piece of fruit, Eve saw more in her hands than was really there. For the first time, she saw . . . *herself*—her hands, her feet, her body.

For the first time, Eve really looked at her body. She considered her skin—the texture, the color, the smell. She felt the hair on her head—long, thick, heavy. She looked down at her feet, looking at the toes, the toenails, her long, shapely legs. Eve was amazed at what she was discovering about herself after one bite of the forbidden fruit.

"Oh my! I *must* share this with Adam," she excitedly said as she ran looking for her husband.

She looked around as she ran through the Garden, seeing things as though for the very first time. Catching sight of Adam in the process of tending the Garden, she ran to him and said, "Adam, I made a new friend today—the serpent."

"Oh, did you now?" Adam rejoined, noticing a subtle change in his mate. "Where is this serpent?" Adam asked curiously.

"Oh, I left him over by the fruit trees. He showed me this marvelous fruit. It is so delicious!" Eve said boldly. "Why don't you try a bite?" She extended the fruit toward Adam.

Adam looked at the piece of fruit. He realized he had never seen this type of fruit before. There was something different about it.

"Where did you get this? We've eaten from all the trees. I don't remember ever having any of this fruit before," he said, confused.

"Oh," said Eve. "This is from *that* tree in the center of the Garden," she explained. "You know, the tree of the knowledge of good and evil. Didn't God say we would die if we touched the fruit?" she asked.

Horrified, Adam breathed, "Eve, what have you done?" as he backed away from her.

TWENTY-THREE

Adam *knew* what God had said. He had shared those same words with this woman whom God created to be his wife. He shook his head in pain and confusion, not knowing what to do or expect from God.

He loved this woman who was flesh of his flesh, bone of his bone. God had joyfully created them to be together so they could have many children and populate the Earth. Oh, what a wonderful relationship he had previously shared with God!

Looking around himself and up to the sky, he realized God would be arriving at any moment to visit, giving him further instructions on what He wanted done in the Garden. Adam knew he had to make a decision.

He refocused on Eve as she asked, "Adam, why did God lie to us? I touched and ate the fruit and didn't die," she said convincingly. "Here." She pushed the fruit toward him. "Try it. It's delicious."

He loved this woman. The decision was made. He bit into the fruit.

In Eternity . . .

"And that's what happened on Earth, spirits," said History Angel Fonorel.

"And it is my one regret," said the ancient voice approaching the pre-born spirits. "I am Adam, the first man created by the hands of Almighty God. God is merciful. That is why I stand before you now," Adam explained, white hair flowing down his back and over his white robes.

The spirits flowed to this kind-faced man.

"What I did was wrong," Adam continued. "I cannot justify my actions by saying that my beloved wife Eve caused me to be disobedient to the Almighty. I chose to be disobedient to the Almighty because I placed my wife and my flesh above what God required of me," Adam sadly explained.

Angel Fonorel stepped back so Adam could stand before these Earthbound pre-born spirits.

"History lessons are important in Heaven as they teach lessons for the present and the future. Because of my disobedience," continued Adam, "I had to work from that day forward by the sweat of my brow. Up until that time," he explained, "things in the Garden tended to take care of themselves. I was merely the caretaker."

"Our Creator, God the Father, the Son, and the Holy Spirit, are all very capable of getting things done on Their Own. But They decided to create human beings to take care of everything on the Earth for Them. God also created us to have fellowship with Him so He could bless and enjoy us." Adam paused as a twinkling flash came forward to ask a question.

"Father Adam," Darwin respectfully asked. "What was it like being the only one of your kind on Earth, you and Mother Eve?"

Adam looked at the pre-born spirit, long ago memories in his eyes.

"By the time God created Eve," he began, "I had already named all the animals and plant life. He had given me a grand home to live in, a place I could go into each evening at the end of my day's work to relax and enjoy. I was able to communicate with all the animals. It was interesting listening to them," he chuckled quietly.

"I had a dog named Erasmus. He kept me company as I walked the Earth taking care of all God had provided for me. Each and every day I spent many hours talking to God about the things He wanted me to do on the Earth. At the time, I was the only one of my kind and the Earth was huge. So one day God made a decision to give me a mate, one who would help me tend the Garden and populate the Earth. That's when He created Mother Eve," Adam continued, thinking back to when God brought Eve to him.

"She was and is the most beautiful of all God's creation. When I saw her I knew she was what had been missing in my life," Adam stated, staring out into space as he thought of getting to know the woman who had been created just for him.

"Children," he said, "when you are allowed to go to the Earth, know that God has created someone just for you. No, not in the same way He created Eve and me.

Nevertheless, God has someone especially for you." Adam concluded his talk with the pre-borns.

Angel Fonorel came forward to thank the ancient man as he walked off into eternity. As he turned to leave, a beautiful young-looking woman took his hand. It was Eve. She had the loveliest mane of shiny white hair flowing down her back.

The pre-born spirits all drew their attention back to the angel as he spoke.

"Children, when you become a part of the Earth-realm, you will have many instances of learning about the things Father Adam has just told you. On the Earth, these lessons will be classified as *ancient* history . . ."

"Angel," interrupted William. "Will we remember any of what Father Adam just told us when we enter the Earth-realm?"

"No, William, you will not," answered Angel Fonorel. "You will be in a learning phase when you reach the Earth. Although Heaven will be ingrained in you, you will have to learn all about God the Father, the Son, and the Holy Spirit as you grow up on the Earth. When you return here for the Judgment Seat of God, the previous knowledge you learned here will be returned to you. God chooses to send you down to the Earth as an infant," he explained. "Some of you will be called to preach the things you will learn here. Some will be writers. Unfortunately, some of you will turn away from everything you will learn here, but God has a purpose for it all. Let's now prepare for our next speaker," Angel Fonorel said as the pre-born spirits became restless from having to pay attention for so long.

TWENTY-FOUR

So, what's the point of learning all this stuff?" John interrupted sulkily. "We won't be able to use any of it . . ."

"John," thundered a voice, cutting off the complaints of the pre-born spirit. Though not completely familiar, this voice had been heard by the pre-borns before. It only spoke occasionally. When it did, the pre-borns shuddered.

"You are being taught these things because Almighty God has ordained that you be taught these things," the Apostle said authoritatively, no room for misunderstanding or argument. "You Earthbound pre-born spirits have an opportunity to go to the Earth. Your assignments are not only to populate the Earth but also to be ministers for the Kingdom of God while you are there," he clarified. "These classes you participate in now are simply to bring before you the things you will participate in and be witnesses to on the Earth."

The Apostle looked at the pre-born spirits with stern love and much joy in his eyes as he spoke.

"My children, I must tell you a story. It is a true-life story about a man that lived on the Earth whose name was Saul. He attended what were classified as the best schools taught by the most anointed teachers, teachers such as Masters Gamaliel and Nicodemus," the man-spirit told the pre-born spirits as he walked before them. "Born into a good family by the grace of the Almighty, his family was able to send him to the best, most prestigious schools of all time. He was fervent for the Word of God, even to the point," the Apostle indicated sadly, "of causing many people to suffer because he was fervently wrong. This man Saul believed that the teachings he followed were the right ones. And they were . . . in theory. But they left out the element of the Son, Jesus Christ. God is merciful and He is faithful, John," he said directly to the pre-born spirit.

His inattentive pre-born mind had drifted away from what the Apostle said to the other pre-born spirits. The little spirit became more alert as the Apostle continued, "One day during the old days on Earth as this man Saul walked with his companions toward the city of Damascus, Jesus Christ, the Son, met him and turned his life around. Saul found out who Jesus was. The Son showed Saul that, while he was persecuting Jesus's followers, he was also going against God, not serving God at all. Saul was devastated and blinded by the truth of Jesus Christ. Saul came to the harsh conclusion that he had persecuted Christ's followers because it felt good to his flesh. He also realized that his flesh profited him nothing. Saul understood he needed to return to being a spiritual creature."

The spirits looked on in wonder as the Apostle explained these deep things.

"You will not remember any of what you are being taught right now. Nonetheless, these things are important," the Apostle continued in his soothing voice. "Children, God has done everything for a purpose—to bring glory to His Kingdom and to bring order into the world. As you see below on the Earth, lives are in chaos because of the sin on the Earth. This is the reason God sent His Son Jesus to save the world. When I was a boy on the Earth," the Apostle reminisced, "I was taught that a Messiah would come. Unfortunately, we took our own preconceived notions and decided who and what this Messiah would be and do for the world. We were the Pharisees. But when I came into the knowledge of God's truth, it revolutionized my way of thinking. I was required to turn from what I realized were my wicked ways and turn to God's ways."

The spirits were very quiet as Apostle Paul shared about his life on the Earth.

"You see, before I became Apostle Paul, I was the man Saul. When Jesus appeared to me," the Apostle explained quietly, tears glistening in his eyes, "He completely changed my life. He showed me Who He was and what He had done for me through His death on the cross. Needless to say, I was appalled by all the havoc I had created for His followers. I immediately asked for forgiveness. He forgave me," the Apostle concluded.

The pre-born spirits let out a collective breath as the Apostle concluded his story, his robes glistening brightly.

"Apostle Paul," Emmanuelle came forward excitedly to ask a question of this powerful saint. "Apostle, will the same thing happen to us?" The inquisitive pre-born wanted to know. "Will we meet Jesus in the same way when we go to live on the Earth for a season?"

"Spirit, only Almighty God knows the time and the season of your salvation on the Earth. At some point, each of you will have a day of reckoning in which you will either choose to walk with the Lord or choose to walk away from Him. Nevertheless, a decision must be made," the Apostle explained as he walked away from the gathering.

The pre-born spirits applauded respectfully as the aged Apostle walked away from their gathering. *What a powerful speaker*, many of the pre-borns thought. What an awesome opportunity to hear from one who had endured so much during his season on the Earth!

Angel Fonorel resumed instructing the pre-borns. Even though they were in eternity, there was so much to learn and so little time to learn it. The speakers they listened to and the things they were told were a portion of Heaven that would be instilled into their very essences. Although they wouldn't remember the things they were being taught, these testimonies were a part of their makeup. These lessons would guide their actions if allowed.

Many Returned Saints were slated to teach the pre-born spirits about life on the Earth. The next speaker the pre-borns were assigned to hear was Prophet Isaiah.

TWENTY-FIVE

H e strode decisively into the History Chamber, robes glistening and swinging as he quickly moved toward the front of the amphitheater.

"Praise the Most High God, pre-born spirits," Prophet Isaiah said with a very warm and welcoming voice. Tall and slender, the presence of the man-spirit filled the chamber as his voice boomed the greeting to the pre-born spirits.

"Hallelujah!" returned the excited chorus of pre-born spirits.

"Very well, then. Let us begin," Isaiah said. "I was a prophet of the Most High God during my sojourn on the Earth. God allowed me to see many of His miraculous works. He also allowed me to see the destruction of many of His people. It does not please God to destroy His own people, the chosen of Israel. However, as the people of God decide they will do as they please, God is so inclined to allow many destructions to fall upon them," Isaiah explained to the pre-borns. "Almighty God sends His prophets into the world with words of grace, mercy, righteousness, and judgment. Judah and Jerusalem fell away from God so badly, it became difficult to distinguish between those who were called by the name of God and those who were not. God willingly gives full mercy and grace to those who seek His face. He stood ready to help Judah and Jerusalem become clean if they were willing to put away their evil doings from before His holy eyes, bless His name. But they would not," the Prophet continued sadly. "They desired to seek their own way so as to not be hindered from doing the will of their flesh. Now, considering you will not remember these things when you go to the Earth as children, you may ask why the other prophets and I have been commissioned to tell you these things. These are events that have occurred through the annals of time, the history you will be exposed to. Jehovah God desires that you know about these things so you will understand the goings-ons of the Earth you will inhabit," explained Prophet Isaiah.

"Prophet, Prophet," called a voice in the midst of the other pre-borns.

Pre-born spirit Beverley glowed brightly as she sought to get the attention of Prophet Isaiah. When he acknowledged her, she asked, "Did you see God while you were on the Earth?"

"Ah, a very good question, Beverley," he assured the pre-born. "God gave me a vision of Himself. *In the year that king Uzziah died, I saw also the Lord sitting upon a throne, high and lifted up, and His train filled the temple. Above the throne stood the seraphims and each one had six wings. With twain he covered his face; and with twain he covered his feet, and with twain did he fly. And one cried unto another, and said, Holy, holy, holy, is the Lord of hosts: the whole earth is full of His glory. And the posts of the door moved at the voice of Him that cried, and the house was filled with smoke,"* explained Prophet Isaiah.

All the pre-born spirits listened in awe as the commanding voice of Isaiah shared the vision.

"Prophet Isaiah," called out James. "Will we have the same vision of God? Why won't we be able to see God in the Earth as we see Him now, Prophet?"

"Brother Isaiah, may I answer the pre-born's questions?" interrupted another booming voice.

All the pre-born spirits shifted their attention to the owner of the new voice entering the chamber. An ancient that the pre-borns saw quite frequently in the presence of the Divine Trio, they immediately knew who their next speaker would be—the great Prophet Moses. The two Returned Saints embraced with brotherly love as Prophet Isaiah relinquished the teaching podium.

"Pre-borns, I entreated the Lord our God to show His glory to me. Almighty Jehovah God said He would make all His goodness pass before me and He would proclaim His name, the name of the Lord, before me. He proclaimed that He would be gracious to whom He would be gracious, and He would show mercy upon whom He would show mercy. But Almighty God also told me I would not be able to see His face because of His holiness. You see, pre-borns, no person can see the face of the Lord and live. The main reason God the Father sent Jesus Christ the Son to the Earth was so God could be among His creation in a form His people could look upon without losing their life from seeing His glory. God is so gracious, pre-borns!

Glory to His name!" Moses exclaimed. "While you are here before your Earth-existence, you are allowed to see the glory of God at all times because you are spirit and able to see the glory of His spirit. When you go to the Earth, you will be in human form as I was. In that form, you will not be able to see the spiritual form of God because the form will be invisible to you. But you will be able to see the glory of God in the evidence of all His creation, in the other humans you will be surrounded with, and nature. You yourself will be a manifestation of the glory of God in the Earth," Prophet Moses explained to the pre-borns.

The pre-born spirits were ecstatic. They were hearing from witnesses who had already gone to the Earth and done some of the same things they would do when it was their season to go to the Earth. There were many more voices to come that they needed to hear from. God Almighty wanted them to know that their life on Earth would not always be one of joy and happiness.

TWENTY-SIX

P re-born spirits," said the Apostle, returning to introduce the next witness to be heard by the pre-borns. "If you will remember, I shared with you my story of when I was on the Earth. Before God gave me the name 'Paul,' I was Saul. I made havoc of the church, entering into every house and haling men and women, committing them to prison. I gained special permission to go and find those who called on the name of Jesus and to bring them bound unto Jerusalem. I was determined to stop the new religion of Jesus Christ. I breathed out threatenings and slaughter against the disciples of the Lord," the Apostle informed the pre-born spirits. "I held the cloaks of the people who stoned to death your next speaker," the Apostle said tearfully. "Thank God for His mercy and grace. For even after all the things I did to hinder the growth of the Kingdom of God and to persecute His people, God forgave me," Apostle Paul explained, humbly bowing his silvery head. "I listened to the same words of the man you are about to hear, but because my heart was hard, I did not receive his words. Now, pre-borns, receive ye the words of Stephen, one who gave his life for the Word of Truth," the Apostle proclaimed, stepping back and allowing Stephen to address the pre-born spirits.

"*The Lord is my light and my salvation; whom shall I fear? The Lord is the strength of my life; of whom shall I be afraid?* The words of King David are words that shall stand the test of time, my soon-to-be brothers and sisters. Many of you shall choose the good thing, the Word of Truth. Many of you shall turn away but will be afforded the opportunity to receive the Word of Truth many times during your sojourn on the Earth. I am Stephen, chosen and appointed to be a deacon during my season of life on the Earth. I was called to go forth and minister the gospel of Jesus Christ. Almighty God used me to perform great wonders and miracles among the people. My calling and appointment were not without cost, though," Stephen explained. "Falsely accused because the words I spoke pricked the hearts of the listeners, I was brought before the council. Their final verdict was to stone me to death. But, my friends, if God Almighty were to ask me to do it again, I would gladly do it all again for the glory of the Kingdom of God," Stephen declared joyously.

"The life you will live on the Earth will be very fulfilling if you have God as the foundation of all that you do. The Word of God is Truth. It is living and able to sustain you through all manner of trial and tribulation. Although you will not remember the very important lessons you are being taught before your season on the Earth, Heaven will be in your heart and in your spirit because this is where you were created. Though man will continually attempt to convince you that there is no God, you will know deep within that there is only one God—Almighty God," concluded Stephen.

He stepped away from the History podium as Angel Fonorel respectfully ushered in the remaining speakers for this segment of history lessons for the pre-born spirits. These great saints of the Most High God were anxious and excited to share the knowledge they had obtained on the Earth with those destined to go to the Earth in their seasons.

"Almighty God has *set thee over the nations and over the kingdoms, to root out; and to pull down, and to destroy, and to throw down, to build, and to plant*," Prophet Jeremiah quietly said to the assembly of pre-born spirits. "Do not think it strange that God has called into manifestation your existence on the Earth. God's thoughts are not the thoughts of man, neither are His ways the ways of man. For as the Heavens are higher than the Earth, so are God's ways higher than the ways of man and His thoughts than man's thoughts. These words from Prophet Isaiah will be relevant in each of the seasons to which you are assigned. God's Word will not return to Him empty. Each Word He utters from His Spirit will *accomplish that which He pleases and shall prosper in the thing whereto He sent it*," assured Prophet Jeremiah. "During my stay on the Earth, I was a prophet. God predetermined my lot in life before He sent me into the womb of the woman who birthed me into the Earth," this prophet explained with fervor. "He ordained me, He anointed me, He appointed me for the work of the Kingdom of God. I was persecuted because I was obedient to God. Many of the people God sent to fight against me did not prevail because God was with me to deliver me," Jeremiah continued zealously, moving to the side of the assembly as the next speaker approached.

"*The law of the Lord is perfect, converting the soul. The testimony of the Lord is sure, making wise the simple. The statutes of the Lord are right, rejoicing the heart. The commandment of the Lord is pure, enlightening the eyes. The fear of the Lord is clean, enduring forever. The judgments of the Lord are true and righteous altogether,*" spoke the voice of the saint known as King David. As he spoke the words of the psalm God had given to him, he smiled at the pre-born spirits as they listened with rapt attention.

"When you enter the Earth-realm, spirits, you will be surrounded by many voices telling you that there is no God. Rest assured, pre-borns! God has sent His testimony into the Earth so that all who are willing and all who are seeking may find Him. *Blessed is the man that walketh not in the counsel of the ungodly, nor standeth in the way of sinners, nor sitteth in the seat of the scornful. But his delight is in the law of the Lord; and in His law doth he meditate day and night. And he shall be like a tree planted by the rivers of water, that bringeth forth his fruit in his season; his leaf also shall not wither; and whatsoever he doeth shall prosper,*" David continued. "Verily I say unto you, children, that when you come into the knowledge of the truth of the Word of God, you will be blessed beyond measure. God will plant you in the place He desires for you to be. You will be as the tree planted by the rivers of water. You will bring forth fruit in your seasons and your fruit will last forever," David concluded.

Angel Fonorel stepped before the assembly of pre-born spirits again as David concluded his portion of the lesson. "Let these words of wisdom and truth sink deep into your spirits," he advised. "You will not remember these words when you enter the Earth-realm as infants. These words will come to you throughout time as you live your life and fulfill the purpose for which God is sending you to the Earth. God will watch over you to fulfill His Word for your life. He will surround you with His Holy Guardian Angels to protect you. Be encouraged, pre-born spirits! God will be with you always," Angel Foronel concluded as he moved the pre-born spirits to the next phase of their training.

Beverley

TWENTY-SEVEN

In the Unseen . . .

Despair laughed mockingly at the petite young colored woman as he floated in the atmosphere above her head. She was so gullible.

"Hmmmph," he scoffed as he invited Misery and Hopelessness to join him in worsening the situation for Anna.

Despair had been with Anna for many years. Yet she had never recognized his devices. Saturating her life with many of his associates—Misery, Desolation, Hopelessness, Anguish, and others—gave Despair pleasure beyond measure. He reveled in filling this young woman's life with more of himself.

Pouring more of his character into this traumatic situation, he laughed zealously as he encouraged his minions to dig deeper with this one. *This could be the very thing to push this poor foolish soul over the edge*, he thought as he rubbed his gnarled hands together.

Despair was not alone. He shared the atmosphere clouding this situation with Anger, Pride, and Self-Righteousness, three demons that had followed Leon Scott for a very long time.

Since being on his own, away from his family in South Carolina, Leon had allowed these three felons from Heaven free reign in his life. Handsome and with the gift of gab in his arsenal, Leon manipulated others to do his bidding with much self-confidence and no remorse. Pride urged him to go the extra mile to get whatever he wanted from whomever he wanted it. Leon willingly complied.

Anna was an easy mark for Leon. He skillfully used his charm to get precisely what he wanted from her. From the moment they met on the D train to Coney Island, Leon knew she would be an easy conquest for him. His instincts had paid off.

Now that he had, though, the thrill of victory had dulled. He was finished with her. He was now ready to move on to his next conquest. With the help of his mother, Beulah, who had flown all the way from Georgia, Leon knew he would be able to start another chapter in his life.

Self-Righteousness deftly influenced Leon and his mother, causing them to believe they were better than young Anna. Looking around the apartment the young woman occupied with her children, Self-Righteousness made sure that Beulah could clearly see that her granddaughter was too good to live in such a hovel. He eagerly persuaded Beulah to not allow that to happen.

And then there was Anger. This demonic presence forged a foothold over the entire situation in the midst of these three emotionally charged adults. Anger called on his associates Antagonism and Resentment to help in the confrontation so he could maintain his position of strength.

Brooklyn, New York: May 21, 1959

"Leon," Anna shouted. "How could you do this to me? Why are you taking my baby, our daughter, away from me?" she asked, tears flowing down her cheeks.

"He's not doing anything to you, girl," said Mrs. Beulah Scott. She was ready to take her new granddaughter out of this filthy dwelling and away from New York. She had already seen enough.

"Child, you have already given him the baby. And you're doing the best thing by giving the baby to her father's family. My son will not be able to care for her. His father and I are better able to take care of her. Just think. She will have a better chance in life in South Carolina," Beulah said convincingly to Anna while thinking in her heart, *Away from you.*

Anna contemplated for a moment. She knew what this meant. Although she had planned to get a divorce so she could marry Leon, she knew in her heart of hearts that Leon had no intention of marrying her. Mother Scott had just confirmed this notion.

"You already have two other children and are married to someone else. I will not allow any grandchild of mine to live under your roof in these conditions," Beulah replied arrogantly to the sobbing young woman.

Beulah, Beuly to most, had had just about enough out of her eldest son, Leon Heyward Scott. *Already married and divorced by age twenty-seven. Now here he is having babies out of wedlock*, she disgustedly thought to herself, *with a married woman, if that didn't beat all!*

She already had one granddaughter whom she seldom saw because of the bad blood between Leon and his ex-wife. This child would not be lost to her, too. She would take this baby back to South Carolina and raise her as her own if she had to.

When he had called her and his daddy, Otis, to tell them he had messed around with a girl and gotten her pregnant, Beulah shook her head. *What was that boy thinking?* she wondered. She didn't know why he had to go away from South Carolina and live in New York anyway. There was nothing but fast women from the South up there. She didn't want him bringing just anything into the family.

Beulah felt sorry for this young woman she was meeting for the first time that day. Nice enough and pretty enough even though she was dark-skinned, she needed to get her act together. No man wanted to take care of somebody else's children. Beulah was not going to allow her son to be a scapegoat-father for Anna's other two children.

Baby Beverley was gorgeous. She had the prettiest light skin and jet-black curly hair on her tiny head. Beuly was going to go ahead and take this baby with her to South Carolina. She couldn't see leaving her here with this young woman. She classified Anna as hot and fast, having baby after baby by her husband and with other men.

"Come on, June-bug," she decisively called her son's nickname as she turned to leave the dingy rooms Anna called home. Beulah glared pityingly at the crying young woman, tears streaming down her face as she reached for her child.

"Honey," Beulah said to Anna as she turned away. "Get your life together. My son's not going to marry you because of a baby. I will not allow it. He's not going to raise your other two children just to raise his own, either. I will see to that," she said flatly, haughtily exiting the apartment.

Beulah quickly left with only the baby. As nasty as that place was, she didn't want to take anything with her from the apartment except the baby. But she had to admit—as filthy as the apartment appeared, the baby was clean and smelled like a baby should.

She wondered what ran through her son's mind as he went about with these fast young women. Lord knows he had been brought up better than that! She did not raise her children to be fast or slick. They had done a good job of picking that up by themselves.

Pleading with Leon, Anna let out a loud, forlorn wail. She never imagined she would allow this man to talk her into giving up her child after she had worked so hard to get him. Life was so unfair! She knew God was angry with her. What was she going to do?

"No, Leon, please! Don't let your mama take our baby! Please! I'll do whatever you want me to do," Anna begged desperately, running behind them out of the apartment to the second floor landing.

Leon looked at this woman in disgust. He wondered to himself why he had stayed with her for so long. How could he tell her she was just a fling to him? That he had only spent time with her to break up the monotony of life here in New York? A fling only long enough until he found the woman he really wanted to be with.

"Look, Anna. Let me go take Mama back to my place. I promise," he said, knowing he was lying. "I promise I'll talk her into changing her mind. She just wants what's best for our daughter," Leon explained, looking over her head into the dingy apartment Anna called home.

His skin crawled from just being here. Leon decided to say whatever it took to make her believe him and to get her to let go of his arm. Slowly, she let go of his arm. She knew Leon was fibbing to her, he always had. But she had to have some hope. She couldn't just lose her baby *and* him. She couldn't.

Silently hanging her head, she forced herself to act as though she believed him. "OK. Call me, hear?" she called as he went down the steps to his mother and their child.

Anna wondered if she would ever again see the beautiful little girl she had birthed. Her heart ached as she longed to feel that baby back in her arms. Why had this happened to her? Was God so angry with her that He would allow such a horrible thing to happen in her life? *God must really hate me*, she thought, wiping the tears from her eyes.

Leon didn't know it but she had already had one child taken from her—her oldest son Willis. She'd had five-year-old Willis with a guy from North Carolina she was going steady with when she left Virginia.

Edward Mullins had come to New York and gotten him about five months ago. Eddie said he wanted to take Willis for a visit with his family. When they arrived in Reedsville, Eddie sent word back to Anna that he was keeping his son and not bringing him back. Now it was just her and three-year-old Gwen. What was she going to do?

Returning to her dingy one-bedroom apartment, Anna peered into the bedroom to check on her toddler. She discovered that Gwen had slept through all the shouting and crying.

"Thank God for small favors," she muttered halfheartedly as she locked the door and left the apartment.

Quickly running outside to the pay phone, Anna saw Leon's car just as it turned the corner away from her street. Needing someone to talk to, Anna rushed to call her sister Evelyn who lived in Flushing. Though younger, Evelyn was so much wiser. She would know exactly what to do.

Anna's tears returned as she fumbled to place the nickel into the slot of the payphone. Closing the door of the booth behind her, Anna considered her situation. Here she was, twenty-four years old in Brooklyn with three babies . . . well, one now. Three years ago, she had married Horace Horton, Gwen's dad, when he moved to New York briefly to find work. Almost as soon as little Gwen was born, Horace went back to Virginia. He said he couldn't stand living in New York with Anna and he didn't want a baby in the first place. Heartbroken, Anna went on a campaign to find her one true love. She thought it was Leon.

Anna knew she hadn't been raised this way, *no*! But real life sure is different from being sheltered while growing up. She couldn't wait to leave Virginia six years ago when she turned eighteen. Riding the Greyhound bus out of Richmond, Anna had told herself she would never return to Virginia. She was going to have fun. Her plan was to go to nursing school and then marry a doctor. She knew she could do that in New York. The city was so open and free, with none of the prejudices of Virginia and the South. She was going to have a blast! But all that was ruined.

When she arrived in New York, she discovered she was pregnant with Willis. Not wanting to get an abortion, she called the baby's father and discovered he had already moved on in the two months she had been gone. And now . . .

The phone rang twice before Evelyn picked up, stopping Anna's reverie.

"Hello," Evelyn answered gaily as she picked up the receiver.

"Evvie," Anna sobbed into the phone, allowing the built-up sadness to overtake her once again as she thought of her dilemma.

"Mae? Mae? Mae!" shouted Evelyn into the phone, realizing it was her sister.

She pitied her sister raising three, now two, kids alone. She had tried to warn Anna Mae to leave that Leon alone—he was no good. Unfortunately, sometimes we have to learn by our own mistakes.

"They took her," Anna sobbed dejectedly. "They took my baby."

"What do you mean?" asked Evelyn, becoming more upset as her sister poured out her story.

"Leon's mother came from South Carolina and took Beverley," Anna sobbed.

"Mae," Evelyn said frantically. "Go home. I will be there shortly." Evelyn hung up quickly. She turned to the man calmly sitting waiting for her to get off the phone. When she looked into his face, she saw something there she hadn't noticed before. What was it? Pride? Self-confidence? She couldn't put her finger on it.

"Richard, you didn't tell me your mother was here in New York," she said calmly to Leon's younger brother.

They had started seeing each other at the same time as their older siblings. She liked Richard well enough, she just didn't trust him. He was a shyster. She could see through the façade he had built around himself. She wished her older sister could see the same thing about Leon.

"Oh, yea," he replied, off-handedly. "She came up to see the baby, that's all," he said, shifting his eyes.

Evelyn had watched Richard for almost two years now. She knew when he was lying or evading the truth. The only reason she hung out with him was because he was always up for a good time and he was handsome. But now . . .

"Oh, really. Just to see? Not to take?" she asked sweetly, knowing he was playing a game with her. She wasn't having any of it.

"Well, I don't know what she and Leon had planned . . ." he started, a sly smile forming on his lips.

"You're telling a story," Evelyn accused. "I can see it written all over your face. What has your brother done?" she asked, sitting heavily on the chair behind her, incredulous at the deceit going on behind her and her sister's backs.

"Look, Evvie," Richard started to explain. "You're a good girl. You have a nice apartment, a good job. I enjoy being with you, but look at your sister. She's got three kids she can't even take care of. All three are by different men. She lives in a pigsty. You know as well as I do that she tried to trap my brother with this baby," he spoke to her rationally.

"But . . ." Evelyn began, wanting to come to the defense of her sister. She loved Anna dearly but knew Richard spoke the truth.

"Wait, Evvie, let me finish," Richard said. "When Leon told Mama and Daddy about Mae, the baby, and the other two kids, they were fit to be tied. My brother had already messed up with his first wife. He had a kid with her and then got divorced. Mama barely sees his oldest daughter! He told Mama how bad Mae was living. Mama couldn't let her grandchild come up like that. So, yes, Mama came to get the baby. But first, Mae gave the baby to Leon, Evelyn. She gave Beverley to him."

While Richard explained, Evelyn cried softly. She felt sorry for her sister but also knew she couldn't change things for her. Anna Mae had to want to change herself. Anna was very headstrong and thought she knew it all. She claimed to know what she was doing, which Evelyn doubted. All she could do was be there for her sister.

"Richard, I understand," she told her friend calmly, wiping the tears from her face. "Could you take me over to my sister's place, please?" she asked. Evelyn knew she would have to help her sister overcome this stage in her life.

TWENTY-EIGHT

LaGuardia Airport, New York

"Son, you are going to have to do better than this," Beulah advised her eldest son. "You can't continue running around with fast women and expect God to bless you for it," she scolded as they walked through the airport toward the boarding gate.

"I'll do better, Mama. I promise," Leon replied as though on cue.

He hadn't meant for this to happen, Anna Mae getting pregnant. He just wanted to have a good time. After all, he had just gotten a divorce and wasn't looking to settle down again yet. Anna Mae was just a distraction he had allowed to go too far.

Beulah didn't know if any of what she said sunk in to Leon's brain. Leon had left home at eighteen and enlisted in the Army for three years. When he came home, he met his now ex-wife Leona, married her, had a daughter, and divorced within four years. Beulah didn't know why they hadn't gotten along. Leona was a good girl from a good family in North Augusta, South Carolina.

Her family was Christian. They all had good jobs. She was a nice light-skinned girl with good hair, just the type of girl Beulah wanted her sons to marry. And her younger son Richard was no better.

136

Every time she looked around, one girl or another claimed to be pregnant by Richard. He probably thought she didn't know his real reason for leaving South Carolina. It was rumored that Richard had at least three babies on the way. He didn't want to take responsibility for any of them.

My goodness, Beulah thought. What was wrong with her children? Especially her sons? Boarding the plane with her pretty little granddaughter in her arms, she thought about the life this child would lead. Instinctively, she knew Beverley would be a smart child—she could see it in her sleeping face.

She might darken up a bit, Beulah pondered. But she hoped Beverley would never be as dark as her mother. *What was June-bug thinking? Messing around with that dark-skinned young woman? And with two children already!*

Lord, have mercy on my children, she prayed silently. She and Otis had not raised their children to act this way. They knew the facts of life—be good or you will suffer. It was just as pure and simple as that.

As the plane took off, Beulah settled back in her seat with the still-sleeping baby. After leaving that nasty little apartment in Brooklyn, she and Leon went to Sears and Roebuck and purchased everything she needed to take care of the baby between New York and Georgia—a couple changes of clothes, diapers, blankets, bottles, and powdered milk. She was set and very glad she hadn't taken anything from that young woman's place. She didn't need to take *anything* with her from New York except the child.

Eternity

"Father, why have You decided to not permit Beverley to grow up with her biological mother?" the Son asked Almighty God. Watching the situation play out below Them on the Earth, He felt compassion for the woman Anna Mae.

"My Son, if We were to allow Beverley to grow up in New York with the rest of her siblings, she would not turn out the way We need for her to turn out," Almighty God explained.

"I have ordained this one to be a mighty warrior for My Kingdom. She will go through many trials and tribulations on the Earth. These things are needed so she will be able to stand firm and do what I have called her to do."

"Will she ever see her biological mother and siblings again?" Jesus wondered aloud.

"Yes, she will, My Son. However, it will be much later in her life. She will go to many places and do many things before she will meet them. At one point in her life, she will completely turn away from that side of her family. But she will turn back to them and bring salvation into their lives," explained the Father.

As she slept in her grandmother's arms, Almighty God and His Son continued to observe Beverley. Beulah Scott would learn to love and dislike this child before it was all over. But it would be this child who would be her salvation as well.

TWENTY-NINE

Bush Field Airport, Augusta, Georgia

Beulah stepped from the plane in an already sweltering Augusta, Georgia. She saw her husband Otis and their daughters Cassie, Barbara Anne, and Lila waving through the windows of the Bush Field Airport terminal. June-bug had called Otis the night before to let him know her arrival time with his four-month-old daughter.

Stepping into the baggage area with baby Beverley, the girls clambered around Beulah trying to get the first glance of the little bundle.

"Aww," said Barbara Anne. "She is so pretty, Mama. Look at how light she is!"

For only the second time since Beulah had taken her from her mother, the little girl opened her eyes.

"Oh my," said Otis. "Look at those pretty brown eyes." He watched as the baby focused on the five faces surrounding her. She glanced from one to the other as she seemed to consider who these people were and why she was here.

Then she looked up into Mama's face and smiled.

"Ummph, must be gas," said a smiling Beulah, explaining away the baby's smile.

"No, Mama," said Cassie, the eldest girl. "I think she's really smiling, like she knows she is supposed to be here."

Beulah glanced at the baby girl again, bundling her up to take her home. She was determined to not let anything happen to this child. And if she had to keep this little one away from her daddy, then that was what she would do. Her son was making some very poor decisions. She wouldn't join him in his mistakes but she would take care of the mistake he had already made.

In the Unseen . . .

Many sets of eyes watched as the baby and her entourage moved through the airport to the waiting car. These demons had been alerted from the moment of conception of this little one. She was one who needed to be destroyed immediately before she could wreak havoc on the kingdom of darkness.

Destruction, Ignorance, Abuse, and Rebellion surrounded the family. They were biding their time until they heard the clarion call from the Seat of Darkness to go in and do what they were called to do. They had each already prepared their associated demons that stood ready to do the bidding of darkness. Fortunately, they were not the only eyes watching this precious one.

High above in the atmosphere surrounding the child and her family, Wisdom, Understanding, and Knowledge soared through the skies as they trailed the vehicle bearing this soon-to-be warrior for the Kingdom of Heaven. They were joined by Protector and Comforter who constantly traveled between the Throne of Grace and the Earth bearing instructions on how they would keep this little one until the time appointed.

These angelic presences knew that time was of the essence. Being under authority, they also knew that their time was not their own. Their time belonged to the Creator of Time, Almighty God. He alone would be the decision-maker on when things would happen according to His time for this child.

Joyce

THIRTY

In the Unseen . . .

Condemnation flitted around Marie Jones' head as she rode the train with her twins toward the Atlanta Amtrak station. He knew which buttons to push with this one. Feelings of condemnation had steadily built in this young woman from before her pregnancy until the present time. The feelings had not diminished in any way.

Guilt and Despair also dogged her every step each time she spoke with her loving parents without telling them what had occurred in her life. Each time she hung up the phone from speaking with them, she felt dirty. She knew of no way to wash herself clean from the guilt she felt.

Once Despair sunk into her spirit, it seemed that all hope was lost. She knew her parents loved her. Unfortunately, she didn't believe that love was strong enough for them to forgive her for the indiscretion that would bring so much shame to her family.

Now that this young woman was on her way home for the celebration of the life of their mortal enemy Jesus Christ, Condemnation, Guilt, and Despair persistently waged their attack against her so she would have no peace in finally coming clean about what had happened in her life.

Atlanta, Georgia: December 21, 1961

"Mama, I'm at the train station," Marie Jones told her mother when she called from the Atlanta Amtrak station.

She was scared to death! Jeffrey and Joyce were now six months old and quite a handful. During the trip down South, many of Marie's fellow passengers had pitched in when both the twins cried from hunger or just needed attention while their mother was busy with the other.

One lady came to Marie's rescue several times. She thought Marie had left her husband in New York while she took the babies home for Christmas. Marie didn't correct the woman. Feeling very condemned, Marie thought the lady would condemn her as well.

She loved those little twins with all her heart. Each had his or her own separate personality. Marie was amazed that they both could be so different and yet have come from the same womb. She thought about herself and her brothers and sisters and could only remember the sameness they all shared. But these two . . .

Marie still hadn't found the heart or courage to tell her parents about her children. As many times as she had spoken with her siblings, she hadn't told any of them either because of the shame. *When does the shame end?* she wondered. Marie felt as though the burden of shame would be hers to carry alone for the rest of her life.

After having the twins in June, Marie had struggled to survive in New York City. Becoming friends with several other single mothers, one of them offered to baby-sit when she went back to work. The only price she charged was groceries and snacks for all the children.

Marie spoke with her parents often but always made sure to call them while she was at work. She didn't want to risk them hearing the babies. Desperately missing her family, she finally worked up the courage to go home at Christmas. This was the one time of the year when they all came together to celebrate the birth of Jesus Christ and family. Marie hoped everyone would be so caught up in the Christmas spirit that not too much would be said about the shame and disappointment she had brought into the family.

"Ree," her mother said, calling her by her nickname. "Daddy's on his way there now. He should be about there, honey," Ethel Jones informed her daughter. Excitement filled her voice since she hadn't seen her youngest child for almost two years.

Ethel and Homer had planned to visit Marie in New York several times. Those plans were quickly canceled by Marie with one excuse after another. First, she was taking some classes she needed to advance in her job as a paralegal. Then she had to go out of state for training for the same advancement. Marie's ultimate goal was to become an attorney.

Finally, Marie's parents decided they would wait until she came home. They knew she was all right. She was just a young girl away from home for the first time and probably really enjoying her newfound freedom. They trusted her and felt good that she was making her way in the world.

Marie took a deep breath, deciding to break the news to her mom before she arrived home with the babies. Marie loved her mother so much. Oh, how she hated to break her heart!

"Mama, I got to tell you something," she began, tears welling up in her eyes. Dread filled Marie's heart as she tried to think of the best way to put what she had to say to her mother.

"Mama, I . . ." She didn't know how to tell her. Yes, she was twenty-two years old and a grown woman. Yes, she was out on her own. But she had shamed herself and her family. How could she tell her?

"Mama," she tried again. This time tears choked her voice. Other than telling her parents she wanted to move to New York by herself, this was the hardest thing Marie had ever contemplated telling her mother. How could she? Maybe she had made a mistake in coming home for Christmas. Maybe . . .

"Honey, what's wrong?" Ethel asked, concern in her voice. "Baby, it's all right," she said, trying to soothe her.

Ethel knew something was wrong. God had woken her early over the past several mornings to pray. By the time she roused herself, Homer was already in the kitchen sitting at the table with a cup of coffee and the Bible. The first morning of the call to pray when Ethel went into the kitchen, she asked her husband, "Honey, what's wrong? Can't sleep?"

"No, Telly," Homer answered, using his pet name for her. "The Lord woke me up to pray for Ree. Something's going on but I don't know what it is. I'm glad she'll be home in a couple of weeks. I miss that child," he shared, deep concern etched across his face.

They prayed together every morning for two weeks, both pouring out their hearts to God concerning their youngest daughter. Their early-morning prayer sessions lasted about one or two hours. When they finished praying, it was already time to get up. Aside from thoughts and worry about their daughter Marie alone in New York, they were refreshed and started their days.

While listening to her daughter on the other end of the line, something flashed through Ethel's mind's eye. Two something's to be more precise. Babies. But that couldn't be. Surely her daughter would have . . .

Well, maybe not. Lafayette, Alabama had its share of out-of-wedlock babies. But none of them had come from Homer and Ethel Jones' children—eight handsome, strapping boys and seven beautiful girls, not a one with a baby out of wedlock. Maybe not until now, Ethel thought.

"Honey, what's wrong," Ethel asked as Marie continued to sob into the phone. "Are you . . . pregnant? Honey, answer me," Ethel said hesitantly, dreading the answer her daughter might give.

"Oh, Mama," Marie sobbed, a faint smile showing through the tears as she thought about her situation. "Mama . . ." Marie shook her head, not wanting to say. "Mama, I have . . . oh God, Mama, I have the babies already. I have twins, a boy and a girl. Mama, I am so sorry," Marie said with a rush, relieved she had finally told but still dreading the outcome of her admission.

Ethel Jones sat down hard, thankful a chair was so close to her. Twins. Twins? Questions flooded her mind. "But Ree, honey, when?" she asked.

"Mama, the babies are . . ." Marie hesitated again, knowing this confession would hurt her mother even more. Hurting her more was the last thing she wanted to do. "Mama, they're six months old," she answered resolutely. It was going to come out when she saw them anyway.

Marie wondered if her parents would ever be able to trust her again. She had gone off to New York to make her way in the world. Her family had all expressed big dreams for her and she had shot those dreams down one by one.

Marie turned around just in time to see her handsome father Homer striding toward her. Oh, how she loved her daddy! As the youngest girl in her family, it seemed as though her daddy had poured all the love he could upon her. Even though he said it wasn't so, everyone knew she was his favorite. Until now . . .

She started to cry into the phone again as she saw him increase his stride toward her. "Mama, Daddy's here. I am so sorry I disappointed you, Mama. I am so sorry . . ." she cried.

Homer grabbed her in a big bear hug that lifted her off the floor. Marie held onto the phone as though it were a lifeline. How could she tell her daddy about the children? *God, please help me!* she whispered in her heart.

She threw her arms around this big burly man she called 'Daddy.' Oh, it felt so good to be in his warm embrace again, to feel his whiskered face against hers. Homer worried as his little girl cried as though her heart were breaking.

"Daddy, oh, Daddy. I'm so sorry," she cried through her tears.

"Baby? Ree, what's wrong?" he asked, worried. He set his daughter back on the floor, the phone receiver still clutched in her little hand. She had forgotten she was talking to her mother.

"Mama, you still there?" she asked. Ethel was crying softly into the phone.

"Baby, I'm still here. Hang up the phone. I'll see you in a little while," she assured her daughter.

Ethel thought back to the flash of the babies in her mind's eye. She was hurt, so hurt, that her youngest daughter had felt she couldn't share this problem with her parents. Even though she and Homer were stern disciplinarians, they had always brought their children up to be honest and straightforward with their parents. How had it come to this?

"Lord," Ethel prayed. "Please help us to love Marie through this time in her life. Father God in the name of Jesus, please help us to love her as you love her, unconditionally, with our whole hearts. Please help her to come through this as gold purged by your fire. Lord, I thank you. In the name of Jesus, I pray. Amen."

After she prayed, Ethel felt better. She wondered, though, how her husband was faring as he faced the truth of Marie's indiscretion.

THIRTY-ONE

Marie hung up the phone and turned to her daddy.

"Daddy, I have something to tell you," she began.

As she pondered the best way to tell her father her secret, flashbacks of childhood ran through her mind. She could remember the many times her brothers and sisters had gotten into trouble and told their parents. She remembered Daddy going out to the woodshed to get a switch from the 'switching' tree when they were younger. As time went on, the switches became belts and the belts became paddles that Daddy made on his workbench. Each of the fifteen Jones children received their fair share of whippings from both Ethel and Homer, Homer being the sternest of all disciplinarians.

Before she could completely formulate what she would tell him, the twins realized they hadn't seen the face of their mother for quite some time.

Joyce, the instigator it seemed, began kicking her legs, causing Jeffrey to cry. As Jeffrey wound up for a good, *'I'm hungry and somebody had better feed me right now!'* cry, Marie turned to her father decisively and said, "Daddy, I've got something to tell you."

Homer followed his daughter's glance as she looked toward the rocking stroller. He had never seen a contraption such as this one. *My goodness*, he thought, *it's big enough to hold . . . two babies!*

He tentatively followed his daughter as she walked over to the stroller. It dawned on him that this was the reason God had gotten him and Ethel up to pray during the early morning hours for the last two weeks—to prepare them for this moment.

"Marie," he said her name, thousands of questions in his eyes. He looked down into the stroller and saw two sets of the deepest, brownest eyes he had ever seen in his life. One of the little things was dressed in blue and the other in pink.

Homer sat on the bench next to the stroller. Joyce and Jeffrey stopped crying long enough to stare back at the eyes staring at them. Grinning toothless grins, their arms and legs flittered about trying to grab the attention of the owner of this new face so they could be picked up.

As Homer considered these babies, he remembered when Marie Anne Jones was born. Both these babies were the spitting image of his precious Ree. His only problem was that he couldn't figure out how she could have had these two beautiful babies without him knowing anything about them.

As Homer turned to her, Marie thought he was going to blast her. Instead, he opened his loving arms to his daughter. Pulling her down onto his lap, tears rolled down his face. He thought of the hardships she must have gone through and must still be going through from trying to care for these two beautiful babies alone.

"Honey," he began, heartbroken but not for the reasons Marie thought. "Why didn't you tell us, Ree? Honey, everyone makes mistakes. We could have helped you," Homer told his daughter as she sat on his lap quietly weeping.

Marie felt even guiltier as she thought of how she had kept these babies from their grandparents in addition to getting pregnant in the first place. Regardless of the mistake she had made, Marie knew her parents would still love these babies, no matter how they had gotten here. She realized she had allowed pride to keep her from allowing her family to help her in the situation she found herself in.

"Daddy, I brought shame to the family. I didn't know what to do. I didn't want you to have to suffer through this because of me," Marie explained.

Homer looked at this brave young woman, his daughter. He remembered when she was eleven and broke her arm falling from a tree she had been told not to climb. Marie walked around for almost two days without telling anyone about her arm. She didn't want to get a whipping as a result of her disobedience.

When she could stand the pain no longer, she told her oldest sister Carrie. Carrie took her to the doctor so their parents wouldn't find out until later in the day. When Homer found out, he whipped Carrie for not telling and promised Marie she would get hers when her arm healed. Marie milked her injury much longer than needed because she hated whippings and would do anything not to get one.

Homer smiled as he thought about that incident. Some things never changed, he realized.

"Honey, we'll make it through this," Homer assured as he set her aside. He reached into the stroller, cradling a twin in each of his massive hands. The twins cooed warmly as they cuddled into the hands belonging to this strange, kind face. They felt at ease with this person and forgot about being fed and picked up. They were receiving the attention they craved.

Homer knew Marie would explain later why she hadn't told anyone about what she was going through. He was hurt because he was just now finding out about these precious grandchildren, hurt because his daughter couldn't find the courage to tell her parents.

Even more hurt because of the reason why she didn't tell them—his reputation as a stern disciplinarian—Homer recognized that his daughter had probably feared admitting what she had done.

That was water under the bridge now. He would not condemn his daughter or these babies. He would love them and help her as much as he possibly could. After all, that's what family was for.

In the Unseen . . .

Condemnation, Guilt, and Despair fervently fought the darkness pulling them away from their once welcoming victim, Marie Anne Jones. They were losing their grip on her mind as she sat with her Earth-father and her children.

"Nooo!" screamed Despair. He had fought so hard to keep this one. He was not interested in losing her, he thought as he scrambled to get a better hold of her mind.

Love, Hope, and Peace settled over the family as the man prayed a quiet prayer of thanksgiving, asking Almighty God for direction as he helped his daughter and these two precious babies. The Hosts of Heaven gathered around the family and pushed back the darkness that had followed the young woman for so long. As light beamed in every direction, the minions of darkness gave up their stronghold and fell away to the pit from which they had come.

Margarette Ann

THIRTY-TWO

In the Unseen, Summitville, Ohio

Angels Candol and Anka stood watch over three-year-old Margarette Ann Wells. Some things had been brewing in and around the Wells household for many days. They observed the demon spirits coming to and going from the Wells farm.

Candol left his post for the briefest of moments to consult with Almighty God in His throne room.

"Almighty, the enemy is building his forces for an attack on this child," he explained. "Should I enlist the aid of more warrior angels at this time, Holy One?" Candol asked respectfully.

"No," answered Almighty God. "The attack is allowed. It is purposed for the strengthening of the family. I will need this family's strength in time to come to be able to send the little one forward," God concluded decisively. God considered the demonic activity proceeding in the household on Earth. Timing was everything in this operation. He dismissed the warrior angel back to his post.

"As You wish, My Lord," replied Angel Candol as he bowed to his King and went back to Earth.

The demonic forces continued to grow. Anka recognized most of the dark angels setting up camp around the farmhouse. In the attic, Destruction had the most prominent vantage point. He barked out orders to the lesser demons. He was the largest of all the demons

"Mischief and Fright," Destruction said gruffly, "set up camp in the girl's room. She has come to an age in which you both can do much damage."

"Yes, my lord," both demons replied obediently. They gleefully set up their battle station in her closet, the place the child hated and feared most.

"CD," called out Destruction to his pet children's imp, Childhood Disease.

He had used this imp much over the centuries to destroy many children. He would use CD to launch an attack on the child this very night.

"Yes, Lord Destruction," the ugly imp answered derisively. He hated children. He would do whatever it took to maim and destroy as many as possible. His body consisted of every childhood disease that had ever plagued the world. He was the embodiment of death for children and very good at his job.

"Set up your station under the child's bed. Begin your destruction of the child tonight," Destruction instructed shortly. "Hit the child with as many diseases as you can muster. We need to totally incapacitate this child before she can do any damage to our master's kingdom."

This child had been targeted from birth by the kingdom of darkness. Satan was present when pre-born spirit Margarette Ann entered the Chamber of Gifts and Talents. He was there again when she spoke with Almighty God prior to being sent to her Earth assignment. Satan was dedicated to ending her before she could begin to fulfill the destiny God had for her. Destruction was willing to help in whatever way he could.

"Anger . . . Abuse . . . Strife," commanded Destruction. "Set up in the master bedroom, the kitchen, and the living room. You will all make your presence known tonight as well," he ordered. "You are to keep the parents in a high state of anger and distract them from helping the child. We must take this child out now," Destruction pointed out determinedly.

Angels Candol and Anka watched and listened from the upper corners of the child's room as the demons set up for a concentrated attack. They had cloaked their position with a holy mantle so the demons could not detect their presence. Suddenly, with a brightness that would have caused a blind person to see, Archangel Michael entered their sheltered area. Immediately, any concerns they shared were calmed.

"Almighty God has dispatched me with a message for you. Fear not, angels of the Most High God, for I have this day touched the hearts of the members of the

Community Church. Even now, they are praying for things they know not of. Be encouraged, for the attack will be ongoing but short-lived. It will not be to the death of any of the inhabitants of this house," said Michael who disappeared as quickly as he had appeared.

Immediately upon Michael's departure, angels Candol and Anka began to pray for the Wells household. Their prayers joined the prayers of the twenty or so saints gathered at the Community Church of Summitville and also the prayers of the Intercessor and His angels in the Heavens.

Summitville Community Church Sanctuary: December 21, 1962

Associate Pastor Dorothy Cooper wrapped up the impromptu Bible study as she prepared those gathered to pray for whatever was attempting to attack their little community.

"The Bible says in James 5:16 that *the effectual, fervent prayer of a righteous man availeth much.* Brothers and sisters, we are the righteousness of God in Christ Jesus. Because of His saving grace we are able to come before the Throne of Grace with boldness and to seek the face of the Lord," she preached. "*Let us therefore come boldly unto the throne of grace that we may obtain mercy and find grace to help in time of need,*" she concluded, motioning for the believers to come forward to pray around the altar. "Sister Lorene," she said to the pianist, "please play some praying music for us." She then gave a wry smile, knowing they were about to enter a heavy time of intercessory prayer.

Dorothy, or Dottie as most called her, had woken up at 3 a.m. with a strong urge to pray. The call was urgent! She almost leaped out of the bed when she realized what was going on. She felt an unsettling in her spirit but couldn't put her finger on the reason.

At 3:15, her phone rang in the kitchen. Immediately, her heart dropped. Calls this early usually meant someone had died. She quickly went through her mind searching to see if anyone was ill or maybe a teenager was out driving somewhere. She couldn't bring anything to mind.

"Hello," she whispered tentatively, quickly answering the phone so as not to awaken her husband Earl who was a light sleeper anyway. Due to get up in about an hour, as hard as he worked, he didn't need any early wake-up calls.

"Dottie, it's me," said the voice on the other end of the line.

"Me" was Clarice Mitchell, head intercessor at Summitville Community Church. Sister Mitchell had orchestrated many amazing prayer conferences over the past ten years. This woman of God was a strong intercessor. She *knew* how to touch the Throne of Grace.

When Dottie realized who it was, she became even more uneasy in her spirit. This was serious.

"Dottie, I had a vision. I saw legions of demons entering town. They were setting up camp to do some real damage," Clarice retold her vision. "As the demons flew over town, they all gathered over one main area but I couldn't tell what area it was," Clarice continued. "But I did see the main demon, Dottie, Destruction," Clarice warned.

Dottie quickly thought back in her prayer history. The last major call for prayer in this town was about ten years ago. It dealt with a busload of children returning from a field trip to Pittsburgh. Bad weather suddenly came up during tornado season and caught the bus on the highway.

God called the prayer warriors together two hours prior to the start of the tornado. They were able to touch the Throne of Grace to waylay the destruction sent to them. By the grace of God, none of the passengers on the bus had been seriously injured. They were all able to come home the very next day. But this . . .

Dottie sprang into action. "Clarice, pick me up. We're going to the church."

Dottie hung up the phone without saying anything else to Clarice. She got out her church directory, turned to the intercessor's page, and started dialing.

THIRTY-THREE

"Aiiiieeeee," little Margarette Ann screamed, attempting to wake up from her nightmare.

She screamed several times before Albert and Emma roused from their deep sleep. Emma, close to the end of her second pregnancy, slowly rolled out of the bed, big with child, in her eight and a half month. Pain had kept her awake most of the night.

Glancing at the clock on her nightstand on her way to see about Margarette Ann, Emma figured she must have finally fallen asleep about two hours ago. It was going to be a long day from 3 a.m. until 9 p.m.

"What's wrong with that girl now?" groused Albert over the din of Margarette Ann's screams.

Emma noticed their daughter's nightmares becoming more and more pronounced. Several times, they'd heard her whimpering or talking in her sleep, saying "No!" to whomever she was talking to during the course of the night. That hadn't been too bad.

For the past four or five nights, though, Margarette Ann began to cry out from her nightmares. Almost every night like clockwork, the child whined and screamed from whatever bothered her while she slept before jumping out of bed to wake her parents to save her. It quickly became old for Albert.

He loved his little Margarette Ann, that was a fact. But these late-night/early-morning episodes were taking away from his sleep. Working every day at the feed store from sunup until well after sundown, Albert worked hard. When he came home from work, he barely made it through dinner without nodding off at the dinner table.

His family needed the supplemental income between farm seasons. After the crops were in and while the land rested during the winter, there was not much income until the next harvest. Every year from November until March or so, Albert and his brothers found work in town at the feed store to supplement their family's income. Margarette Ann waking up in the early morning hours was not something he needed when he had a full day ahead.

Glancing over at the time, Albert exclaimed, "Three a.m.! Emma, get that kid quiet so I can get some sleep!"

Emma shuffled as quickly as she could to her daughter's room. "Why don't you get up and do it yourself?" she muttered angrily under her breath as she trudged down the hall. Albert acted as though this were her fault. He had at least gotten some sleep since he went to bed at seven or so. She had yet to get a good rest at night since these nightmares started.

Sometimes, she was just so tired of his constant whining and bellyaching. As the so-called 'master' of their home, Emma thought he took the role too seriously, especially now that she was so late into this second pregnancy.

She didn't know what caused these nightmares in their daughter. Margarette Ann didn't watch anything scary on TV at night—or any other time for that matter—because they limited her viewing. She played all day either by herself or with her cousins who came over daily. Good and tired when she went to bed at night, the little girl often fell asleep at the dinner table. Emma had no idea what was going on.

"Unnhh," Emma groaned as a sharp pain took her breath away.

She'd been having sharp, infrequent pains around her midsection for the past week or so. Her water hadn't broken yet. When she spoke with Dr. Frank, he told her to try to take it easier than usual. So close to having their second child, she didn't want anything to happen to this precious bundle.

Margarette Ann shrieked again, this time as she barreled out of her room, headed to her parent's room. "*Daddy*," she caterwauled as she hurriedly brushed her mother out of the way. What bothered Margarette Ann the most were the eyes glowing in the darkness of her room. Yellow, green, red—all she saw was their gleaming scariness. And she didn't like it.

In the Unseen . . .

CD had slept beside the feverish child all night, lazily stroking her fevered brow as he heaped his ugly diseases one by one upon her fragile body. When her fever spiked at a hundred and two degrees, he harshly slapped her awake, all pretense of gentleness gone.

Mischief chose that exact moment to fling the closet door wide. He stood there drooling, breathing out curses at the child. Margarette Ann screamed the first scream. She screwed her eyes closed as tightly as she could, hoping to blot out the image she had just seen. Sweat pouring from her little body, she pulled the quilt up and over her head. As she opened her eyes under the blanket, she saw more ugly eyes there with her. Trying to get away from those scary eyes, she screamed a second time.

Reaching for her, CD's claws barely touched but scratched her skin. She yelped in pain and fear as he reached for her, grabbing strands of hair as she shook her head trying to get rid of the monster in her bed.

Fright had become quite strong since Lucifer had convinced him of his new name. He later discovered he had been lied to. However, he liked his new personality much better. He loved his job of frightening little kids and did it extremely well. In partnership with Mischief, Fright usually had a good belly laugh from his assignments that kept him until it was time for the next target. On this night, he chased the child Margarette Ann from her bed. He only did it so she could raise a ruckus in the little farmhouse and create turmoil for the family residing within.

Jumping out of her bed, Margarette Ann scurried to close her closet door. Mischief cornered her by her toy box. His foul smell enveloped her as he threatened to touch her with his claws. "I'm going to get you, Margarette Ann!" he yelled threateningly at the child, jumping toward her, startling her.

The color drained from her face as Margarette Ann ran to her bedroom door to get away from these monsters invading her room again. They had never been this bad before. She had always been able to say, "In the name of Jesus," just as Granny Dottie had taught her and they would leave. But not tonight. Too afraid to do anything but scream, scream she did.

When she tried to open her bedroom door the first time, Fright held it closed so he could terrorize the frightened child a little more. Quaking with fear, she repeatedly tried to pull the door open with the unmoving doorknob. While Fright held the door closed, Mischief mesmerized the child into a trance of fear.

In the Seen . . .

"Aiiiiieeeee," she screamed the third time, finally breaking free from the trance. Flinging her bedroom door open, Margarette Ann ran from the room as though her life depended on it.

"*Daddy*!" she screamed as her mother reached for her.

"Margarette Ann," Emma cried as her daughter barreled past her. She twisted around just in time to see the child careen through her opened bedroom door.

From the bed, Albert quickly turned on his bedside lamp just in time to see his daughter leap, almost from the doorjamb, into his arms, frantically throwing her arms around his neck. Sleep vanishing from his mind and body, Albert comforted his little one, worried as he tried to figure out what was wrong.

Emma rushed into the room in time to see her daughter gratefully hugging her dad's neck, trying to burrow closer to him, thin body quaking with fear. From what, her parents did not know.

"Emma, she's burning up," Albert alerted his bewildered wife.

As he soothed their child, Margarette Ann started to murmur in her fever-crazed state.

"Monsters, Daddy. Monsters," she explained in a frightened, little girl voice.

Albert glanced up at his wife, understanding dawning on him as he realized what his daughter was saying.

"Monsters? Emma, what's going on here?" he asked his wife, quickly becoming angry.

Bewildered, Emma put her hand on her daughter's forehead.

"Honey, I think she has a high fever. Maybe that's why she's delirious," she explained.

"It's not the fever!" Albert shouted. "It's you! What are you letting her look at on TV all day?"

Emma could not believe he would blame her for their daughter's nightmares and everything.

"Albert, you know Margarette Ann doesn't look at TV all day. She plays outside by herself and then the kids come over to play with her," Emma said emphatically. She was becoming frustrated with all the stuff going on. What with the new baby almost here, hardly getting any sleep, and having pains almost constantly, like now.

"Unnhh," she groaned, grabbing for the dresser beside her. Making her way to her side of the bed, Emma sat down hoping to release some of the pressure of the pain.

"What's wrong with you? Is this your way of getting out of our discussion by faking a pain? Well it's not working!" Albert yelled as he laid Margarette Ann on the bed in his spot, got up, and pointed a finger directly in Emma's face.

"Albert, what are you talking about? You know I've been having pains going on two weeks now!" she yelled. "How could you believe I was faking this pain, Albert?" she screamed, becoming more and more upset. "How could you?" she sobbed, tears rolling down her cheeks.

In the Unseen . . .

Strife hovered just above the family laughing his head off. He loved making people go at each other, especially the so-called *happy* couples. They were always so positive, so happy. Well, he would see about that! In all his ugly demonic ways, Strife was very good at what he did. He threw several more darts toward Albert Wells as he paced the floor of their bedroom, becoming angrier and angrier.

In the Seen . . .

"I don't need this garbage, Emma!" he shouted. "I work hard every day for this family. I don't deserve this treatment. I have been good to you! Nothing is ever good enough," he cursed toward her, ranting and raving out of his mind.

Emma looked toward Albert, wondering how this could have happened between them. She knew they loved each other with all their hearts. She knew she had never told Albert that what he was doing wasn't good enough. She bowed her head and said in her heart, *Lord, what do I do?*

She heard the still quiet voice as it answered, *Bind!* Well, it couldn't hurt even though she probably should have done it way before now. She struggled to her feet and lifted her hand to point in the corner of the room. "In the name of . . ." she began, shouting as much as she could to get the attention of whatever demon had dared to infest their home.

In the Unseen . . .

Before she could get the name out, Mischief and Fright attacked the sleeping Margarette Ann again. Flashing their ugliness in front of her fever-glazed eyes, they slunk back into the shadows of the room. They hung around only long enough to give Margarette Ann a good scare.

In the Seen . . .

"*Daddy*," she screamed, jerking from her fitful slumber. "*Daddy!*"

Albert put his hands over his ears as though in intense pain. Strife called out to Anger, "Now! Hit . . . him . . . *now!*" he yelled.

Anger flung himself on Albert in a full frontal attack. Albert became even more agitated than before.

"Can . . . you . . . please . . . *quiet . . . that . . . child . . . down!*" he said menacingly between clenched teeth. It was becoming harder and harder to bridle his anger.

Emma became very frightened. She had never seen Albert act this way before. She whispered softly, "Lord, please help us." As she whispered this prayer, she looked into her husband's face. He looked as though he were in pain. Emma summoned the courage to whisper another quick prayer. "Father God, please help us in the name of . . ."

Again, before she could utter the name of Jesus, another attack was launched against both her and her husband. Emma felt a sharp stabbing pain in her lower back. The pain seared hotly around her midsection causing her to double over. Clutching her stomach, she felt the baby leap vigorously inside her body. For the briefest moment, concern filled Albert's eyes. Then Anger attacked again.

"Look at you, Emma. You're pathetic," growled Albert. "You think you can fool me into thinking you're in pain so I'll stop yelling, don't you? Well, it's not going to work," he shouted menacingly, standing over her, pointing an accusing finger in her face.

The look on Albert's face was enough to frighten even the bravest person. But at this moment, in pain and vulnerable, Emma was not that person.

THIRTY-FOUR

Summitville Community Church

Dottie threw open the doors of the church and rushed to the altar, the urge to pray great. She had called fifteen homes before Clarice picked her up. She knew it would be at least twenty minutes before the closest prayer warriors arrived. She knelt before the altar in anguish.

"God, you have hidden the reason from me for this great urge to pray. Lord, please help me pray by the power of Your Spirit for whatever need there is in this community."

She knew the Lord had called them to pray for someone or something in their small community. She just didn't know what. As Dottie cried out to the Lord, Clarice joined her. They both praised the Lord for guiding them and bringing the other prayer warriors safely to the church. The two women worshiped for about ten minutes before others began to file in. Some were still half asleep. All were more than willing to assemble together to pray.

Dottie went to the podium and opened her Bible for a word as she prepared those gathered to pray.

Wells Farmhouse

Abuse entered the room silently. He looked to Strife who gleefully gave him the nod to have his way with this family. Abuse wrapped his tentacle-like arms around Albert's shoulders.

"That screaming is driving me crazy . . ." Albert shouted to the atmosphere in the room as Insanity took over his mind. Darkness clouded Albert's mind like a shroud. He couldn't think. All he knew was that he wanted the screaming to stop.

"*I can't take this anymore . . .*" Abuse whispered into Albert's ear.

"I can't take this anymore . . ." shouted Albert as he strode toward the bed.

Another pain tore through Emma, rendering her helpless to calm Margarette Ann. She saw the desperate look on her husband's face as though through a fog. Another pain hitting her with the force of a train slamming into a car caused her to faint.

Margarette Ann screamed deliriously. She struggled to get away from those eyes, those ugly red, yellow, and green eyes that were everywhere, but she couldn't.

Albert reached the side of the bed where his little girl lay. He looked down at his tormentor, the one causing him so much pain right now.

"*This screaming has to stop . . .*" Anger and Abuse whispered into his ears simultaneously. Destruction laughed in the background. He would win this battle. This little girl would not preach about Him, not if Destruction could help it.

"*This . . . screaming . . . has . . . to . . . stop!*" Albert yelled as he picked up a pillow.

Summitville Community Church Sanctuary

Sister Lorene Wagner started playing the piano. At first she played softly. Suddenly, the impulse to play songs about the blood of Jesus and victory came upon her.

> *What can wash away my sin?*
> *Nothing but the Blood of Jesus.*
> *What can make me whole again?*
> *Nothing but the Blood of Jesus.*
> *How precious is that flow,*
> *That makes me white as snow,*
> *No other fount' I know,*
> *Nothing but the Blood of Jesus.*

I know it was the blood,
I know it was the blood,
I know it was the blood for me.
One day when I was lost,
Jesus died on the cross, and
I know it was the blood for me.

The Blood that Jesus shed for me,
Way back on Calvary,
The Blood that gives me strength,
From day to day
It will never lose its power.

The voices of the saints filled the sanctuary of the Community Church. Unknown to those gathered, the sound of their singing amplified throughout the community into the farmland surrounding the church.

Angels of the Most High God joined in the much-loved choruses, causing the songs to have more volume than the small group of people could give them. The songs reverberated through the town to the little farmhouse that housed Albert, Emma, and Margarette Ann Wells and their unwelcome guests, the demons from the throne of darkness.

Candol and Anka, Margarette Ann's guardian angels, were joined by hundreds of angels sent by the worship of the saints. They shined brightly as the prayers strengthened the angels as well as the occupants of the house.

Albert looked from the pillow to the face of his daughter over and over. Why did he have this pillow? Why was Margarette Ann screaming? What was wrong with Emma?

Over and over these questions came to his mind but he couldn't make a decision.

"Shut that blasted singing out of here!" cursed Destruction.

The din of the saints and angels singing those songs about the blood and victory caused his flunkies to lose their concentration. Many of them held their hands over their ears to block out that dreadful singing.

Destruction rose out of the house to see what was going on. He couldn't believe his devilish eyes! Everywhere he looked, angels of the Most High God, in their full splendor, were singing the songs he hated about that nobody Jesus and His blood.

"You will not win!" he shouted at the angels, shaking his fists at them for emphasis. "This is my territory! This is my time, blast you!" he cursed at the loudly singing angels.

He flew back into the house in time to see Candol and Anka laying their hands on Margarette Ann to soothe her. Mischief and Fright were chained in the corner. CD had been thrown out of the house into the middle of the sleeping cornfield.

Albert looked at his peacefully sleeping daughter. He looked at the pillow and said to no one in particular, "Let me put this under her little head."

Emma stirred as another contraction hit. Warily, she called to Albert, "Honey, I need to go to the hospital; my water broke."

Albert rushed to her side, not quite sure what had gone on. "Sweetheart, I'm so sorry. I don't know what came over me." He remembered flashes of the past hour or so but couldn't remember how it started.

"*Nooo!*" yelled Destruction. Yet again, he knew he had lost. The angels of the Lord advanced on him threateningly.

"No, this is my time, I tell you. This is my time. She's mine," he whimpered as the angels of the Lord forced him and his demons to leave through the walls and floors.

"Victory is mine, victory is mine,
Victory today is mine!
I told Satan 'Get thee behind!'
Victory today is mine!"

The saints at Summitville Community Church rejoiced as the burden lifted. The prayer warriors danced around the altar as the sun came up. Another battle won for the glory of God!

Emmaline

THIRTY-FIVE

Charlotte, North Carolina: May 27, 1964

Mama, Alton's getting out of prison today," Maybelle told her mother Emmaline with a sigh. Today was Little Emmaline's fourth birthday. They had a big party planned for her.

"Ummhmm," replied her mother noncommittally, wondering where her daughter was going with this conversation.

It was four years to the day since Emmaline's son Jimmy rescued his baby sister from her husband, Alton. Maybelle and Little Emmaline almost lost their lives that day because of the beating Alton inflicted on Maybelle and by proxy, Little Emmaline. Thank God he hadn't succeeded in his plans of doing away with either of her precious little girls!

Emmaline had to admit that her little namesake was a scrapper, that was for sure. Emmaline Ruth Johnson had come into the world fighting to keep her life. Every day she fought to show anyone interested that she was going to come out on top.

"Mama, Alton's mom called to ask if Alton could come by to see me and Little Emmaline today. She says he is really sorry for what he did and wants to make it up to me and Little Emmaline," Maybelle explained.

Emmaline thought back to that dreadful day four years ago when she and her husband arrived at the emergency room to see their daughter. Had their daughter-in-law not been in the ambulance with Maybelle, they would not have recognized their own child.

Alton had beaten their Maybelle so badly! Her face was a swollen mass of bloody pulp on her head. Her face, lips, and eyelids were swollen twice their normal size. Hair was pulled out of her scalp in various places in plugs, leaving gaping wounds all over her head. Blood was everywhere!

Everyone, family and doctors included, wondered how Maybelle could have possibly survived the brutality. It brought tears to Emmaline's eyes just thinking about it. When her parents met the ambulance at the hospital, Maybelle was in severe pain and had lost much blood. Through it all, she remained conscious to everyone's surprise. Upon seeing their daughter, Stanley and Emmaline cried, partly from joy that she and the baby were alive but mostly with anguish that Alton had beaten Maybelle so viciously.

"Honey," she asked, forcing herself out of her reverie, "what exactly does Alton mean by 'make it up' to you?" She hoped he didn't mean what she thought he meant.

"I don't know, Mama," Maybelle said hesitantly.

Since that awful day, Maybelle's family had rallied around her and Little Emmaline and become fiercely protective of them both. When Alton's parents came to the hospital to see the baby, Maybelle's brothers made sure they were never left alone with Little Emmaline. When they requested to see Maybelle, Emmaline stood guard over her daughter with as much ferocity as a lioness protecting her cubs.

Finally allowed to visit with Maybelle for a few moments, Henry and Annie Johnson were appalled by what they saw. They found it hard to believe that their son could do what had been done to Maybelle's body. Granted, Alton *had* changed since the incident in Nashville. They wondered if it was possible that he had changed *this* much.

"Mama, we're not getting back together if that's what you're worried about," Maybelle assured her mother who breathed a sigh of relief. "But I do want him to know that Little Emmaline and I are still standing despite his attempts on our lives."

As they ended the call a few moments later, Emmaline thought about how much she loved hearing the strength in her daughter's voice. After her stay in the hospital, Maybelle recovered slowly but steadily. She followed the doctor's advice and never looked back. Emmaline watched her daughter grow stronger and wiser during the last four years. Maybelle had done remarkably well.

Maybelle returned to school for her Bachelor's degree in English so she could teach. She finished her course work in two years while raising Little

Emmaline alone. She never considered dating anyone because she simply didn't want to be bothered.

Maybelle thought about what she and her mother had just discussed. Out of the corner of her eye, she saw the little face peeping around the corner. She continued to stand at the kitchen sink as though deep in thought. She did not want Little Emmaline to know she had been found out.

Turning her back to the child as though to do the dishes, the shy little voice finally spoke, asking softly, "Mama, is my daddy coming over here?"

Maybelle didn't keep any of the horrible details of that day from the child. Today though, she wished she had. She did not want her daughter tainted by what Alton had become after his experience. She neither knew what kind of attitude he had after prison nor was she willing to find out.

Although Alton's mother said he had changed, Maybelle still remembered the worst beating she had ever suffered. She remembered the pitying yet skeptical looks in Alton's parents' eyes when they visited her in the hospital.

Although in a drug-induced haze, Maybelle never forgot the questions Henry and Annie asked her that day. When she and the baby were finally able to go home from the hospital, they had continued the same line of questioning as they prepared for Alton's trial that sent him to prison for four years.

"Maybelle, are you sure Alton did this? What did you do to him? You know how much of a temper he has now after his incident, honey. Was he drinking? Did you say something to set him off? Honey, is Little Emmaline Alton's baby? What other reason would he have for beating you like this?" The last two questions hurt Maybelle the most.

Maybelle would never forget those questions or the way they made her feel as her mother and father-in-law earnestly broached the subject with her. With time, the pain of the questions eased. Maybelle tenaciously went on with her life.

When Annie Johnson called her a week before, though, those same questions came back to mind. Maybelle forced herself to forget about them as she told Annie she would consider Alton being able to come and visit.

Putting all of it out of her mind for the moment, she turned to her pretty little chocolate drop of a daughter who came into the kitchen.

"Little Emmaline, I don't know yet if we should allow him to come and visit us. What do you think we should do, sweetheart?" Maybelle asked her daughter. Little Emmaline closely resembled the father she had never met, the father who had attempted to stop her life from being.

Little Emmaline sat at the kitchen table quietly considering her mother's question. In church since birth, this little one had wisdom beyond her four years, sometimes causing her mother to wonder who the Lord had given to her to be a mother over.

"Mama, why did Daddy do this to us?" Little Emmaline asked thoughtfully.

Discussing the incident before with her, Little Emmaline didn't say very much. Much of what was told to her, she kept in her heart. A curious child who was often closed-mouthed about many things, Little Emmaline never had much to say.

"Mama, is he the same as he was before?" Little Emmaline asked seriously in her tiny voice.

Maybelle smiled gently at the curious little girl. She wondered the same thing.

THIRTY-SIX

Hanging up the phone, Emmaline Carter smiled to herself. Maybelle June Johnson was a strong young woman and a remarkable teacher in Charlotte. Tireless in her efforts to help her students learn to speak and write English correctly, she was an example to everyone she met of how to overcome any obstacle.

And now this man who had almost killed her and their child was trying to come back into her life? *Hmmph, not if I can help it*, Emmaline thought to herself.

In the Unseen . . .

Division and his partner Strife split their time between the two women who were about to speak on the telephone. Emmaline Carter and Annie Johnson played important roles in the scenarios about to occur in the city of Charlotte concerning their two children, Alton and Maybelle.

The two demons had driven a wedge between these two for the past four Earth-years. Now that Alton was in town, it was essential that they remained divided. Little Emmaline was an integral part of the plan Almighty God had for Charlotte and these two families. The Forces of Darkness were committed to keeping that plan from coming to pass.

Holy Guardian Angels Echol, Axel, and Virdon were well aware of the cloud of confusion these two minions had placed over the women's minds. Cloaked from their sight in the atmosphere, Echol and Axel positioned themselves while Virdon attended to Little Emmaline. Echol stationed himself with Grandmother Emmaline and Axel with Annie for the removal of the confusion. Time was of the essence.

In the Seen . . .

Emmaline picked up the phone to call Alton's mother Annie. She hadn't spoken with her since Little Emmaline's last birthday. Communications between the two were strained since the beating. They both wanted to maintain a good relationship with each other because of the connection of Little Emmaline. But every time Emmaline looked at her daughter, she withdrew from the relationship.

"Hello," Annie said as she answered the phone.

"Hello, Annie," Emmaline replied distantly. "How've you been?" she asked. She didn't know whether she cared to hear the answer or not.

"Oh, Emmaline," Annie responded tentatively. She didn't know how this conversation would go. She remembered the last conversation with Emmaline; they had both decided it would be better if they remained at a distance. "I'm fine. How are you?"

"Look, I'll just get to the point," Emmaline said matter-of-factly. "Why does your son need to see Maybelle and Little Emmaline?" Emmaline asked. She waited for an answer. She wasn't going to beat around the bush. Alton was a sore subject with her.

"Emmaline, Alton's changed. Prison really opened his eyes," Annie explained.

She knew her son was wrong for nearly beating Maybelle to death, but he had paid the price for his actions. Now he wanted, needed to know he was forgiven by his soon-to-be ex-wife and her family.

"Emmaline, please," Annie pleaded. She knew Maybelle would do what her mother wanted her to do. Annie wanted her son to do what was right by Maybelle and their daughter.

Annie Johnson had spent the last four years of her life coming to grips with the fact that her son had snapped and Maybelle had not done anything to cause his actions toward her. She regretted the line of questioning Henry and she had put Maybelle through. Now she wanted to make things right. She needed Maybelle and her family's cooperation in order to do that.

"Annie, look," Emmaline began. She was tired of the emotional struggles she had battled for the last four years. "Your son practically killed my daughter and in the process, their daughter," she said, bitterness rising up inside of her. "Just because he served four years for that crime doesn't mean he's changed. It simply means that maybe they didn't give him enough time!" she spouted sarcastically.

Annie gasped in shock. They were Christians. Their families had attended the same church for years. Always taught to forgive and forget, it was obvious that Emmaline had done neither.

"Emmaline, I'm willing to forgive you for that remark," Annie replied condescendingly. "We are supposed to forgive as many times as we need to forgive so God will—"

"Hold on, Miss High and Mighty," Emmaline cut her off. "Have you forgiven the boy that crippled your son so he couldn't even walk for a time, Annie?"

She knew Annie had remained almost obsessively bitter for a long time because of Fletcher Conroy, the boy who had stolen her son's dreams. Alton's dreams of becoming a professional basketball player and ultimately a doctor were shattered that horrible day. Annie had cried long and hard after the trial. Her son's attackers were set free to do the same thing to someone else without having to serve any real time for their actions.

"Well, that's different. That boy did that for revenge!" Annie shouted into the phone, justifying her actions. "Alton could have been crippled for life because of that boy!" Annie continued ranting. Her voice rose in anger as she recalled an image of her son lying in a hospital bed after the beating.

Then the image of Alton changed into one of Maybelle lying in a hospital bed after being beaten. *What if Maybelle had lost her life*, she wondered in that instant. *Maybelle* could have died. *The baby* could have died. Alton would only have been crippled as a result of the beating he had received.

My God, Annie thought. *What have I done, Lord?*

For more than four years, she had carried this thing within her concerning her son. Was she so blind she couldn't understand why Emmaline felt the same as she? She couldn't compassionately go the extra mile with another woman whose loss would have been even greater than her own? What was wrong with her?

Suddenly, they both realized they were acting just alike concerning their children. They were still revisiting emotions that had caused their friendship to be on shaky ground after all this time and didn't realize it until now. It was almost as if scales had been pulled from their eyes.

In the Unseen...

Echol and Axel blew the cloud of Confusion from the women's minds. The Earth did not quake, thunder did not clap, nor did lightning flash. But the stark realization of their actions over the past several years hit them both with a force that caused them to rock on their heels.

Each of them had allowed a cancer, Anger, to eat up their friendship because of the actions of another. Emmaline and Annie felt different as the Holy Guardian Angels of God ministered to their spirits, causing them to pray.

In the Seen . . .

"Oh, God, please forgive us," Emmaline sobbed into the receiver. She knew better! God had brought her through so much! Yet she had held this grudge against her friend all these years.

"Annie, can you ever forgive me?" she asked her old friend.

"Oh, Emmaline, can you ever forgive me?" Annie sobbed in response. "All this time I've put all the blame on you and Maybelle, not wanting to blame Alton. I should have blamed the devil because it was old slew foot that got this whole mess started."

"And Emmaline, you're right. I never did forgive that boy for what he did to Alton. I've allowed hatred and resentment to grow and fester in my heart toward that boy. Oh, God," Annie cried in despair. "Please help me forgive that boy whom I have hated all these years," she prayed, anguish in her voice.

Both women clung to their telephone receivers as though to a lifeline, trying to reconcile their feelings for each other and getting it all out.

"Annie, I know it wasn't your fault what Alton did to Maybelle," Emmaline started again. "I just wanted to blame someone, too. I should have been there more for you. I love you. Always have and will," Emmaline continued, weeping quietly now as her heart and eyes opened to what had transpired four years before.

"Emmaline, I know Alton is just getting out of jail," Annie began, not really sure what she was going to ask her friend. "But he seems to have changed so much. I know his heart is broken. Every time he looks at pictures of Little Emmaline, he cries when he thinks about what he almost did," Annie explained as another torrent of tears flowed down her face.

Emmaline quietly listened to her friend and fellow in-law. *God,* she prayed in her heart, *please help me to say and do the right thing.*

THIRTY-SEVEN

A nnie, is Alton there with you right now?" she asked.

"Yes, he is Emmaline," Annie answered. "He lives here on the weekends. During the week, he lives in that rehab facility on the edge of town. He's learning more about dealing with anger. It's a wonderful program run by the Assemblies of God."

Emmaline considered as she measured her words before responding.

"Annie, could Stanley and I stop by just to speak with Alton before he goes to see Maybelle and Little Emmaline? There are some things I want to say, need to say to him to get things out in the open." She waited for Annie's answer.

Annie considered what Emmaline had just done. Emmaline had given Alton permission to see her daughter and granddaughter, but not before she and her husband had seen and spoken with him. Annie wanted to do the right thing but didn't know if Alton was ready.

Trust, Annie heard in her spirit as she hesitated before answering. *Trust*, she heard again.

"Emmaline," Annie began. Praying silently in her heart, Annie experienced conflicting emotions within her heart and mind. It caused wariness at the thought of that first contact between her son and the people he had hurt so much.

"Annie, I can't promise I won't say an angry word to Alton," Emmaline interrupted, answering the unasked question. "All I know is I intend to speak to Alton with as much love as I can about the things he did that hurt me."

Satisfied with her answer, Annie consented to Emmaline and Stanley dropping by to see her son. As she hung up the telephone, Alton walked into the kitchen. He had heard his mother's portion of the conversation. Annie could tell he had been crying as well.

"Mom," Alton began. He did not know what to say to this woman who had sacrificed a friendship to stand by his side. "Mom, I'm so very sorry," Alton continued. He felt inadequate as he apologized for the consuming anger that had taken over his life for so many years.

"Honey," his mom said quietly, "Mr. and Mrs. Carter are going to allow you to see Maybelle and Little Emmaline. Before you do, though, they want to speak with you first," she explained. She watched his face the entire time she talked. "Miss Emmaline says she wants to say some things to you to get them off her chest," Annie continued. She wanted to spare her son the hurt that might come from his mother-in-law. But more than anything else, Annie wanted him to be man enough to accept whatever was said.

Alton considered before commenting. Emmaline Carter was like a second mom. He had loved her almost as long as he loved Maybelle—she was just that type of person. He acknowledged that she was still angry and hurt by what he had done.

He remembered how she had wept during the trial but had never said a word to him. More often than not, she only looked at him pityingly during the proceedings, shaking her head in disgust whenever their eyes met.

"Mom . . ." He looked in his mother's eyes, apprehension in his own. "I know Mrs. Carter is angry. She has a right to be. But what will I say to her? What will I say to Mr. Carter?" Alton asked, unsure of what was about to happen.

Alton had had four years to think about what he had done. To this day, he still couldn't believe he had loved Maybelle so much and yet treated her so badly.

"Son, God has forgiven you. Dad and I have forgiven you. Now you need to give the Carter family the chance to forgive you," Annie said. She knew in her heart that this was God's will concerning this situation.

As she patted her son's face, the doorbell rang. Mother and son looked at each other resolutely, sadness in their eyes as Annie answered the door.

Growing Up is Hard to Do . . .

Beverley

THIRTY-EIGHT

In the Unseen . . .

Anger and Self-Pity clung to Beverley as she listened to her grandfather's eulogy being read. The two demons were assigned to keep her on the path the kingdom of darkness had laid out for her. Anger ate at the child, filling her with more of himself as she thought about events leading up to this day.

Before Otis Scott passed away, the family and hospital staff prevented Beverley from seeing him. She never got the chance to tell him goodbye, or how much she loved him, or any of the things she needed to say to him.

"Against hospital rules and regulations," some said.

"She's just too young to see Otis in this condition. It will scar the child for life," others said.

The more everyone kept her away from Otis, the lower she sank into Anger and Self-Pity. No one seemed to understand or care about her emotions. Anger and Self-Pity capitalized on the family's disregard.

Enjoying the funeral service, Self-Pity sat on the back of the pew massaging Beverley's head with gnarled talons. Looking around the crowded sanctuary through beady blood-shot eyes, he noticed there was not a strong presence of the Heavenly Host at the gathering. Detecting only a few white iridescent forms here and there, Self-Pity observed more dark menacing forms in the sanctuary than the other at this event.

Catching a glimpse of his cousins Turmoil and Despair and his old friend Anguish, Self-Pity saw many of his kind flitting around the grieving family. They emitted their evil perfume like a fine mist, saturating the atmosphere above the humans.

With such a small company of holy angels, Self-Pity experienced no hindrances as he diligently fed Beverley's mind with thoughts that no one else cared for her the way her grandfather had cared for her. Doing an exceptional job of keeping the girl's mind focused on her own troubles, he didn't allow any thoughts concerning anyone else's troubles to come through.

Edgefield, South Carolina: November 16, 1972

"Enter, Deacon Scott, into your rest. We all loved you but God loved you best," Pastor Cleveland Barnes intoned over the remains of the dearly departed, Otis Sylvester Scott.

The congregation wept, some quietly and others not so quietly. They all reminisced about the man they knew and loved. Beverley looked around at the huge gathering of people in the church. Family and friends gathered in the sanctuary of Dry Creek Missionary Baptist Church in memory of their beloved friend, brother, and deacon.

Turning her head back to the front, Beverley caught sight of cousin Flora Mae Peterson just as she flopped to the floor in a pool of black silk while viewing the remains of Daddy. Cousin Flora Mae served as the main "swooner" during regular church service. She showed her best during funerals.

Far from serving as the only swooner, Mrs. Alma Williams joined cousin Flora Mae on the floor as she stepped forward to view the remains. She had already lost her wig once during the service when her body jerked from being hit by the Spirit. Usher Sister Kathleen White stealthily stepped forward and replaced the wig as it came off again when Mrs. Alma slid down to the floor. Sister White even took the time to make sure it was set on Mrs. Alma's head correctly.

Beverley looked at Pastor Barnes speaking from the old pulpit, Daddy lying in the coffin in front of the altar. Multicolored flowers banked all around the coffin. The smell at the front of the sanctuary was both overwhelming and sickening.

The church was packed with many people. Many of these people Beverley knew. There were even more that she didn't. Daddy was very well known and loved. He would be sorely missed in the community.

Pastor Barnes droned on about what a good man Daddy had been and what a powerful legacy he left for his family. Beverley caught bits and pieces of the message as she zoned out from the happenings around her: "Passed on to glory . . . life cut short by emphysema."

Otis's two sons, Leon and Richard, two of his daughters, Cassie and Lila, and Beverley all sat on the front row on the right side of the flower-filled sanctuary. Eyes downcast and tearful, Otis's children mourned the loss of their patriarch who was "called home" as people of the Baptist persuasion fondly said.

On the second row on the same side of the sanctuary sat Otis's baby sister, Ida Mae Collins, nieces, nephews, and various other relatives. They were all heartbroken because he had been taken away from them.

Not in attendance were his wife of forty-nine years, Beulah, and his daughter Barbara Ann who "couldn't stand funerals." Beulah was at home in bed, angry that Otis would leave her like he did. She wasn't the only angry one in the family.

As white-gloved pallbearer Deacon Eldridge Turner stepped forward to close the lid on the coffin, the resulting thud gave a clear sound of finality. Beverley stood up from the front pew with the rest of the solemn mourners. They all prepared to move the coffin down the aisle and through the doors of the church to take her beloved Daddy to the grave someone had dug out in the cemetery.

Thirteen and heartbroken, Beverley marched stiff-legged down the aisle in her black collared, multicolored taffeta dress and black patent leather Mary Jane's. Partially in defiance but fully in anger, she followed the people who had kept her from seeing Daddy before he passed away.

She had loved Otis Scott all of her life. The one thing she had loved most about Daddy came to her mind when she was allowed to look into the casket at his remains—the whiskers.

She loved to feel his whiskers at the end of the day. He usually brushed them against her cheek as he hugged her when he came home from work at the mill. As she looked at his corpse in the casket, she saw that someone had shaved his face clean. She would never feel those whiskers again. She missed those whiskers.

As they prepared to bury Daddy, she wanted to jump into the casket with him. She didn't want to be left here to contend with Mama. Questions invaded her mind: *Why Daddy? Could I in fact go with him? Why do I have to be left with Mama?*

At the gravesite, Pastor Barnes picked up a handful of dirt as he finished the eulogy. "Earth to earth, ashes to ashes, dust to dust. Lord, into Your hands we commend the spirit of our brother Otis Sylvester Scott, for Thou hast redeemed him, O Lord God of truth."

All those in attendance said a final "Amen."

Beverley stood at the edge of the grave looking at the casket as it slowly lowered into the ground. This was final and she knew it.

Why? The question reverberated through her mind as she turned away from the grave. Entering the car the funeral home had sent for her and her family, Beverley was so very angry.

After returning to the house, Beverley quickly shed her church clothes for work-clothes, grabbed Daddy's old wood-chopping jacket, and went outside behind the house.

Frustrated, she chopped wood. She didn't want to be bothered with all the people coming to the house after the funeral. These people were coming over for three reasons—to eat, to talk, and to cry. She didn't want to do any of those things. She just wanted to chop wood and think about Daddy and the life they had shared.

THIRTY-NINE

Halfheartedly chopping wood on that dreary November day, Beverley reminisced.

She remembered many mornings sitting on Daddy's lap, sipping coffee from his saucer as he blew it cool and sipped it with her. From about the age of two, whenever she smelled coffee, Beverley knew Daddy was getting ready to sit down for breakfast. Oftentimes, she would awaken out of a deep sleep and run to the kitchen to have her morning coffee with him, no matter how early.

Beulah constantly scolded Otis for "giving that baby coffee" and spoiling her. There was nothing Beverley could want that Otis would not find a way to provide for her.

By the time she was five, Beverley had her own saucer to sip from when Daddy shared his morning coffee with her. Rarely eating from her own plate, Beverley ate food from his plate because it tasted better than what Mama put on her small plate.

Everything was better when shared with Daddy. Some of the happiest times of her young life occurred while she was with him.

"Otis, you're gonna spoil that child rotten," Beulah often said. But Otis continued to let his sweet baby girl sip as much coffee as she wanted and do whatever she wanted. She was his girl and everyone knew this.

Beverley shared the closest relationship with Otis. He loved his sons and daughters and his children loved him but Beverley was his shadow.

Whether he was in the field plowing or harvesting or driving to town, Beverley was always with him. By the time she was seven or eight, Beverley knew more about the process of butchering a hog or cow than Otis's older children. Neither his youngest son Richard, who was still at home, nor any of his daughters had either the time or the desire to be with him in the field or the farm.

When she turned nine, Otis taught Beverley to drive the old Mercury. Long-legged and lanky, Beverley drove often and well. Otis's daughters had no interest in learning to drive. He had a special pillow for her to sit on as she drove. She quickly outgrew it. Sitting right next to her, Otis explained everything as she slowly drove down the unmarked roads close to their home. He helped her negotiate turns and taught her to park well before she was ready for a driver's license.

She loved riding with him every other day as he drove to Vaucluse to pick up the slop (buckets of leftovers) his white friends and acquaintances gave him for the hogs he raised. Many of Beverley's best friends lived in Vaucluse. Since there were few if any colored families where they lived, all her best friends tended to be white. Those were the best of times.

Hot angry tears coursed down Beverley's cheeks as she thought about Daddy . . . her daddy! Even though Leon was supposedly her biological father, Beverley had never acknowledged him as such. As a matter of fact, she'd always hoped she had been adopted. That would at least explain why she never felt close to Leon. Daddy, Otis Scott, was the only daddy she had ever known. She planned on keeping it that way.

Continuing to chop wood through her anger, hurt, and tears, Beverley thought back to when Daddy went into the hospital for the first and last time. He had become very sick with emphysema, an illness that had dogged him for many years. During his last visit to Dr. Horace Matthews, the family doctor, he was immediately transported to Aiken County Hospital to intensive care. Mama came home that day with the sad news that Daddy was in the hospital and not expected to "make it."

"Make what, Mama?" Beverley had asked curiously, not sure what the term meant.

Beulah looked at the child she and Otis had reared from four months old. Working as a nurse's aide, Beulah had dealt with death but not this closely and not with a child in her own family. She didn't know how the child would take it. But she wasn't concerned with that because it was all out of her hands anyway.

"Yer daddy's gonna die, child," she explained to the girl, angry tears filling her eyes. There was no other way she could think to put it, God help her. She watched the child's face as reality sunk in about her Daddy. Beulah was so angry.

In her mind, his illness could have been prevented. Over the years, she had often begged Otis to stop smoking. He never did. Even when she hid his cigarettes, he went out and bought more. He cut their life together short because of tobacco. Beulah didn't know if she could forgive him for that.

As the information sank in, Beverley ran outside as though chased by the devil.

"Nooo!" she screamed, slamming the screen door open as she ran outside. She looked up into the sky where that God was supposed to be.

Why couldn't He take Mama instead? Why did it have to be Daddy? These questions and others jockeyed for position in her mind as she ran behind the house, down the hill, through the horse pasture, to her secret place—the spring. She had to get away from the bearer of the bad news. She had to be alone and this was the place she came to be alone.

She loved her little secret place. She spent many hours here watching the water course through the ground, babbling as it coursed through the path it had made over many years. The only person who had come down to share it with her had been Daddy.

Beverley heard Mama's voice calling.

"Bev! I say! Beverley! Come back here, child! We have to take your daddy's stuff up to the hospital," Beulah shouted in Beverley's general direction.

Everyone knew her hiding place. Few bothered to go down there to get her. Living as far in the woods as they did, they could yell to their hearts' content to get the attention of someone who was out in the woods away from the house.

Beverley considered the information Mama had given her—going to the hospital to take Daddy his things. Maybe she would have a chance to see him. She solemnly made her way back up the hill to the house.

Daddy is dying, she thought, making her way to the house to prepare for the ride to the hospital with Mama. Why? What had he done? Was God punishing him?

The most she remembered from church about God was that He was a punishing God. If you sinned, you were punished. That punishment usually meant death and most people ended up in Hell. That's what she was taught and she believed it. Sometimes they were also taught that a few people got to go to Heaven to be with God. But you had to be *really* good to go there. Kind of like Jesus, the Little God, the Sunday School teachers taught. She wondered where Daddy would go.

After all, he did drink a lot of that scuppernong wine when Mama wasn't looking. And he would sneak a cigarette or two or more a day. Beverley began crying as she realized that Daddy would probably go to Hell for those two things.

While riding toward the hospital, Beverley determined in her heart that she would join Otis Scott in Hell just so she could be with him again. After all, Heaven wouldn't be much fun without Daddy.

Beverley couldn't help wondering what life would be like without Daddy. She didn't like the picture. They had never had a lot of money. But with Daddy they didn't need a lot of money. He was always able to provide what they needed when they needed it. What would happen now? Who would farm the land? Who would butcher the hogs and the cows and sell the meat for money?

Arriving at the admissions ward, Nurse Leona Burke sadly informed Beulah that Otis had taken a turn for the worse. As a result, Dr. Matthews had moved him to the intensive care ward. Nurse Leona knew and loved the Scott family. She had worked with Beulah for years and knew how devastating Otis's illness was for the entire family.

Dr. Matthews came out just as Nurse Burke finished discussing Otis's worsening condition. Horace Matthews shook his head sadly as he approached Beulah Scott and their granddaughter, Beverley. If only they had caught this thing sooner, he reflected. They might have been able to do something more effective than just watch the man die. As the emphysema hit the end stages, the disease escalated and cut Otis down before they could do much else.

Dr. Matthews soberly approached Beulah, his right hand outstretched. He drew her and Beverley into a nearby visitor waiting room before he allowed her to go in and see her husband.

"Beulah," he said sorrowfully. "I don't know what to say except the truth. Otis is not going to make it much longer. I don't believe he will even make it through the end of this week, Beulah," he shared, wishing he didn't have to pass this sad news on to her and her family. "My best advice to you is to enjoy the small amount of time you have left with him and start making arrangements," Dr. Matthews said with a note of finality.

Beverley stood by Beulah's left shoulder as the doctor spoke with her grandmother. He never looked at her, never once said a word to her. Beverley felt as though everything happening around her was happening to someone else. She felt alone, abandoned, as hot tears flowed freely down her quivering face.

Beulah called Richard to come to the hospital to get Beverley and take her back to the house. Beverley wordlessly looked at the adults surrounding her, fervently wishing they would let her see Daddy. Finally, Beulah looked at her and said the words that broke her heart: "Bev, you're too young to go in there to see your daddy. The hospital won't let us take you in there, child." As she said this, Beverley's body quaked from the pent-up tears threatening to burst her heart open with grief.

Over the next several days, when Otis's eldest son and daughters arrived from New York, they were all able to go in and see their daddy before he passed away. Beverley was not allowed and remained on the outside looking in, filled with an unbearable grief.

And now he was gone.

Nothing else mattered to Beverley as she chopped the wood. It didn't matter what she did now that Daddy was gone. She didn't care anymore and no one could make her care. She continued to chop wood, stopping every once in a while to stack it against the shed. They could always use wood, she sadly contemplated as she looked at the growing stack. And so, she chopped some more.

FORTY

Beverley glanced toward the house several times while chopping the wood. She never saw the two men looking out at her—Richard and his older brother, Leon, whom everyone called June-bug. They looked out of the screened porch at her, discussing her.

"Man, you gonna take her back to New York with you, aren't you?" Richard asked his older brother. A decision had to be made. Beverley didn't recognize Leon as her daddy but he was.

"I don't know, man," Leon pondered. "You know Maggie just lost another baby. We're trying to make this marriage thing work. We don't need Beverley underfoot full-time while we are doing what we need to do," he explained to his younger brother, hoping to justify his decision to not take his daughter with him.

Richard continued to reason with him.

"Leon, she's your daughter, man. She's lived with Mama and Daddy since she was a baby. Mama's getting older. Bev needs to grow up around kids her own age. You can't just keep her out here in the woods, Leon," he rationalized.

"Look at your other girl, Mildred," Richard continued. "At least she is growing up with her mother and they live around more people. I think you'll be making a big mistake if you leave her down here with Mama," Richard concluded, shaking his head.

Richard knew what it was like living out here. So did his brother. They had lived it. Richard didn't want his niece to have to go through what he had already lived through, especially since Daddy wasn't going to be around any longer. He had to figure out a way to convey this to his older brother. He just had to.

Leon suddenly became angry. He felt judged and didn't like it. Although it wasn't the best decision, it was the only decision he was prepared to make. He wasn't prepared to bring Beverley back to New York with him right now—he just wasn't. What was he going to do? What could he do?

He and Maggie had only been married for five years. She'd had three miscarriages in those five years and was greatly discouraged about not being able to give him children. She welcomed his daughter every summer without fail. He could tell that Maggie really cared for little Beverley. But Leon felt that their lifestyle just didn't include having a teen around full-time.

"Man, you just don't understand," he said angrily to his brother. "Look, you got kids you don't even see! So how can you judge me?" Leon asked nastily, hitting his younger brother below the belt. He decided that he would not be bullied by anybody into making a decision he was ill-prepared to make.

"All right, man," Richard said, backing down. "I'm not judging you. I'm just telling you—Beverley is your kid and you're responsible for her. You know what? Just forget it. I'm done," Richard ended, leaving his brother on the porch.

Although the conversation was over, Leon continued to consider his youngest daughter out in the yard despondently chopping wood. *Yes*, he thought. She would probably be better off here in the South. Mama would have more time for her and could keep a better eye on her. He would leave her here he finally decided as he went through the kitchen to check on his mother.

Later on that night, Beverley lay in the big bed in the middle room, the house quiet and still. After all the visitors left, she silently went back into the house. She bypassed the kitchen and Mama who remained in her bed still angry with her husband for leaving her.

Collecting her nightclothes from under her pillow, Beverley went through the kitchen to fill up the wash pan so she could take a quick wash-up. She took the pan into the little closet they called a washroom. There was only one source of running water in the house, a pump in the kitchen. The house had no bathroom or toilet. Instead, they used pots to do their business after dark and the outhouse during the day.

The only time Beverley was afforded the opportunity to experience modern conveniences was when she went to town to Aunt Ida Mae's house or when she spent the night with her cousin Gloria.

Beverley washed up quickly and put her nightclothes on. She threw the water out the back door and went through the darkened house to her bed. She lay there contemplating the events of the past couple of weeks. Daddy was gone. Today made it final.

She missed him terribly, more than she thought she would. She had loved that man and knew beyond a shadow of a doubt that he loved her. Why did he have to drink and smoke so God would punish him and send him to Hell?

Looking through the window blinds she had left open, Beverley rolled over onto her left side, gazing at the night sky. She closed her eyes for what she thought was only a moment. When she opened them again, she couldn't believe her eyes! There was Daddy standing on the front porch!

He didn't look anything like the corpse she had seen in the casket at the funeral. He looked so handsome, wearing a plain short-sleeved shirt and dungarees. And he had his whiskers. He smiled at her through the window.

Sitting up in the bed, Beverley attempted to wipe the sleep out of her eyes. Was she dreaming or was she awake? She didn't know the answer to that question and didn't care. All that mattered was Daddy had come back.

"Daddy," she asked, hope filling her heart. "Is that you?"

"Yes, baby, it's Daddy," he assured her. "I want you to do something for me," he said with a gentle smile, love filling his eyes.

"OK, Daddy," she replied eagerly, happy to hear his voice again.

"Take care of your mama," he requested. He repeated the request, "Take care of your mama."

Then he was gone.

Beverley sat up in the middle of the bed. Daddy had asked her to take care of Mama. She pondered this request from her beloved Daddy. Why would he ask *her* to take care of Mama?

More than anyone else, Daddy knew there was no love lost between Beverley and Beulah. It was a well-known fact within the family that when Beverley was born with very light skin, Beulah was ecstatic. She couldn't wait to get her hands on her new light-skinned granddaughter! Beulah quickly went to New York to get her so she could raise her. As the child grew older, her skin became darker. The difference caused Beulah to shun the child.

Otis noticed but hoped his wife would get over her prejudice against the darker-skinned toddler. She didn't. As the child grew older and darker, it became obvious that Beulah only tolerated her. As the other lighter-skinned grandchildren came along, Beulah favored them more and Beverley less.

This was the main reason Beverley and Otis became so attached to each other. Otis took the little dark-skinned girl with him everywhere he went except work. When he went to Aiken to visit his sister and her family, Beverley always went and played to her heart's content with her cousins. When he went off to drink and smoke with his friends, Beverley was his confidant and never told his secrets.

So why would he tell *her* to take care of Mama? She drifted back to sleep pondering this question a little more but couldn't come up with a reasonable explanation. When she got up the next morning, she quickly told Beulah about the visitation. Still in bed supposedly mourning, Beulah turned her back on the child, admonishing her to not tell tales about the dead.

Beverley considered her grandmother's back sadly. More than ever, Beverley wished Beulah could have been the one to die and not Daddy. The moment when Beulah turned her back to her, Beulah became the evil, wicked old grandmother. She was not "Mama" anymore.

Beverley contemplated the turn of events in her life and unconsciously began to count down the days until she became eighteen. At eighteen, she would no longer need to look at the back of this woman whom she had grown to despise.

Eternity

"Father, what is to become of the child Beverley?" asked the Son. He had observed all the turmoil the child had gone through since birth. She had been rejected and had now lost her only friend on the Earth.

"You will see, My Son," said Almighty God. "This one is strong and will accomplish all I have sent her to the Earth to accomplish. You will see," promised the Father.

Margarette Ann

FORTY ONE

Summitville, Ohio: March 1973

Margarette Ann Wells heard her father's footsteps. She dreaded each step as it ominously approached the bathroom door. Judging by his behavior, it was obvious Albert had stopped off at Scooter's Bar on the way home from work again as he frequently did of late. Margarette Ann grew increasingly scared as Albert drank more and more before coming home.

Industriously, fourteen-year-old Margarette Ann had already fed her younger siblings—ten-year-old Cindy, seven-year-old JR, and four-year-old Annie. In the process of getting them bathed and put to bed before their father got home, she kept an eye on the clock as she quickly moved about the house. There would be yelling and cursing if she didn't have everything done by the time Albert Wells walked through the front door of their tiny farmhouse.

Her after-school chores included seeing to the younger ones when her mom went to work at the hospital before her dad came home from his job at the steel mill forty-five miles away in East Liverpool. Working hard six days a week, Albert barely supported their growing family on his paycheck alone.

When her mother went to work right after Annie was born, Albert went on a week-long drinking binge. Because the farm had finally stopped yielding the crops needed to support his family, Albert oftentimes drank until he passed out to prevent thoughts about his problems.

He figured it was bad enough he had to go to work for someone else. When their situation called for Emma to work, Albert saw it as the final blow to his already damaged ego. After the loss of the farm, Albert became surly. Here he was with a wife and four young ones and he couldn't even make a living off the land. This constant thought disgusted and depressed him.

Albert stopped going to church around this time. Since he wasn't going, he barely permitted Emma to go with the children. When Margarette Ann turned seven, Albert began verbally abusing his family when he got drunk. He started calling Emma names if she was slow getting things done around the house.

His next step of physically abusing Emma quickly ended when he woke up one night staring down the barrel of Emma's daddy's shotgun. Emma held the gun and her parents stood behind her should she require any help. That night Albert found he wasn't as brave as the liquor made him.

He easily found a more willing and sure victim in his oldest daughter, Margarette Ann. He could yell at her, swear at her, threaten her—she did whatever he asked. He could come in drunk after work and this one would buckle down in fear and make him feel as he was supposed to feel—like a man.

Pretty soon, when the other children came along, Albert terrorized all of them in the evenings after work. He felt no remorse. These were his children, born for his pleasure! He would treat them any way he wanted, he reasoned. He felt powerful as he wielded his anger at life on his children. Soon, though, that wasn't enough.

Emma began to find Albert repulsive in more ways than one. She shunned his drunken intimate overtures as they progressively became more and more abusive during times of intimacy. Albert quickly tired of her behavior.

He frequented the bars in the surrounding towns. Amazingly, he remained faithful to his marital vows. As he increasingly drank and physically abused his children, he subconsciously knew that the situation had to reach a peak. It was as though he couldn't stop himself . . .

In the Unseen . . .

"Molester, come forth," the command came out of the darkness surrounding the Wells house. The Prince of the Power of the Air held court and divvied out the assignments for this season concerning Albert Wells.

"Yes, my lord," came the heavy reply. The deep voice of Molester reverberated in the Halls of Darkness as he stood before his master. Molester was ugly beyond belief. Because he was so hideous, he rarely showed his face. This was acceptable since only his actions were needed to accomplish the plans of darkness, not his face.

"It is time for you to make your presence known in the Wells household," his master explained.

The prince had watched for some time now as the situation deteriorated in the once Christian family. *Now the man no longer attends church services*, the devil sneered.

He had bombarded this family with anger, abuse, cursing, debt, and all other manner of evil since the birth of Margarette Ann. At one time, they had been able to resist the onslaught. As time went on, the devil kept the pressure up and increased it.

He knew the destiny of Margarette Ann. She was to be a preacher just like her grandmother except even more powerful. Satan was bound and determined to not let that happen.

Because of the way her life was unfolding, the child had stopped believing in God. After being enrolled in a Catholic school to receive a religious education, Margarette Ann found more verbal and physical abuse in school because of her shyness. The nuns at the school targeted Margarette Ann because she did not desire to participate as much as the other children.

Margarette Ann never said a word. She suffered in silence. She believed the God she had heard so much about, the God Granny said loved her so much, had deserted her. She couldn't see Him in anything concerning her. Beaten at home and beaten at school, Margarette Ann was afraid to say anything about any of it, afraid she would receive more beatings if she did.

Satan sent Suicide to the child once she turned twelve and could understand. The urge around her to commit suicide was strong. Fortunately, something always held her back from the act. Margarette Ann began nicking herself with a little penknife she found. She experienced strange pleasure from cutting her body in places only she knew about.

One night she placed the dull edge of the blade across her wrist. She imagined pressing the blade through her skin to the vein. In her mind, she could see the blood squirting out of her body. Then she thought about her mama finding her dead and couldn't bear the thought.

Margarette Ann seemed to withdraw from life as Albert's abuse continued and worsened. She attempted to keep the younger children from going through what she went through by getting them to bed early before their father got home. It worked for the most part.

Satan had tired of playing around with this family. He needed something significant to happen to drive the child over the edge and even further away from God.

"Molester," he commanded, "this is what I have for you to do in this household." He conspired with this expert demon.

In the Seen . . .

Meanwhile in the Wells house, Anger and Profanity were having a wonderful time with Albert and his children. Albert had come home earlier than usual, more drunken than usual.

"Margarette Ann," he yelled, crashing through the front door of the house. He threw his belongings everywhere as he entered the house, bellowing for his oldest daughter. "Mar-ga-rette Ann," he yelled again, emphasizing each syllable of her name. Albert wanted to make sure she was good and scared by the time she stood before him.

Margarette Ann cringed as she heard the voice she had come to fear.

"Oh, no," she whispered in dismay. "He's home early!" She cringed again as he yelled her name even louder the second time. She hadn't quite finished feeding the children and getting them ready for bed. JR and Annie had already eaten. They were sitting in front of the TV in their pajamas looking at Lassie.

"Turn that so-and-so television off," Albert cursed as his two youngest children scrambled to get out of his way.

Annie trembled, tears rolling down her pale cheeks as Albert strode over to her. She wanted to scream but remembered the last time she screamed and how his huge hand had slapped her across her face.

Margarette Ann hurried to the living room in time to snatch Annie off the floor as JR ran to hide behind her. Her dad stood there with a look of triumph. He knew he had won another round of "scare the kids to death."

That was the name he had given his drunken games with the children. Albert knew he would get away with every bit of harassment he poured out on his kids out of frustration.

Albert learned to skillfully threaten his children in a way they dared not tell his wife what went on when she wasn't at home. And it worked well. In the beginning of the terror, the children were able to spring back from his bouts by the weekend as though nothing had happened. As time progressed, the children became more and more scarred by the emotional and physical abuse.

Albert taught himself to never leave marks on "Emma's precious children," as he snidely referred to them. She had threatened to leave him more than once if she ever found out he was abusing his privileges as a father. And of course he didn't want to look like a failure as a father in addition to his other perceived failures.

So he learned different tactics for terrorizing them. One evening while feeling particularly carefree, he locked the youngest in the woodshed for an hour after dark. Annie screamed until she was hoarse. Albert laughed his head off as Margarette Ann, sounding like her mother, begged him to let little Annie out of the woodshed. She hadn't done anything, Margarette Ann kept telling him. But he'd decided it was his right to do what he wanted to do to and with his kids when he wanted to do it. He continued his rampage.

"Get those kids in the bed, Margarette Ann. And get my dinner on the table," he commanded the frightened girl.

Margarette Ann quickly scurried down the hall holding Annie with Cindy and JR in tow. She made quick work of sponging Cindy off since she hadn't had a bath yet. She had the younger three in bed in a little over fifteen minutes before her dad yelled out her name again.

"Margarette Ann . . . get my dinner!" he yelled at the running child.

She quickly thought, *What have I done to deserve this?*

FORTY TWO

Margarette Ann could not understand how or why her dad had become such a mean-spirited man. He treated her mom and his children like so much garbage. He had been doing this for about three, maybe four years. As she scampered to the kitchen to heat her father's meal, she thought back over her life.

When she was between six and eight, she remembered her dad as sweet and loving. She was the only child then. Life was good. They attended church on Sunday followed by family dinner at either a grandparent's house or at one of her aunt's or uncle's homes. They always ended up staying over well into the evening after homemade ice cream and cake.

Those were good times, Margarette Ann remembered. She spooned steaming gravy over the boiled potatoes and chicken on her dad's plate, adding green beans and a good-sized hunk of cornbread. She hurriedly set it on the table as her dad grunted his way into the kitchen. He sat down as she placed a glass of iced tea on the table by his plate.

"Get that blasted iced tea away from me, you little . . . go out to my truck and get me a beer," he ordered the frightened child. He wanted to curse at her but restrained himself.

Without realizing it, Margarette Ann attempted to remind Albert, "Daddy, Mama don't like you bringing . . ."

Before she finished the statement, Margarette Ann realized her mistake.

"What the . . ." Albert stood up angrily from the table. His action caused the iced tea to slosh over the sides of the glass and onto the table. "This is my house! I am the man of this house, little girl, and you would do well to remember that," Albert roared as he menacingly yelled at her across the table. He started around the table but suddenly changed his mind as pure rage entered his heart.

"Go get me a beer out of my truck, girl, before I do something to you."

Albert sat back down, abusive thoughts filling his mind. He drank in the thoughts and emotions he experienced. He allowed them to consume him in much the same way he consumed the food on the table before him.

The girl quickly ran outside to his truck. She got what he demanded and ran back to the kitchen, quickly setting the can on the table.

Not wanting to create any more confusion, Margarette Ann quietly said to Albert, "Daddy, I'm gonna go take my bath so I can go to bed if it's all right with you. I'll wash your dishes when I finish, Daddy."

A funny look crossed Albert's face as he stared at his daughter.

"No," he said harshly. "You stand right there 'til I finish my food," Albert ordered. "Then I'll tell you when you can take a bath," he said as he stuffed another forkful into his mouth.

Taking a swig of beer before continuing his meal, Albert relished the wave of fear coming from his daughter. He felt the power of her fear. He would show her, he would show them all, he assured himself confidently. He was tired of feeling less than a man in his own house. He would show Miss High and Mighty Emma Wells he was still the man around here.

In the Unseen . . .

Frustration buzzed around Albert's head as he ate his food and drank his beer. Stewing in his mind was the contemplation of what he would do to further scare his daughter. Frustration knew each dirty button to push to manipulate Albert as he became more and more bothered at not being able to do what he wanted to do in his own house.

No stranger to Albert, Anger accompanied Frustration as Albert finished his meal. Anger had worked on Albert for quite some time. He could see that all his work had not been in vain. He could see that the full fruit of his deeds was ready to manifest. This family was ready to be destroyed. It was only a matter of time.

In the Seen . . .

Albert finished his meal. He angrily shoved the dishes across the table toward the frightened child. As she washed the dishes with her back to him, he slowly drank the beer. He did not want to become any more intoxicated than he already was. Albert enjoyed the moment of intense fear and angst he was causing Margarette Ann. He wanted the moment to last for a while.

As Margarette Ann finished cleaning the kitchen, Albert glanced at the clock on the wall above the sink. *Humph,* only seven o'clock. Four hours before Emma came home from work. Plenty of time to make this the most memorably frightening night of Margarette Ann's miserable fourteen years.

Margarette Ann turned apprehensively from the sink. She never knew what to expect from her father anymore. He grew progressively more unpredictable as his drinking increased and he became angrier with life.

"Daddy, I'm done," she said quietly, casting her eyes to the floor.

"Go take your bath then," he answered snidely. He continued sitting at the table nursing his beer.

For one split second as he swirled the last bit of beer around in the can, Albert wondered why he acted so mean and hateful to his family. If he were to be honest, he didn't know why he did half the stuff he did to his family, especially his kids. Sometimes he felt good doing these things. Other times he felt so bad, he cried himself to sleep before Emma came home from work. Tonight was not one of those nights.

Albert listened as Margarette Ann turned off the water in the tub. He heard the bathroom door close quietly as she prepared to get into the tub. He waited.

Margarette Ann hung her pajamas on the back of the bathroom door. She hadn't heard her dad leave the kitchen so she guessed he was still drinking his beer. *Why,* she wondered, *is he acting this way?* None of them had done anything to him. Yet, he treated them all so badly.

As she climbed into the bubbles in the tub, she heard her dad's footsteps coming down the hall, hopefully going off to bed. Many nights he just fell into the bed in a drunken stupor, still wearing his filthy clothes. When Emma arrived home, she'd take a look at the sleeping form of her husband in disgust and pity. She would often opt to sleep on the couch instead of disturbing him.

Margarette Ann listened as his footsteps came closer to the bathroom door. Expecting the steps to continue past the door, she relaxed a little as she allowed the bubbles to close around her thin body. She never heard the door open but she felt her father's eyes.

Jerking upright but not enough for her upper body to be exposed, Margarette Ann shockingly realized that Albert was in the bathroom.

"Daddy, what is it?" she asked. She felt uncomfortable as he stared at her.

"Get out of the tub and go to bed!" he yelled. "*Now!*" he commanded, emphasizing the word.

Startled, Margarette Ann prepared to get out of the tub. Realizing she would have to get up to get her towel, she respectfully waited for her dad to close the door.

"What are you waiting for?" he shouted. He knew the problem but enjoyed her discomfort. "Hurry up!" he rushed her as he continued to stand in the doorway.

"Daddy, I was waiting for you to close the door because my towel is over there," Margarette Ann explained, pointing to the towel rack on the wall by the door.

"Oh, I'm not going anywhere, little girl," he said boldly. "So don't you sass me," he said as she protested. "As many times as I've changed your diaper, I've seen your naked behind before. Now get out of the tub," he said defiantly, daringly. Albert felt a surge of power as his temper flared.

"Daddy, would you please give me my towel, then?" Margarette Ann pleaded. She did not know what else to do.

"Get it yourself," he replied belligerently.

Margarette Ann slowly stood. She attempted to cover as much of her nakedness with her face cloth as she could. It didn't help. She suffered embarrassment and felt belittled as her father's eyes tracked her every move. Grabbing for the towel from the rack, Margarette Ann reveled in the privacy it offered as she wrapped it around her body. Albert watched his daughter, wanting to stop yet wanting to continue. He felt it was wrong, knew it was wrong. As always, he couldn't help himself.

Joyce

FORTY THREE

Alabama: June 1973

Big Mama, Jeffrey is changing so much," thirteen-year-old Joyce shared with her grandmother, Ethel Jones. "All he wants to do now is hang out with those old boys at home. And they're horrible," she explained. Her ponytails bobbed as she animatedly discussed her brother with her grandmother.

Ethel knew about the thugs Joyce spoke of. Ree had already warned her about the changes coming over both Jeffrey and Joyce. Ree had caught Jeffrey a number of times with bundles of money and bags of drugs he delivered for some thugs in their neighborhood. Marie was at her wit's end trying to figure out a way to get her children out of that atmosphere.

Not that Joyce was a goody-goody by any means. Ree had come home from work several times to discover Joyce with an apartment full of friends, boys and girls, some much older than she. As time went on, Joyce also began sneaking off after sweet-talking her mother into letting her spend the night at a girlfriend's house. Of course, there was never a girlfriend. But Joyce found ways to hang out all hours of the night with a fast group of kids.

Ethel considered her newly-teenaged granddaughter. Since she had found out about these two children thirteen years ago, she and Homer had never looked back.

211

All of Marie's brothers and sisters and their families pitched in to help Marie with the upbringing of the twins. Every three or four months or so, someone traveled from Alabama to New York to help Marie with the twins for a couple of weeks or to bring the twins back and forth between the two states, allowing Marie to grow in her job as a paralegal.

An extremely tight-knit family, all their relationships grew even stronger as time went on. The twins spent every summer and various other holidays throughout the year with their grandparents. They were able to grow up with their assortment of cousins in Alabama.

Since the day Homer picked up his youngest daughter and her twins at the train station in Atlanta, the love never stopped pouring out from them to Marie and these beautiful babies. Many extended family members believed Ree had "messed up" her life by becoming involved with some "old jack-leg gigolo" in New York and having babies without being married. Some of her elderly aunts and uncles advised Homer and Ethel to just let her lie in the bed she had created and not give her any help.

Homer and Ethel, however, had a different opinion concerning their youngest daughter. Protective to a fault concerning Marie and her children, Homer and Ethel closely guarded them from the bad opinions of those family members. The damage had already been done. There was no need to condemn them any further. God had a way of straightening things out in even the toughest situations.

In spite of her mistakes, Ree had done quite well for herself. Having acquired a good job as a paralegal in a Manhattan high-rise, Marie was able to not only care for herself and her children, she was also able to send money home on a regular basis to help the family. Ethel and Homer banked the money Ree sent so they could put it toward the twins when they came for their frequent visits.

This summer, though, Ethel and Homer perceived a definite difference in Jeffrey. After celebrating the twins' birthday during the annual family reunion, Ethel and Homer noticed Jeffrey's sullen attitude. The more everyone tried to get him to participate in the activities they'd planned for the reunion and birthday party, the more he withdrew.

Jeffrey had a newly developed oldness (the old folks would say, "he has an old spirit about him") that Ethel and Homer couldn't figure out. Many of his cousins complained that Jeffrey wasn't any fun anymore. They said that all he talked about was death and dying, stuff they weren't interested in.

Ethel was worried, that was certain. She and Homer prayed about their grands all the time, especially these two who didn't have an earthly father around them in New York. When the twins came South for their visits, they had more than enough father figures to be around—their uncles and, especially, their Paw-Paw. Ethel and Homer made sure the twins were surrounded with love and discipline at all times so Marie wouldn't have to worry about them getting on the wrong path.

And Marie did her part. She didn't date much in the twins' early years after having been dealt a raw hand by their father. She'd just recently started seeing a very respectful young man whom she'd brought home with her for Christmas the year before.

Samuel Jenkins was an exceptionally nice young man. Originally from South Carolina, he had lived in New York for about five years. He drove for New York City Transit on the train system. He made good money and was not afraid to spend it on Ree and her two children.

Dating Marie for over a year now, Samuel loved Jeffrey and Joyce as though they were his own. Attending the family reunion this year with Ree to drop off the children for the summer, he made a great impression on the whole Jones family.

"Honey," began Ethel, breaking out of her reverie to finish their discussion. "Boys will go through their changes as they try to find their way to manhood," she explained. "Look at your uncle Rufus. Child, we had a time with him! He thought he was some kind of sugar daddy to all the girls in school. You should have seen him. He'd played the field like nobody's business until he fooled around and tried to talk to a girl who had four older brothers. They tore Rufus's tail up before he got away from them." Ethel laughed at the thought of her son receiving his comeuppance. She was also trying to make sense of why Jeffrey was acting the way he was.

But Joyce knew differently.

"No, Grandma, it's different. Jeffrey is selling drugs! I even saw him hanging out with a boy that has guns. Grandma, I'm scared for him."

"Guns? What you say, child?" Ethel questioned Joyce. Her heart pounded at the thought of her grandson handling guns.

"Yes, ma'am," Joyce said respectfully. "I saw him with Oscar Brown on 33rd Street just last week. They were back in an alley. I saw him holding Oscar's gun and looking at it like he wanted to use it. He was holding it like this," Joyce explained as she took a comb and held it in both hands like it was a gun. She pointed it toward the window as though studying how to shoot the birds flying past the window.

Ethel sat down on a chair at the table. Now this was upsetting! She would talk to Homer about this. They would let Ree know about it as well. As she sat there listening to Joyce, a very bad feeling wound its way around her body. She considered the things that could happen if Jeffrey got his hands on a gun. She knew nothing good could come of it.

"Samuel," Ree said into the telephone handset. "I don't know what I'm going to do with Jeffrey or Joyce. They're hanging out with the wrong people. I have to work. They're getting too old to have a sitter, but I don't know what to do," she said, venting to her friend.

"And I don't want to send them South to live permanently with my parents, either," she said, anxiety in her voice. She was exasperated as she shared with Samuel the things the twins were going through a couple of weeks after taking them South for the summer.

She enjoyed the relationship she shared with this man. Samuel Jenkins was all a girl could dream of and she enjoyed being in his company. Handsome and hardworking, Marie quickly learned he was someone she could trust. She didn't hesitate in sharing her hopes and dreams with him.

Very respectful and always the gentleman, Samuel really cared for Ree. He considered asking her to marry him. He loved her like crazy. He even loved her two kids. He realized that everyone makes mistakes—he had made quite a few in his lifetime. He wouldn't hold the twins over Ree's head. She was a good woman. After meeting her family last Christmas, he knew she came from really good people. And he wanted her in his life.

"Ree," he interjected, "let's get married. You know I love you, girl. And I love the kids. Let's just do it."

He had talked about getting married before. Ree would never allow herself to believe that a good guy like Samuel would want to marry her and take on her two children. She had thought about it, even daydreamed about her wedding. She just couldn't allow herself to consider the possibilities.

"Samuel, get serious," she replied. "These are not your children. You would probably be better off with someone who doesn't have the baggage I have to bring into a marriage," she said, trying to talk him out of his proposal.

Samuel wouldn't be dissuaded this time. A decision had to be made. He was determined to marry this woman.

"Ree, remember what Reverend Allen preached about last Saturday evening at the singles' meeting?" he asked. "You know, about the man who finds a wife finds a good thing?"

"Yes, I remember," Ree answered softly. She wasn't sure where Samuel was going with this line of reasoning.

"Well, I believe God has brought us together to give me a wife, you a husband, and your children a father," he explained matter-of-factly. "You know there are no coincidences with God. He does everything for a reason," he said softly.

Ree considered what he said. When she became pregnant, she knew her life had changed completely. As she made the decision to keep her two babies, she also made a decision that would affect all of them for the rest of their lives.

The twins' real dad had nothing to do with them. After she gave birth to the twins, Marie discovered he was married. He was on a mission to have as many extramarital flings as he could without getting caught. Unfortunately, she was one of those flings.

Fortunately, though, she had taken the lemons life had given her and made two pitchers of good lemonade. Both sweet and tart at the same time, her children were her reason for being at this time.

And now, here was a man who wanted to share her life and the lives of the two precious bundles of joy God had given to her. Ree cried as she thought about her prayer to God Who she thought was still angry with her. She had asked for a man to love her and her illegitimate children like they were his own. God had sent just that man.

"Mama, it's Ree," Ree said breathlessly as she phoned her mother. What a day this had been! After Samuel proposed again that night, she had accepted. The two had gone to city hall, applied for a license, and gotten Reverend Allen to marry them a week later.

Ree decided they would have a more formal wedding at Greater Tabernacle Baptist Church where she had grown up when they went to pick up the kids down South. They hadn't told anyone, her parents or his. They wanted to savor the moment, just the two of them. Now it was time.

"Mama, guess what I done went and done did?" she said, using as much bad grammar as she could to get her mother to laugh.

"It *must* be good if you done went and done did it, baby," Ethel laughed. The grammar thing was a joke throughout the whole family. Though only able to complete the eighth grade, Ethel had always spoken *good* English. She expected her children to do the same.

"Mama, Samuel and I are married!" she shouted into the phone, not able to hold it any longer. She and Samuel had shared the most joyous three weeks together as man and wife, not sharing with anyone else but themselves. Now Ree wanted the whole world to know.

"You've done what, honey?" her mother asked, shocked beyond words.

Of course she was happy for Ree after meeting the young man who was now her son-in-law. But again, this crazy child had done something so monumental without telling anyone. Ethel could hear Samuel in the background chuckling as Ree laughed melodically.

"Mama, where's Daddy?" Ree asked. Hearing silence from the receiver, Marie knew her mother was crying since she was the most emotional mother of all times.

Ethel cried quietly into the phone as she handed it to her husband. Homer looked at his wife, worried something was wrong because of her tears.

"Hello," Homer said into the phone, a question in his heart. "Ree, what's wrong, honey? Is everything all right?" he asked.

"Daddy, everything *is* all right! Samuel and I are . . . married!" Ree explained excitedly.

Homer's heart pounded as he comprehended his youngest daughter's declaration. *Married?* His little Ree? To that Samuel Jenkins boy? This was good.

"Honey, when? You never said anything about this. Let me speak to Samuel."

Ree handed the receiver to her new husband. Kissing her softly on the lips, Samuel beamed as he put the phone to his ear.

"Mr. Jones? It's me, sir," he said respectfully to Ree's dad, his new father-in-law. He could hear Ree's mom crying in the background and praising the Lord. "Mr. Jones, Ree and I got married three weeks ago. We just wanted to spend some time together before we told either of our families, sir," Samuel explained.

Homer Jones considered everything he had been told over the last few minutes. He respected this young man for loving his daughter and her two children. He respected him even more for marrying her.

"Well, son, first off, I guess you need to call me Dad," Homer said with joy in his voice. "Second, son, welcome to the family! Let me speak to Baby Girl again." He nodded his head as he thought about the happiness this would bring to his family. "Ree, you know you have to have a wedding here or your mama will never let this rest, don't you?" Homer informed his daughter, both of them joyously laughing.

"Yes, Daddy, I know. Samuel and I have talked about it. We would like for you and Mama to make arrangements with Pastor Killian for us for August when we come to pick up the kids. Mama, tell my sisters I want them to stand with me. We'll get Samuel's brothers to stand with him with my brothers. Daddy, I am so excited!"

Homer could tell. He felt the excitement through the phone coming from his daughter. He couldn't wait to tell her brothers and sisters.

"Honey, do you want me to tell Jeffrey and Joyce for you?" Homer asked. He thought the children should be told as soon as possible. He didn't know what effect it would have on them.

Ree became silent. *Joyce will take it well*, she thought. Her daughter already loved Samuel and called him "Pops" whenever he came to the house. Jeffrey, however, was a different matter.

"Daddy, is Jeffrey there now?" Ree decided. This was a major hurdle she would have to get over in order for her happiness to be complete.

"Yea, Shuge," Homer answered, calling her by one of his many pet names for her. "He's sitting out on the front steps. Let me get him."

Homer looked out the door at the boy. He wanted to help him because he loved him with all his heart. During this visit, though, it seemed as if Jeffrey had turned away from the older man. Jeffrey acted as though he didn't want to be bothered with anyone.

"Jeffrey, son, it's your mama," Homer said quietly to the boy, apprehensive of the way the boy would react.

When Jeffrey heard his mom was on the phone, he perked up before he could stop himself. He missed her and missed being in New York with his buddies. Maybe she was calling to say she would be there to pick them up earlier than planned.

"Mom," he said into the receiver, gladness in his heart and on his face. "Mom, how are you? I miss you," he said with his changing, thirteen-year-old voice. "When are you coming to get me and Joycie?"

"Honey-babe," Ree said gaily to her son. "I have a surprise for you and your sister." Marie paused, searching for the right words to win her son over in this moment of truth. "Samuel and I got married, Jeffrey," she quickly breathed out before she could change her mind.

FORTY FOUR

Jeffrey stared at the receiver in his hand as though it had grown a mouth, hands, and legs. He felt like he had been slapped as the breath left his body. *Married? Mom? Why?* He was the man of the house, wasn't he?

He took care of things. He watched out for Joycie. He even had a job running errands for Eddie Purdie, the thug who lived in that real nice brownstone down the street from their apartment building. How could she do this?! They didn't need a man in their house. He was the man of their house.

"Why?" Jeffrey intoned the word. He felt dead inside. This Samuel guy was all right but Jeffrey didn't need a dad in his life. For thirteen years, his mom, sister, and he had made it by themselves. They didn't need some man coming into their lives trying to be the man of the house and a dad to him and Joyce.

"Why, Mom? I'm the man of the house. You're always saying how I keep things in order. Why?" Jeffrey repeated. He needed to know the answer, but at the same time, didn't want to know.

"Honey, it's not about you being the man of the house. I love Samuel. He loves me and you and Joycie. He wants to help take care of us, Jeffrey. Don't you understand?" Ree asked, hoping and praying she could help her son see her side of the situation.

Samuel motioned to her to let him talk to his new stepson.

"Jeffrey," Samuel began. "Son, please don't think I'm coming in trying to change anything in your life. I just want to make it better for you, Joyce, and your mother," he explained to the wall of silence on the other end of the phone line.

"First of all," Jeffrey said, immediately belligerent, "don't call me 'son.' I am *not* your son. I am not anyone's son except my mom's! Understand?" He challenged Samuel with what little authority he could muster to his voice.

"Yes, Jeffrey, I understand," Samuel answered. It was wiser to give in until he got on better footing face-to-face with Jeffrey.

"Second of all," Jeffrey shouted in rage, "we were doing just fine before you came along. I was taking care of things for my mom. We don't need you, man!" Tears began to roll down his face. Dashing them away with the back of his hand, Jeffrey squeezed the receiver, wishing it were Samuel's neck.

Standing behind the boy, Homer put his hand on Jeffrey's shoulder in support. Jeffrey shoved the phone into his grandfather's hands and ran out of the house. Homer took the phone. He knew the boy was hurting. He also recognized that Jeffrey would need time to sort things out on his own.

"Samuel," Homer said into the mouthpiece, "don't worry, son. And tell Ree not to worry, either. He'll be fine. Let me go to him. I'll get back with you. OK?" He felt a strong urge to pray before he went out to the boy.

"Daddy," Ree cried into the phone as she took it from Samuel. She knew her son was hurting. "Daddy, what should we do?" she asked, feeling the distance between her and her son right now.

"Honey, don't worry," assured Homer. "I'll take care of this. Just enjoy yourself with your husband. We'll talk more about this," Homer said, ending the conversation.

Ree and Samuel looked at each other as she hung up the phone.

"Babe . . ." Samuel looked at his new wife, her cheeks stained from the tears she shed for her teen son. "All we can do is pray and ask the Lord for guidance. He hasn't failed us yet," he assured her as he took her petite hand into his.

"Jeffrey, Pops said for us to come straight home from school today so we can pick mom up from work and go to dinner," Joyce reminded her twin.

Jeffrey had acted strangely ever since returning from down South. He acted as though he hated their new stepfather Samuel Jenkins. Joyce was crazy about him. He was so funny and helpful most of the time. And he always brought a smile to their mother's face.

"He's not my pops and I'm not going straight home. I'm not going to dinner with 'the family' either," Jeffrey said sarcastically. He voiced his displeasure at having to play the happy family with this man who had come to take over as man of the house.

Jeffrey refused to attend the wedding when his mother and this man came to Alabama to pick them up after summer vacation. He hadn't said two words to his new stepfather in the four weeks they had been back at home. He wasn't planning on saying anything to him at all except, "*Get lost!*"

"I'm tired of him trying to tell me what to do. I didn't want Mom to get married in the first place. I will *never* accept it," Jeffrey said, argumentative and petulant at the same time.

Jeffrey had not accepted Samuel. He was doing everything he could to drive Samuel away. Nothing seemed to work. He began hanging out more with Eddie Purdie and his crew, taking on more responsibilities as a runner for Eddie's organization.

Bankrolling about two grand a week, Jeffrey kept the money hidden in his room until he needed it. He was one of Eddie's best couriers and his weekly pay showed it. None of the other couriers made as much as he did. He had plans for this money.

He didn't know how he was going to get rid of this Samuel Jenkins character, though. Although he didn't want to hurt his mother, Jeffrey just didn't believe they needed this man in their lives.

Jeffrey ran off down the street away from his sister. He wanted to get to Eddie's so they could talk. Eddie was like a big brother to him. He helped him with his schoolwork. Eddie was really smart like that. That's why he was such a good businessman.

"Hold up there, young blood," Eddie said as Jeffrey charged into his apartment. Eddie lived in a super nice brownstone around the corner from Jeffrey's third-floor walkup. 55 East 76th Street was like a palace to Jeffrey. Eddie's lifestyle at the age of twenty-five was something Jeffrey hoped to climb to by the time he was twenty. And if he continued with Eddie, he knew he would reach his goal. He looked up to Eddie Purdie. Jeffrey knew Eddie would find a way for him to get Samuel Jenkins away from his family before it was too late.

"Hey, Jeffrey, what's up little dude?" Eddie asked. He cared what went on with this young man who had become a big part of his life. "Somebody chasing you, boy?" Eddie asked, looking toward the door in case he had to make a quick move.

"Naw, just running away from my twin," Jeffrey said, catching his breath and looking around to make sure they were the only two there in the ultra-modern apartment. As he looked at the furnishings Eddie had acquired over the years, Jeffrey dreamed more and more of becoming like Eddie, his idol, his mentor. "That man wants to go out to dinner as a family. I'm not going," Jeffrey said defiantly.

Eddie considered his young friend and remembered twelve years or so ago when he was in the same predicament. He had never known his father. His mother was a prostitute and he was a surprise.

Dealing with the many pimps that came into his mother's life, Eddie was determined to never be under the thumb of any of those so-called "uncles" or "father figures" his mother frequently brought home. He knew how Jeffrey felt. He wanted to help him take care of the situation. Jeffrey was very important to his organization. He didn't want any flies in the ointment of the mechanisms.

"J-man, I've been meaning to talk to you about something." Eddie pondered how this would affect young Jeffrey and what his response would be. "There are ways to get this man out of your life if you are willing to take the chance of your mom finding out you are behind it." Eddie offered.

"What, Eddie? What are you talking about?" Jeffrey asked, brightening at the mere thought of something to get Samuel Jenkins out of his life for good.

"Well, Jeffrey, if you wanted, we could arrange an 'accident' to happen to your stepdad. It could be either a drive by or someone could 'rob' him while he is on the train," Eddie offered. He looked at Jeffrey's face to see what emotions the boy experienced while considering Eddie's proposal.

Jeffrey sat at the dining room table where all the drug transactions took place for this small-time drug lord. Eddie had at least $2500 a day, seven days a week, coming in. He paid his runners well for their efforts. In all the time Jeffrey had worked for him, only one person had tried to scam Eddie. Eddie quickly took care of the offender by having one of his goons break an arm and a leg on the scammer.

Jeffrey thought about Eddie's offer. He could have it done and look clean to his mother. It was definitely something to think about. Having Eddie as a mentor, Jeffrey matured a lot quicker than some of the friends he used to hang out with. He had seen some things his mom wouldn't even let him watch on TV. He knew about life and he knew about death. But he wasn't sure if he wanted Samuel Jenkins out of his life bad enough to have him "accidentally" killed.

"Let me think on that, Eddie," Jeffrey replied. He wasn't sure but was willing to give it some thought. "Hey, I gotta go," he said as he went back toward the front door of the apartment.

"All right, young blood. I'll catch you later," Eddie promised, answering one of the many phone lines around the dining room table.

Jeffrey ran down the stairs to the street. He really didn't have to go since he wasn't planning on going to dinner with his family. *But maybe I will go*, he thought. *Maybe I will see something that will help me make a decision about this man,* he thought as he jogged toward their apartment building.

Jeffrey arrived just in time to see his mom going through the front door of the building, two bags of groceries in her hands.

"Hey, lady!" he yelled across the street. "You want a hand with dose groceries?" His mom turned around and smiled in his direction. He had loved that smile for so long. It always brightened his day no matter how dark it was.

"Ooh, a handsome young man to carry my bags," his mom played along. She daintily handed the bags to him and curtsied cutely. "Oh, thank you, kind sir. How gallant of you!" she exclaimed.

Jeffrey held the door open for her and grinned. The elevator was out again, as usual, so they headed toward the steps. He answered the usual questions about school, homework, and such. As they reached the third floor, the door swung open as Samuel greeted his bride of less than six months.

"I knew I heard that voice," he said as he swung Ree off the floor.

Jeffrey observed his mother and this man Samuel Jenkins as they interacted. His mom seemed so happy. He loved to see her smile. Over the years, Jeffrey knew it hadn't been easy for her as a single mother. She always had to work so hard to support him and his twin. But as a courier for Eddie, he had it covered.

Jeffrey had found a way to access his mom's bank account and add money every once in a while. He added it in small enough amounts so she wouldn't get suspicious. It worked out well. When it was time to buy presents and stuff, he always told her he had a little knock-around job giving him enough for the presents. He enjoyed being the man in their little house. He enjoyed taking care of his mother and sister. He didn't see why they needed this man to do anything. Jeffrey wanted to get rid of him.

"Jeffrey, go change clothes," his mom said, breaking through his reverie. "We're going out to dinner this evening as a family."

Jeffrey had to admit his mother had never looked prettier. Since Samuel Jenkins had come into her life, his mom had lost the worry lines. She actually smiled now. But Jeffrey wasn't going to let that stop him from doing what he felt he had to do—get rid of Samuel Jenkins.

In the Unseen . . .

Destroyer observed the interaction between the boy, his mother, and his stepdad. He knew he only had to push a little for Jeffrey to go over the edge.

"Hatred," Destroyer called to his minion waiting patiently for the right time to come forth with this family.

"Yes, my lord Destroyer," Hatred replied, bowing before this powerful demon. Like his name suggested, Hatred hated everything and everybody. There was no loyalty or love anywhere in his slimy stinking soul. He intended to keep it that way for all eternity.

"Throw something at the boy. Cause him to make a decision about getting rid of the man. Fill his heart with such hatred for the man he will forget about his love for his mother. Cause him to do whatever it takes to get the man to leave their home. Do you understand?"

"Yes, lord Destroyer. I will empower him with raw hatred for this man, such hatred he has never felt before in his short, pathetic life, my lord," Hatred promised.

Hatred moved toward the boy and whispered in his ear, "Don't you want to have dinner with just your mom and sister?"

In the Seen . . .

"Mom, why can't you, Joycie, and I go out to dinner alone? We haven't spent *any* time together, *alone,* since we came back from down South," he asked, completely ignoring Samuel.

Samuel stood back, knowing where this conversation could go if he were to step in. He decided to let Ree take care of it. He understood why the boy disliked him—he was a man. The boy felt he was the man of the house and that was the way it should be. He didn't know what to do because he really wanted things to work out with Ree and the twins.

"Jeffrey, Samuel wants to take us out as a family, honey," his mom explained, flashing her eyes, trying to help him understand. Marie wanted this family thing to work out. She had dreamed of a man such as Samuel coming into her life to help her with the children and to have a family. Now that he had, her son didn't like him. And now that she was . . .

"Mom, why do you keep trying to make us a family with this man? I neither trust nor like him and I wish he would go away," Jeffrey yelled at his mother. Ree was taken aback. Jeffrey had never yelled at her before.

Samuel stepped forward now. This boy was yelling at his beloved wife. That, he couldn't bear.

"Now, son," Samuel began. Jeffrey cut him off before he could go any further.

"I am *not* your son!" Jeffrey countered, fire in his eyes. Hatred welled up in his heart as he thought about Eddie's suggestion. Jeffrey made his decision—he hated this man enough to see him gone.

Suddenly turning sweetly to his mother, Jeffrey asked, "Mom, can I change in a few minutes? I have to go do something really quick."

"Sure, son," Ree said, glad the fire was out for now. "Just hurry up, OK?"

"OK, mom," Jeffrey promised as he ran out the door of the apartment. He hurried around the corner to Eddie's brownstone apartment, hurrying so he wouldn't change his mind. When he arrived at Eddie's door, he knocked on the door once and walked in. He had it like that with Eddie. "Eddie," Jeffrey called, not seeing Eddie in the living room. "Eddie, it's me, Jeffrey," he called again.

"Hold on, J-man," Eddie called from the bathroom. He stuck his head out the door with toothpaste around his mouth. "Hold on, little dude. Let me finish up in here," Eddie said, closing the door.

Jeffrey hung out in the living room waiting for Eddie. A bundle of nerves, he clenched and unclenched his fists as he thought about the retribution he was about to shower on Samuel Jenkins. He would show him who the *man* was.

As Eddie walked into the living room, he could tell his young friend had made up his mind. He had already contacted the thug who would do the job because he knew how much the boy hated his stepfather.

"Eddie, I want it done," Jeffrey said, lifting his head boldly, making eye contact with his mentor.

As he made the request, Jeffrey realized there was no turning back. He wanted Samuel dead.

FORTY FIVE

After a very filling soul-food meal at Queenie's Restaurant on 103rd Street in Flushing, Samuel, Ree, and the twins went outside to take a stroll down the street toward the subway station.

"Anybody for ice cream?" Samuel asked, holding Ree's hand as they slowly walked.

Having received the best news of his life, Samuel was on cloud nine. Ree was expecting a baby, his baby. He had never felt this good in his life. Even the fiasco with Jeffrey paled in comparison with the news Ree shared with the family at the restaurant.

"Samuel, twins," Ree had said, a soft, shy smile playing around her lips. "I have something to tell you."

The twins looked first at each other and then at their mother. Samuel, just as unsuspecting as the twins, looked expectantly at his wife as well. "What is it, Ree?"

"I am going to have a baby!" Ree exclaimed. A shout of joy came from Samuel as he realized what this meant—he was going to be a daddy. Not just to the twins, his own baby as well.

"Mom, you're going to have a baby?" asked Joyce, incredulously looking from her mother to her stepdad. "But how? Aren't you too old?" Joyce asked seriously.

Jeffrey sat in horrified silence. He hadn't thought about this. He would have to stop the hit against Samuel and just live with it. The hit was supposed to go down tonight on their way home.

Eddie figured if it happened while the family was together, no one would suspect Jeffrey had anything to do with it. But Jeffrey couldn't let it happen now. He realized his mom must really love this man to have a kid with him. And it would be his fault if the kid did not have a dad to grow up with.

"Jeffrey, son," Ree asked, concerned since Jeffrey hadn't said anything after her announcement. "Are you all right? Don't you have anything to say?"

"Umm, congratulations," was all he could get out of his mouth. He looked from his mom to Samuel who was beaming like the moon. What was he going to do? He couldn't let it happen now, could he?

"Mom, I don't feel so good," Jeffrey said, not looking well at all. "Can we go home now?" he asked, hoping they would miss the guy Eddie was sending to take Samuel out tonight on their way home.

"Jeffrey, you do look a bit sick," Ree agreed, feeling his forehead for a temperature. Sensing none, she looked at Samuel, signaling it was time for them to go home.

Samuel paid for the meal, left a tip, and led the family out to the street. When they hit the sidewalk, Jeffrey looked around to see if he recognized anyone that would be a threat to Samuel.

As he turned to look at Samuel and Ree, he saw him. C-Murder Crawford quickly approached Samuel, a knife in his hand. All Jeffrey could do was react.

"Nooo," he yelled, grabbing Samuel by the shoulders and spinning him away from C-Murder. As C-Murder's fist came down with the knife, driving it deep into Jeffrey's back, Jeffrey looked into Samuel's eyes, a stricken look on his face as he breathed his last words, "I'm sorry."

The knife found its way to Jeffrey's heart with no other route. C-Murder quickly released the handle of the knife and spun around, running back in the direction from which he had come. None of them remembered seeing the face that committed the crime. All they saw was Jeffrey's face as he passed from this life to the next.

In the Unseen . . .

"Nooo," bellowed Hatred. The set-up had been perfect. C-Murder had hidden in the alley the family would pass as they left the restaurant headed toward the subway. He couldn't miss. But he did. Destroyer was furious.

"There will be Hell to pay," shouted Destroyer, contemplating his next move. The man was supposed to die, not the boy. At the very last moment, the boy had obviously changed his mind. He succeeded in saving his mother's husband while losing his life.

In the Seen . . .

"Oh my God," Ree screamed as she gathered her son into her arms. "Somebody call an ambulance, please!" she shouted as blood ran through her fingers from the wound in her son's back.

Samuel and Joyce stood back, stunned at what had just occurred.

"He saved my life," Samuel repeated over and over. He finally sprang into action as he realized Jeffrey needed medical attention quickly. Running back toward the restaurant they had just left, Samuel wondered at the strength his wife was showing in the face of disaster concerning one of her—their—children.

God, please let the ambulance get here in time to save Jeffrey, he silently prayed, running into the restaurant to use their telephone.

Joyce felt as though she too had been stabbed when her brother collapsed to the ground. She recognized the face of the guy who stabbed her brother. He was one of the thugs Jeffrey hung out with. Why would he want to stab her stepfather and instead stab her brother? Something wasn't right but she couldn't put her finger on it.

Joyce ran to her mother and brother as her mother sat on the ground cradling Jeffrey and screaming for help. People milled around trying to see what had happened in the diminishing light. Joyce looked at her twin just as he opened his eyes, tears flowing from the corners down onto the pavement.

"I'm sorry," Jeffrey said faintly as his life's blood coursed from the wound in his back, blood gurgling from his mouth.

Joyce put her ear next to his trembling lips as Jeffrey said those two words again, "I'm sorry."

Why would Jeffrey be sorry unless . . . no, that couldn't possibly be the reason. She knew Jeffrey had changed a lot over the past year or so but it couldn't possibly be what she was thinking. In fact, she wouldn't let herself think that. Not Jeffrey, not her twin.

Joyce held her brother's hand as her mother cried and rocked Jeffrey like he was a little boy again. Marie stopped rocking when she felt her son's body quiver then become very still. Not wanting to believe but knowing it was so, Marie screamed one long heart-wrenching cry of agony as she realized her son, Jeffrey Earl Jones, had taken his last breath.

Joyce felt the slackness in her brother's hand as she held onto it. She looked at her mom's face as she cried, sobbed, asking God to bring Jeffrey back. Joyce looked at her brother. His eyes glassy, his jaw slack, Jeffrey had stopped breathing. Joyce crumpled to the ground as she realized that her brother, her twin, was dead.

Emmaline

FORTY SIX

November 1975

Mama," shouted sixteen-year-old Emmaline Johnson over the din of the pre-Thanksgiving activity in their kitchen.

Her mom, Maybelle, was cooking up a storm. Her younger brother and sister, eight-year-old AJ Jr. and twelve-year-old Cardrina, were in the way more than helping as Maybelle prepared the sweet potato and apple pies she was making early to put in the freezer for Thanksgiving a week away.

"Mother," Emmaline shouted again, trying to get Maybelle's attention to ask her the most important question of her life.

Things calmed down for a moment as Maybelle shooed Cardrina and AJ out of the kitchen so she could hear what Emmaline wanted. Her little Emmaline had grown into a lovely young woman. Quiet, shy, and as smart as Einstein, Emmaline was tall at five foot seven in her stocking-feet. She was lanky compared to Maybelle and her mother and sisters.

Emmaline Ruth Johnson was a beautiful dark-skinned girl with short, thick, coarse hair. Her mother had finally allowed her to relax her hair so Emmaline could take care of it herself as she got older.

"Yes, ma'am," Maybelle said to her oldest child, a teasing glint in her eyes.

When Emmaline Johnson wanted something, she knew exactly how to go about getting it. She was more determined than any of the other children and did not back down. Maybelle often teased her that as disciplined and authoritative as she was, she should probably be a drill sergeant. The girl was hard to turn away and went for what she wanted.

"Mama, can I go to the Thanksgiving dance at school with Bobby Joe Hall?" Emmaline blurted out before she lost her nerve. Once she blurted the request to her mother, shyness overcame her, causing her to cast her eyes to the floor. Emmaline couldn't believe that Robert Joseph Hall, captain of the basketball and football teams and one of the handsomest boys at North Charlotte High School, had asked her out.

Emmaline just couldn't believe it. She thought he was dating someone else. Not being a part of the *in* crowd, she didn't know and really hadn't cared until now. Because she had been teased for years by other students and sometimes the teachers, Emmaline had shunned any activities except academics at school. Naturally tall, she was good at basketball but chose not to go out for the team because the other girls ridiculed her physical appearance.

Thought to be a snob because of her shyness, Emmaline didn't have many friends. She and her best friend, Sonora Ann Huffman, were like two peas in a pod. They enjoyed the same activities and were both highly intelligent. Neither Emmaline nor Sonora ever really put much thought into boys simply because they just didn't trust them.

As a matter of fact, because of her height, a lot of the boys called Emmaline "Em-zilla," referring to her long legs and arms. She'd had her share of days running home from school crying because someone had made fun of her dark skin or thick, coarse hair. She'd not had an easy time of it but was determined to make the best of it.

"Bobby Joe Hall?" Maybelle asked. "Do I know his parents? Where does he live?" she questioned, not trusting any boy around her baby. She had high hopes for Emmaline. She would not let a boy come between her girl and her dreams and ambitions.

"Mama, you know Mrs. Rita from church? He's her grandson," Emmaline explained. "His family moved here year before last from Chicago. He's the captain of the basketball *and* the football team," Emmaline beamed dreamily, ecstatic that he had asked her out.

Emmaline had seen for herself that Bobby Joe was one of the good guys. She had never known of him making fun of her or anyone else and he seemed so nice. When he approached her at school the other day, she actually looked around to make sure he was talking to her, really talking to her, when he walked up and said, "Hi!"

She'd almost run away. Instead, she forced herself to be calm so she could figure out what he wanted. She anticipated that he wanted help with his math or English homework as many of the other students often did. Emmaline had an established reputation as a good tutor who was willing to help anyone with schoolwork.

When he invited her to the dance, she'd leaned back against the locker so she wouldn't sprawl to the floor from shock. This handsome boy was asking her out? *There must be a catch*, she thought. Nobody cute ever asked her out. She felt destined to date only undesirables in school. Now Bobby Joe Hall was asking her out?

She had the presence of mind to timidly say, "Yes," before they both had to go to class, he to chemistry and she to math. All during class, she barely focused on what Mrs. Conner taught. Her thoughts were in the stratosphere as she pranced around on cloud nine. Just as she was doing now as her mother tried to get her attention.

"Emmaline! Emmaline!" her mother said for the second time. "Girl, what's got into you? I said 'yes,' you can go to the dance with this boy. But I want to meet him before he takes my little girl anywhere," she warned Emmaline, smiling.

"I can? Oh, Mama, thank you! Thank you! Thank you! Thank you!" Emmaline bubbled ecstatically, grabbing her flour-dusted mother and dancing her around the kitchen table. She heard the front door close as her dad, Alton, came in from work. Oozing with excitement, Emmaline ran to tell her father the good news.

Maybelle had never seen her daughter so excited and happy about an after-school event. Emmaline usually stayed away from those things because she thought they always turned into something that could cause emotional pain from the teasing she always seemed to experience. Maybelle knew her oldest daughter feared being rejected because of what she knew concerning her birth into this world.

But life has a way of changing how we see things, Maybelle thought as she smiled at her daughter's happiness. Her life was proof of that . . . and so was her husband's. Alton was a changed man. Since his four years in prison for almost killing Emmaline and her mother, he had made a total change. Two years after he returned home from prison, he and Maybelle decided to get back together under the watchful eyes of their families.

Maybelle's brothers made it abundantly clear to Alton that if he even so much as looked as though he would raise his hand to hit either their sister or niece, he could go ahead and reserve a spot with the mortician. They let it be known that they would gladly go to prison to protect Maybelle and Emmaline, but they didn't have to worry about that happening.

After prison and anger management therapy, Alton made up his mind to be the husband and father he should have been from the beginning. He started by attending church regularly. After re-establishing his relationship with God, he eventually decided to go back to college to see if he could salvage his lost dreams.

Following the devastation of the beating so many years before while still in college, Alton never believed he could get anywhere with his life. He thought that all hope was lost and he would just be a cripple for the rest of his life. But God blessed him. He was able to turn his life around. He was so glad he had.

God blessed him through college. Alton received a Bachelor's degree in Chemical Engineering from Lehigh University in Bethlehem, Pennsylvania. He graduated with honors at the top of his class.

After graduation, Alton went to work for Carrier Corporation in Charlotte. The company was good to him and paid for his master's degree in chemical engineering. Alton and Maybelle were finally happy. And they intended to keep it that way.

Emmaline ran to her dad as he walked down the hall toward the kitchen. Alton, eyes shining brightly with happiness at the thought of his beautiful bride, children, and life, opened his arms wide to receive his jubilant daughter. Giving him a big hug, Emmaline excitedly told him about the dance and the boy who had asked her to the dance.

"Wait a minute," Alton said with sternness in his voice and the severest glare he could muster toward his daughter. "I didn't say anything about you going to any dance with any boy," he said, teasingly.

"But Daddy, it's not just any boy. He's Mrs. Rita Hall's *grandson*, the one who moved here from Chicago. Daddy, please! Bobby Joe is sooo nice," Emmaline emphasized. "He's the captain of both the basketball *and* football team, Daddy. Please!" she pleaded, justifying why this wasn't just any date.

Emmaline looked at his face, hoping he was joking but not really sure. She looked from her dad to her mom and back again as she considered what was going on. Both her parents hid their humor well as they "discussed" the problem.

"Well, honey," Maybelle said as she and her husband continued to play with their daughter. "I had told Emmaline yes. But if you don't think it will be a good idea, I can change my answer," she said, glancing at their daughter, a woeful look on her face.

"But, but, Mama . . ." Emmaline said, trying to make sense of this change in developments.

"Emmaline," her dad began. "I don't know this boy. And you know I have always been a little suspicious of anyone who lives in Chicago. This boy might be trying to take you for a ride, you know," Alton said matter-of-factly, unaware he was speaking prophetically. "Does he have good grades? What does he look like? You know those high-yellow boys are nothing but trouble. All they want is a little dark chocolate on the side."

Finally, Emmaline caught the humor of the situation. Her dad was light-skinned or "high-yellow" and her mom was dark-skinned or "dark chocolate." She caught the glint of humor in her dad's eyes and understood that he and her mother were joking with her.

"Dad," she said, exasperated. "Stop teasing! This is serious!"

"Aw, come on, baby girl, we were only joking. I guess our little girl is growing up, huh, hon?" he asked his wife.

"Yes, she is. Emmaline, are you going to need a formal for the dance or just a nice dressy dress?"

"Gee, Mom, I don't know. I'll have to ask around to see what everyone else will be wearing. We've got about a week before I will need anything. Thanks, Mom and Dad!"

Emmaline happily danced down the hall to her room to start planning for her date. She would be attending a dance, with a boy, a good-looking boy at that. What dances were they doing now? She had no clue. Soul Train would be her major TV viewing until the dance.

She decided to call Sonora to see if anyone had invited her to the dance. She hoped someone had. Sonora was so sweet and her very best friend. Even though they both wanted boyfriends, they didn't want to just be someone's joke of a date or anything like that.

Emmaline was happy she was finally going to go out on a date, a real date. Even though Bobby Joe's parents would take them to the dance and pick them up, it was still a date.

Sonora answered on the first ring. "Hello," she said, excitement flowing through the phone to her friend.

"Sonora, it's me, Emmaline. What'cha doin'?" Emmaline asked, thinking about her impending date.

"Emmaline," Sonora screamed through the phone. "Sheldon asked me to the dance!" she shouted excitedly. This had turned into a banner day for them both.

FORTY SEVEN

Eternity . . .

"**F**or I know the thoughts that I think toward Emmaline Ruth Johnson," said the Lord. "Thoughts of peace and not of evil, to give her an expected end," continued Almighty God as He considered the happiness of the girl as she chatted away to her friend on the telephone.

God had continually observed this little one after her parents settled down to make a go at their marriage. He allowed all manner of maturity builders to happen to the entire family: the man Alton, the woman Maybelle, the girl Emmaline, and the rest of their family members.

Emmaline was coming of age. The things destined to affect her during this season of life would influence her greatly as she entered the military and later joined His Army of Holy Soldiers.

"Father," said the voice of His Son, Jesus Christ. "What is to happen to the little one Emmaline Ruth Johnson in this next season of her life?" He asked, concerned for the fate awaiting her.

"Just watch, My Son," Almighty God said confidently. "Even though there are things coming her way designed to break her heart and destroy her mentally and emotionally, she is strong and will overcome. The enemy is gearing up to take her down. But this one has the strength of the Ancient of Days within her. She will conquer all that will transpire."

In the Unseen . . .

Ridicule, Rejection, Discouragement, and Pride sat high in the atmosphere over Bobby Joe Hall's room as he schemed with his best friend, Sheldon Murray. It was time for the ultimate ruination of Emmaline Ruth Johnson and her friend Sonora. These two would cause their downfall to materialize.

"Will Rape be joining us today, Lord Pride?" asked Ridicule as they planned their attack on the two girls. Rape was a very big part of their plan.

"No, imp," answered Pride. "He only shows up on the day of the attack. He is more like a special guest for the invasion. We only need him as the *piece de resistance* on the day of the dance. Don't worry—he will show up in all his glory for this feast," promised Pride.

Satan had attempted to get rid of Emmaline Ruth before she was born but the Almighty had pulled her through. Satan decided that if he couldn't get to her physically, he would work an emotional and mental strategy with her. He would win one way or the other.

In the Seen, Bobby Joe's bedroom . . .

"Man, she fell for it," Bobby Joe Hall chortled to his best friend and cohort, Sheldon Murray.

They had plotted for weeks to ask who they considered to be the ugliest girls at school to the Thanksgiving dance. They were "but-her" or "butter" girls—nice body, "but her" face.

In their estimation, nobody in school cared one way or the other about these two girls. Smart but homely, nobody else wanted to date them. Bobby Joe and Sheldon figured they would get some good Boy Scout points with the appearance of taking them to one of the minor dances of the school year. Plus, they would get a good laugh if they could get everything to happen just right that night.

With the plans they had for these girls, the boys were confident they would have a good time at each girl's expense. Sheldon, who grew up with both Sonora and Emmaline, would not have thought of doing something like this on his own. He had a good coach in Bobby Joe Hall, though.

Bobby Joe was notoriously recognized at David G. Farragut High School in Chicago for pulling pranks on less popular students. Always popular in sports, he had other students groveling just to get a smile from him. Knowing the power of his charm, he capitalized on his good looks and made sure everyone thought of him as smart, good-looking, and kind. Unfortunately, only two of those words accurately described Bobby Joe. And he was no less devious after moving to *lame* Charlotte, North Carolina with his family. He was still up to his old tricks.

After all, it was his fault his family had moved in the first place. Following that little incident with Rosalyn Chambers on homecoming night, Bobby Joe's parents felt it was best for the family to move if they were to either keep Bobby Joe alive or out of jail by the time he was eighteen. Who would have thought there would be such a big stink over him giving her that little pill during the homecoming dance and then taking her home?

He didn't see what the harm was. All the guys were doing it. So now he had to get back into the swing of things with this bug of a girl, Emmaline Johnson. She would never know what hit her. Bobby Joe snickered as he thought about how happy Emmaline had been when he approached her with the invitation.

"Yea, she almost fainted when I asked her to the dance, man," he gloated with Sheldon. "But man, she is one ugly chick! She is *butt-ugly*, dude!" Bobby Joe said, laughing at his own joke.

"Hmmph!" snorted Sheldon. "So did Sonora. Man, I thought she was going to float from the floor to the ceiling when I asked her. Boy, I almost got sick from the look on her ugly mug. Yecch!" He faked barfing at just the thought of her ugliness.

Sheldon wasn't a bad kid. Attractive and very athletic, he showed great skill on the basketball court as well as the football field. He had known Sonora and Emmaline for many years, had played with them when they were all kids. He couldn't see the harm in what they were planning. But he didn't know all that Bobby Joe had planned.

Bobby Joe and Sheldon considered themselves to be two of the most upstanding guys in the entire school. They were good looking, athletic, and hard workers. Surely, it would be OK if they had a little fun with these two undesirables.

"Did you tell Jenae who you were taking to the dance?" Sheldon asked Bobby Joe. In their own minds, they both had girlfriends who were just as good looking as they were.

Sheldon had already spoken with his girlfriend, Sussie Frye. She had given him the go-ahead to do what he wanted on that night. She would be out of town with her family for Thanksgiving and didn't care one way of the other. As ugly as this little nobody was that Sheldon planned to ask out, Sussie was confident he would be there for her when she returned from her mini-vacation.

"Yea, I told her. She'll be out of town that weekend," Bobby Joe replied. He had told Jenae Brown what he was going to do. As the most popular of the students in the twelfth grade, they were known for the jokes and hijinks they normally played on the underclassmen. Besides, they usually got away with their antics.

Bobby Joe and Sheldon continued to plan their night of trickery and deceit with the girls. Bobby Joe had already contacted a friend back in Chicago who would supply them with the needed additives for their dates. He was sure it would be a night to remember for all concerned.

This is the Army, Babies!

Emmaline

FORTY EIGHT

E mmaline, we don't want you to go into the military, honey," Maybelle Johnson tearfully pleaded with her daughter. She trailed behind her daughter as she went through her bedroom, packing a few of her belongings to go to boot camp at Fort Jackson, South Carolina.

Emmaline had looked forward to this day for a very long time. She wanted to hurry and get out of Charlotte. Her mother didn't understand all she had gone through, all she had endured here in her hometown.

Maybelle knew neither of the rape that fateful night two years ago with Bobby Joe Hall nor of the resulting pregnancy. Emmaline had been drugged and raped that night following the Thanksgiving dance. Two months later, she'd had an abortion from the night that should have given her the best memories of her life. All she had to remember of that night were nightmares.

Neither did Maybelle know anything about Emmaline being viciously picked on most of her life there in Charlotte. Emmaline had never told her parents of the emotional turmoil she had suffered from people she had known all her life. Her parents never knew that once people discovered she was the daughter of Alton

Johnson, she was rejected and ridiculed on all sides. She could never hold her head high because of that incident.

"Nobody wants you, Em-zilla," she was told.

"Your own daddy didn't even want you," they ridiculed her.

Because of rejection and ridicule, Emmaline had been forced to run home many days. She never told her parents about it. She didn't want their pity. Although all these things had driven her almost to the point of suicide many times, something always held her back.

Emmaline looked at her weeping mother. Since her dad had passed away from a heart attack a year ago, Maybelle Johnson had not been the same. She loved her children rightly enough. Sadly, something prevented her from giving them all her heart. It was as though her heart had gone to the grave with her beloved Alton.

Maybelle never mistreated Emmaline, Cardrina, or AJ. She simply spent so much time doing good for everyone else. It was as though Emmaline, Cardrina, and AJ were afterthoughts for Maybelle.

"Mom, I'll be right at Fort Jackson for twelve weeks for training. I'll do all my training there, both basic and advanced. I'll try to make sure I get an assignment to Fort Bragg if I can when I finish so I'll be close to home, Mama. I promise." Emmaline knew in her heart that she was lying to her mother. She had already decided that her first assignment would be in Europe, Germany, so she could put as much distance between her and Charlotte as possible.

There were so many things Emmaline wanted to tell her mother but couldn't find the courage to say. Bobby Joe's rape two years ago after the Thanksgiving dance was only one of the things she wanted to tell her about. The whole date thing had all been a game, a plot, to shame her and Sonora, her life-long friend.

They were both raped that night. Sonora had also gotten pregnant that night. Like Emmaline, Sonora never told her parents what really happened. Her family shipped her down to Georgia to get her away from the shame.

When her mom and dad questioned Emmaline about that night, she was too ashamed to tell the truth about what happened with Bobby Joe. Her dad had questioned her, trying to get her to open up. He knew there was more to what she had told them but didn't pressure her. Emmaline had honestly wanted to open up but something stopped her.

After Alton had the first of three heart attacks the next year, Emmaline wanted more than ever to confide in her dad. Instead, she allowed the abuse from her classmates to continue because she didn't want to cause her parents any more worry. She didn't know how to stop the abuse and couldn't see a way out of any of it.

When Alton finally succumbed to heart failure in November of 1976, Emmaline was devastated. She couldn't take any more of the anguish she was forced to endure in school. With her dad's untimely death, she now didn't have a champion even if she chose to tell her dad about her struggles.

She was finally going to tell her dad what had been going on when he died. She was going to tell him how she had become a scapegoat of sorts at school because she wouldn't and couldn't speak up for herself because she felt so worthless. Ugly, black, skinny—Emmaline felt she was worthless to everyone around her, especially to her family—mostly to herself.

Although her grades would have given her a scholarship to any school of her choosing, Emmaline started looking at the different branches of the military. She decided she wanted to get away from Charlotte for good. There was nothing but heartache for her there and she wanted out.

"Mama, don't worry about me. You know I'm a fighter. I'll make it," she promised her weeping mother as she finished packing her bag. As her recruiter was picking her up in fifteen minutes, Emmaline said a brief goodbye to her brother and sister.

Cardrina had fallen into the same trap as Emmaline. Regrettably, the trap had ensnared her. Cardrina was five months pregnant and had quit school at the age of fourteen. She wanted out of Charlotte, too. She had begged Emmaline not to leave her there. Emmaline felt she could do nothing but leave her younger sister and her family so she could find a life for herself.

When Emmaline knocked on Cardrina's bedroom door, the door swung open to reveal the pregnant young girl lying across her bed bawling her eyes out.

"Em, please don't leave me here!" Cardrina pleaded frantically. "I don't want to be here anymore!" Cardrina begged.

Emmaline looked pityingly at her younger sister. If there was a God, she could probably thank Him for allowing her to get an abortion after she was raped. Poor Cardrina didn't realize she was pregnant until it was way too late to have an abortion. She was stuck with an unwanted child. Emmaline had neither needed nor wanted a child, especially one born of rape, just like she was.

But Emmaline doubted if there was really a God. Look at what happened to her parents. Just when things were going well for them, her dad died. He was only forty-nine or so. It just wasn't fair.

Emmaline went to her sister's bed and sat down on the edge. She took Cardrina's hand and rubbed it the way she had done when they were little and one or the other was frightened of something.

"Drina, I got to get out of here. Girl, it feels like I'm drowning," she confided in her younger sister. "I hate Charlotte and most of the people that live here. I am sick of the Hell in this place. I tell you what. No matter where I go when I finish training, I will ask Mama to let you come and live with me. OK?" Emmaline offered her younger sister. She loved this one that looked so much like her. It was almost like looking in a mirror whenever she looked into her face.

Cardrina brightened up when Emmaline made the offer. "You will? You promise, sister?" Cardrina asked, hoping against hope that she would also be able to leave Charlotte.

Cardrina had been raped several times as well. She knew that no one would do anything about it because, as had always been said, she was ugly, black, and skinny just like her older sister. And just like Emmaline, she had spent most of her school-going days running home all the way from school from bullies and the *pretty* people, those who thought they were all that. She was tired of Charlotte, too.

"Yes, Drina-Mina, I'll have you come and live with me," Emmaline promised her sister. Surely in this world there was some place for those who were not as pretty as the *pretty* people. Surely . . .

Emmaline heard a horn blow in the driveway. It was probably Master Sergeant Cloussen, her recruiter. She hurried to AJ's room to say goodbye to her little brother. He sat up on his bed when she came into his room and wiped at his eyes so she wouldn't see the tears he shed because "Sister" was leaving him.

"AJ, I'm leaving now," she said softly. She looked around his room so he would not be embarrassed.

AJ leaped off the bed and threw his arms around his sister's neck. Both of them speechless, they hugged as though they would never see each other again. Emmaline cried in her heart for the family she would miss when she went to the Army. But it couldn't be helped. Every time she rode around town and looked at some of the places in which she had suffered abuse, it caused her to relive those moments again and again. Sometimes, she felt she would go crazy from the memory.

"AJ, I'll see you in about eight weeks for basic training graduation. Grandpa Stanley already promised to bring the family down to Fort Jackson. Don't worry, squirt, you'll see me again. I'll even call home when I can. OK?" Emmaline promised her brother, trying not to let the tears fall from her eyes. It was hard. She and her brother and sister were closer now than they had ever been before.

Emmaline loosed her hold on her little brother and turned toward the door to his bedroom. "Hey, squirt. Take care of Mom and Cardrina for me, will ya?" she asked as she walked through the door, not waiting for an answer.

Emmaline hugged her mom, her best friend in the whole world. Emmaline knew how much her mother cared for her. She had proved it before Emmaline was born by shielding the unborn Emmaline so her late husband couldn't kill both of them.

Emmaline had heard all the stories and had loved her mother unconditionally and beyond measure all these years. Leaving her was not easy. But it was something she would have to do in order to maintain her sanity and find her identity.

"Mom, I love you with all my heart," Emmaline said, finally sobbing at the thought of leaving her beloved mother. "Mom, I have to do this. Please understand," she begged Maybelle.

Maybelle pulled back to look up into the eyes of her wonderful first-born child. Maybelle knew there were things that had happened to this young woman, things she could do nothing about. All she could do was let her go.

"Go, child. Do what you have to do. My love will go with you. Even more importantly, God will go with you, Emmaline Ruth Johnson," Maybelle said, knowing her daughter didn't believe in God the way she did. Since her daddy had gone home with the Lord, Maybelle had felt Emmaline pulling away from the Lord. She continued to pray she would find her own relationship with God. She knew only He could keep her safe.

Emmaline grabbed her bags and went out the front door of the only home she had ever known. She saw the faces of her brother and sister as they looked out of the windows facing the street. As Master Sergeant Cloussen put her bags into the trunk of the car, Emmaline turned to face the house. She lifted her hand in a short wave before she got into the car. Today was the first day of the rest of her life.

Joyce

FORTY NINE

Jamaica Queens, New York: June 20, 1979

P reparing to leave for Army basic training, Joyce looked at her younger sisters and brother. Sharon was five, Angie was three, and Allen was one. They gathered around Joyce's suitcases, not quite understanding where JoJo was going as she packed her bags.

"You coming right back, right JoJo?" questioned five-year-old Sharon, brown and gold streaked eyes big in her pig-tailed head.

Joyce looked at her little sister thinking how much she would miss her much-younger siblings. After Jeffrey died, much of her sanity when she wasn't on the run came from having to take care of little Sharon right after her birth. Even though they had different biological dads, Sharon looked much like Jeffrey and Joyce.

Looking at Angie picking through the things she had just packed and baby Allen crawling around her room, Joyce smiled fondly at "her" babies. These two looked just like Pops. She loved them just as much as she loved the twin with whom she had shared their mother's womb but was now gone. To where, she didn't know.

"I'll be back in a couple of months, Pretty Thang," Joyce answered. Because Sharon had no real concept of time as yet, Joyce didn't bother to explain what "a couple of months" meant. "But I'll call you and write you and let you know where

I am," she assured Sharon and Angie, the only two really paying attention to her. Both little girls nodded their heads in agreement. To what, they knew not. They only knew they would miss their big sister.

Joyce looked forward to going into the Army. Since the recruiters came to her high school for career day, she had planned everything out. She knew her decision would be one she would have to take seriously. But she was prepared to make the decision and many more to follow it.

Even though she loved New York and her family, she was sick of the city and sick of being under her parents' rule all the time. She was ready for adventure on a grand scale. She knew there was more to life than what she faced each and every day of her life—babysitting, same old friends for years, more school if she decided to go to college, and her parents.

Finally graduated, she wanted something different, something she knew she wouldn't find in New York. She certainly wasn't inclined to go to college right now, especially in New York. She wanted to experience freedom she had never had before.

After talking further with Army recruiter Staff Sergeant Sanborn, Joyce discovered she could serve in the Army and get a college education at the same time if she wanted. The Army would pay for it. And the Army would allow her to go to different places, overseas places, she had always wanted to travel to.

While celebrating her eighteenth birthday last week down South with all the grandparents and cousins, Joyce informed her family that she had signed up to serve in the United States Army. Surprised gasps filled the humid country air as her family realized she wasn't joking. Music and conversation stopped in the field behind her grandparent's home.

Pulling out the paperwork she had completed at the Army recruiting station prior to coming South for the yearly family reunion, Joyce shared her ASVAB scores and other information showing where she would go for basic training and what job she would pursue as her specialty with her stunned family members. She gave a big slow grin as a feeling of accomplishment settled in her heart. She was going into the Army, her biggest adventure yet.

Samuel, her stepdad, stared at her, tears welling in his eyes. Of all his children, Joyce was the most adventurous. Always willing to go and do what no one else had ever done, Joyce was bold, brash, and beautiful. Samuel was glad God had made her his daughter.

Since Jeffrey's death five years ago, Joyce had been in sort of a self-destruct mode. Sometimes disappearing for days or weeks at a time, no one ever knew what she was up to. When she finally made an appearance, though, she would nonchalantly come into the house as though she had never left. They knew the girl loved her family, but

Marie and Samuel had almost given up hope with her after some of her escapades. Samuel decided the Army just might be the thing Joyce needed to get on the right track with her life. Lord knows she had already searched with no good results.

At fifteen, Joyce came home with her head covered, claiming to have found religion at an Islamic mosque in Queens Village. She called herself "Amira Bahja Mohammed" and would only answer if they referred to her by her new name. She kept that mindset for seven or eight months until she discovered she stood the chance of being one of many wives when she was chosen to be married. That didn't sit well with her. She quickly renounced the Islamic faith.

At sixteen, she went from Islam to a Pentecostal holiness church and stopped wearing pants or any clothing that were *manly* in nature. Women were advised not to wear any makeup, perfume, jewelry or anything that drew attention. During this time, she constantly rebuked her mother for wearing slacks and dressing her little sisters in pants, giving them a warped mind. Marie suffered in silence because she wanted her oldest child to find her way even as she had. However, Joyce only continued with that movement long enough to discover that the men were able to dress decently but the women had to appear drab. That was their code of belief.

At seventeen, she disappeared for two months during the summer of 1978 and was found living in a Rainbow Family Commune in upstate New York. She enjoyed the communal living until she discovered the leader of the commune, Father Good, was having illicit relations with everyone under his leadership—men, women, boys, and girls.

From this fiasco, she came home and vowed she would not serve anyone or anything because there was no God. As a matter of fact, she knew there couldn't be a God. A real God wouldn't have allowed Jeffrey to be killed like he was.

Joyce remained devastated by the loss of her brother. A part of her was lost forever on that crucial day five years ago. No one seemed to understand the loss she felt in her heart from not having Jeffrey with her any more. Her mom and dad seemed to have moved on. She couldn't make herself come out of what she had felt since that day.

They never found the person who killed Jeffrey. Soon after his funeral, though, strange envelopes addressed to "The Mother and Sister of Jeffrey Jones" occasionally arrived at their apartment. Enclosed in the envelope inside of a card were wads of cash money. Never a return address, no one ever called to explain where the money came from or what it was for. Samuel and Marie decided it must have come from the killer. They started the Jeffrey Earl Jones Foundation for Youth to help young people in their neighborhood find their path in life.

During Jeffrey's funeral, many people showed up that Joyce had seen around the neighborhood but didn't know their names or who they were. One guy in particular who showed up cried almost as hard as the rest of the family. Joyce didn't know who he was but thought he must have been very close to Jeffrey.

On the occasions when she took her younger sisters to the park, many times, Joyce noticed someone else there who seemed to be watching over them. He was a nice-looking guy who appeared to be in his twenties or so. She thought she recognized him as the guy who cried at the funeral but wasn't sure. He always sat opposite where she sat waiting on the girls to finish their play. He never came closer to where she was. A few times, she started to approach him. But when she walked toward him, he always got up and left the park.

Joyce felt there was a connection between her brother and the man but never knew what it could be. When she started dating and hanging out with the wrong crowd, she found that guys wouldn't bother her the way they messed with her friends. She didn't know whether Jeffrey was protecting her or if someone here on Earth was looking out for her.

Samuel looked at his daughter as she made her announcement. He had long quit referring to Joyce as his stepdaughter. She was his daughter—that was the way he felt about her. He went to her and hugged her, telling her how proud he was.

No, he didn't want her to go into the military. However, one thing he had found out about his women was this: they were all headstrong and had to learn from their own mistakes.

He stood with her at the reunion and glowed as only a proud father could. Her grandparents and the rest of the family were shocked that Joyce wanted to go into the military. But in a way, they were all thankful. They knew how much trouble she could get into in the city. Everyone hugged her and told her how proud they were.

Homer remembered the day he had met this little one at the Amtrak station in Atlanta. When he had gone there to pick up Ree, he had no idea he would also be picking up his twin grandson and granddaughter at the same time.

As he first laid eyes on them, Joyce was the one kicking and screaming because no one paid her any attention. She let out a bellow to let him know she was somebody and he would do well to pay attention to her.

"Well, baby," he told her as he hugged her. "With that mouth of your'n, you should be able to make a good soldier in that Army. They'll be lucky to have you. Good luck, shuge," he said teasingly, unshed tears glistening in his eyes.

The family laughed at Homer's joke because they all knew it was true. Joyce had proven over the years to be the most verbal of the family. They all knew this particular quality would serve her well in the Army.

But there was one family member very hesitant in coming forward. Marie hung back, tears gathering in her eyes as she realized the power of what her daughter was doing. She was going into the Army. Her *baby* was going into the Army. Ree looked at Joyce as all their family members surged forward to hug their soon-to-be soldier.

Joyce, though proudly aware that she had made the right decision, was nonetheless anxious at the new ground she was about to cover. Looking around, she felt someone's eyes on her. Before she found the face, she knew the eyes were her mother's.

Joyce and Marie had always been connected in this way. They could be on a crowded New York City street and always search each other out, no matter how many people stood between them. Joyce looked at her mother's eyes and saw the unshed tears. She knew her mother would never understand why she felt the need to do this. But she also knew her mother would not stand in her way of searching out this path in her life.

She wanted to explain to her mother how she felt—as though something were missing from her life and she had to find it. She still missed Jeffrey.

People had told her after Jeffrey died that it would become easier and she wouldn't miss him as much. She had found this to be untrue. She missed him now more than ever.

Sometimes she dreamed about him and the things they did when he was alive. Other times, she dreamed about him as though still living and they were the same age. She imagined the shenanigans and the trouble they would get in together. She missed her twin and wished she could see him.

Joyce was thankful they looked so much alike. She could always look in the mirror and see his face, but it wasn't the same. Joyce knew the Army was something Jeffrey would have wanted to do. She would fulfill the dream for them both.

What she continued to ask herself, though, and what she still searched for the answer to was, *Why?* Why did Jeffrey have to die?

In the days, weeks, months, and years after his death, the *why* of his death was still the most prominent question in her mind. She remembered seeing the guy with the knife about to stab her stepfather. Instead, Jeffrey grabbed Samuel, turned him around and took the knife in his own back.

Had he planned their stepfather's murder that day? Or had it been a case of random violence? None of Jeffrey's old friends recognized the description of the guy who came out of nowhere to bring about the devastation leading to Jeffrey's death.

Joyce agonized over the fact that she would never know the answers to any of these questions until she saw Jeffrey again and asked him the questions that had dogged her for five years. She didn't even know if she would ever see him again. He was lost to her.

Joyce went to her mother as family and friends cleared a path between them. When they finally reached each other, they sobbed because they knew the day Joyce said the oath of enlistment into the Army would be the first day of the rest of her new life. There would be no turning back for either of them.

Joyce and Ree held onto each other as though holding onto a life raft. They both thought that if they weren't careful, the tears they cried would drown them. They had had many milestones in life. This was a major milestone they would have to face together.

Ree looked at her now eldest child, the twin who survived. Joyce had been a very deep child and was now a very deep young woman. She had been through many things since the death of her twin, her soul mate from birth. Ree had watched and prayed for this daughter who seemed to be running headlong into destruction at a speed she couldn't understand.

At eighteen, Joyce was a beautiful, petite young woman who had experienced things her southern cousins could only dream about. Now she was going into the military, a career no other woman in their family had chosen—her daughter the pioneer.

"Joyce, I am very proud of you, honey," Ree wept. She held her closely as only a mother could. "I know you will do wonderful things."

Now as Ree watched Joyce preparing to leave for the airport to go to South Carolina for basic training, her heart pumped with dread and longing as she prepared her daughter for a voyage she would have no part in except to pray. And pray she would.

Margarette Ann

FIFTY

"Mama, why didn't you ever help me?" asked eighteen-year-old Margarette Ann Wells. Hurt and disappointment infused Margarette Ann's heart and mind as she looked sadly at the woman she called mother. This woman had known about her father's abuse all those years and had never done anything about any of it.

"I just don't understand, Mama" Margarette Ann reiterated, packing her bags, preparing to leave for boot camp that day. She wanted to understand, she really did.

Looking around the room that had served as her torture chamber for the majority of her still young life, Margarette Ann remembered the nights Albert Wells had come into this room to molest her. She remembered the tears she shed as she cried out for someone to help her. She stopped believing in God during this season of her life. After all, a real God couldn't possibly let the things happen to a child that had happened to her.

She swung her mind away from the memories of it all. Life has a way of setting things straight, she guessed. She was going into the military. She would change her own destiny.

"Mama, I'm going into the Army and that's that," Margarette Ann said decisively. Her mother begged her not to go when she found out Margarette Ann had signed up for the Army to get away from home.

She had already signed the paperwork and was flying to Columbia, South Carolina for twelve weeks of training at Fort Jackson. She couldn't wait to get away from home. For seven of the last eight years, Albert had molested her and Emma knew it. She couldn't stay in this disgusting, fear-filled house another moment with a man who had treated her as her father had.

"Mom, you need to get some help," Margarette Ann advised the sobbing woman. "Don't let him do this to the others. Please!" Margarette Ann insistently requested.

"Margarette Ann, honey, you have to understand," her mother began. "That's just the way it was. Divorce was unheard of. No one wanted to go to a counselor to let their dirty secrets out. We just had to sit back and endure," Emma explained as best she could.

Once Emma began working evenings at the hospital, it didn't take long for her to realize that while she was at work, Albert got drunk and beat the children. There just wasn't much she could do about it. They both had to work to keep the family going. Unfortunately, she worked while he was alone at home with the children.

And it was true—no one wanted to get a divorce or counseling. How embarrassing it would be in their community with her mother being a minister as well!

When Emma discovered the abuse going on in their home, she stopped going to the family church where she and Albert had grown up. Living in such a small community, she knew someone would eventually know what was going on in their house. She couldn't run that risk.

Once Albert started doing other things to Margarette Ann, it was more than Emma could bear. Short of killing him, though, she was at a loss on what to do about the situation. She knew if she killed him, she could go to prison. After that, it was anybody's guess what would happen with her children.

She certainly didn't want them to go to his parents for fear the same thing would happen in that home. Emma felt caught between a rock and a hard place. But she didn't know the depths of braveness in her oldest daughter.

Margarette Ann finally stood up when she turned seventeen. She started by telling Albert he could not do those things to her anymore. She was tired of being physically, mentally, and verbally abused by her drunkard of a father. When Albert insinuated her younger sisters wouldn't mind, Margarette Ann found the strength and the courage to threaten him with the shotgun she had kept hidden for about a month in her closet. And she was prepared to use it.

"No, Dad," she warned him that day. "You will not hurt Cindy or Annie as you did me because I don't mind killing you. You stole something very important from me. I will not allow you to do the same to my sisters. Please don't try me, Albert. You mean nothing to me. Your death means even less."

Albert backed down and did not pursue the matter any further. The look on his daughter's face told him she was not playing with him and was very serious. He watched Margarette Ann with a brand new respect after that day, a respect borne from her not allowing him to get away with the abuse any longer.

Now that she was going away to the Army, it concerned Margarette Ann that he would be able to get to her sisters in her absence. But she had a plan for that as well.

"Mom, please don't allow your husband to do to Annie and Cindy what he did to me. I didn't deserve the way he treated me and neither do they. Please, Mom, get some help," she pleaded with her mother again. Margarette Ann hoped their talk would help even though deep inside, she knew it wouldn't.

Emma sat on the side of Margarette Ann's bed, head down. Crying profusely, she understood the harm she had allowed to invade her home. Irreversible damage had been done to children she had birthed into the world. As the truth permeated her mind, she regretted not doing anything about the situation before it got worse.

"Mom, Jerry is driving me to the airport," Margarette Ann informed her mother, breaking through the reverie Emma had lapsed into. Jerry was the cousin she had grown up with who was always there when she needed him.

"He'll be here in a few minutes. I'm going to go and say goodbye to Dad," Margarette Ann said, closing her suitcase.

Margarette Ann went out into the hall and looked at the house she was leaving, probably for the last time. It had not been a home to her for a very long time, probably about right when the abuse started. She was determined to never come back here unless there was a death, preferably her father's.

She touched each photo of her and her brother and sisters lovingly as she looked at the pictures of them through the years. Looking at the pictures of her parents, she wondered when everything went wrong in their marriage. She would never put a child through what she had gone through. She wondered what made her parents, good people when they married, put her through what she had been through.

She had boxed up her personal photos in her room along with some of the things she wanted to have with her from her childhood. She realized as she packed that there was not much she wanted to remember from her childhood. She took only enough to show she had survived. And that's what Margarette Ann was—a survivor. She had made it through.

Jerry came into the house as she walked down the steps. Taking her suitcase, he told her he would wait outside in the truck. As she walked into the kitchen, Albert looked up from the cup of coffee he drank. After their confrontation last year, Albert had given up drinking anything alcoholic. He now stuck to hot coffee and iced tea. Realizing his daughter would kill him if he tried anything again, he became paranoid. He wanted to keep his faculties about him. Alcohol only made him weak.

As his oldest daughter stood in the doorway, Albert looked into her eyes only long enough to let her know he recognized her and hadn't forgotten their conversation. He hadn't been able to look into her eyes any more since the confrontation. She had proved to be the stronger of them. He respected her for that.

"Well, I guess y'er Mama and I will try to make it to your graduation, Margarette Ann," he said, turning his attention back to the steaming cup of coffee. He said it more to himself than to her. He wasn't sure how she would react.

"Don't bother. When I leave this house, the only other time I want to see you is when you're in your coffin so I can spit in your face," Margarette Ann said calmly, slowly, to make sure he understood every word she said.

No malice in her tone, Albert glanced at his daughter warily. She had a new strength about her he never dreamed she would have. There had been times over the years Albert had felt sorry for treating her as he did. Through it all, though, he kept telling himself that he couldn't help what he did to her.

"I told Mom to get help and to not let you do to my sisters what you did to me. Please don't let me hear from my sisters that you are abusing your privilege of being a father if that's what you can be called. I will go to prison if I have to," Margarette Ann warned him, the expression on her face unlike any he had ever seen before. "Not only that," she continued, "but while I'm riding to the airport, I'm going to tell Jerry what went on in this house all those years. So rest assured, Albert Wells— you may have gotten away with it concerning me, but I will not allow it to happen to another little girl in this house."

Margarette Ann finished her goodbye to her dad without allowing him to say another word. Albert watched her diminutive figure as she left the house, possibly for the last time. A startled expression on his face, Albert realized he couldn't be angry with her. He knew his actions had been wrong. He just couldn't help it, he kept telling himself.

He also knew that, when Jerry returned from the airport, he would tell many of the family what Albert had done to his children. He would have to face it. He hoped that one day Margarette Ann would find it in her heart to forgive him, but he doubted it.

Having said goodbye to her brother and sisters before they left for school that morning, Margarette Ann Wells walked out of the house to Jerry's truck, triumphant. She looked forward to Army basic training. She knew it would be hard and she hoped she would make it. But even if she didn't, she would not come back to this town or to this house until her father was dead. Today was the first day of the rest of her life.

Beverley

FIFTY-ONE

Aiken, South Carolina: March 8, 1977

Y ou're really going to do this, huh?" Beverley's best friend Janie asked.

Janie helped Beverley pack the few meager belongings she was allowed to take with her to basic training. Janie just couldn't understand how Beverley could leave home and go into the military. None of their crew ever left South Carolina. It was home. They couldn't imagine going anywhere else to live . . . except now.

"Girl, you heard what the judge said," Beverley told her. "Either the military or jail. Can you see me in jail? I almost didn't make it those couple of hours I was in lockup from that Teresa thing. It's either kill, be killed, or else. And I don't like the sound of the 'or else.'" Beverley explained.

Janie thought about what Beverley said. She knew it was hard on her. They ran with a fast crew. The trouble they got into progressively worsened. It seemed as though they couldn't keep their noses clean for some reason. Many of their crew was serving time right now, male and female. Janie didn't want to have to serve any time. She definitely didn't want her best friend to have to serve any time. Neither of them needed a record.

"I guess I understand," Janie conceded, tears in her eyes, "but I sure will miss you, girl."

"Look, girl. I got to get out of here. My dad and stepmom took Roxy to New York because I wasn't doing right by her," Beverley said about her year-old daughter Roxanne. "I've got to figure out a way to get her back. That's my kid. I don't want her to grow up like I did with my grandparents. That's not fair to her," Beverley explained, eyes starting to tear.

As she thought about her situation, Beverley wondered how she had even made it this far. When the school found out she was pregnant at sixteen, the guidance counselor, Mrs. Barbara Hyatt, tried to talk Beverley into quitting school.

"Honey, you'll have to take care of this child. You can't graduate from high school and take care of a baby at the same time," Mrs. Hyatt had advised, well-meaning though she thought she was.

Beverley knew if she didn't graduate from high school, there would be no hope for her. She had already messed up her dream of becoming an attorney. Because of her bad, although passing, grades, she couldn't even apply for a basketball scholarship at this point. No, she had to be out there with the fast crowd. Now she was paying for it.

But she did it. She graduated from high school after having her baby. Her grades weren't as good as they could have been, but she made it. The other two senior girls who had also become pregnant in their senior year ended up dropping out of high school. Beverley didn't. She knew she had to complete this one thing.

Looking back over the past year and a half, Beverley regretted many of her decisions. The only choice she didn't regret, though, was the one to have and keep her baby. When she saw that little face in labor and delivery, she immediately fell in love. She was the prettiest little girl Beverley had ever set her eyes on.

Roxy was very light-skinned at birth, whiter than anything else that was for sure. The only way the nurses were able to tell she belonged to Beverley was by looking at the tips of her ears. Roxy was born the same way her mother had been born—light, bright, and almost white with a head full of jet-black curly hair. She was beautiful.

Beverley now wished she had done right by her daughter. Young and dumb, she couldn't stay off the streets long enough to take care of herself much less a baby. It cut her deeply when her dad and stepmom came from New York and took Roxy back with them. History was repeating itself through her. She had to correct it.

And now she was going into the Army. One day in September of the previous year while walking downtown Aiken, Beverley happened to pass by the Army recruiting station. Her thoughts immediately went back to the day when her high school had sponsored a military recruiting day before her class graduated. What really intrigued her was the Army band playing at the end of the presentations. When the recruiters left, she began considering the Army.

What was it all about? Could she go into the Army and make a life for herself and her child? Her Uncle Richard told her the Army was "not the place for women," which intrigued her even more. There had been women soldiers singing with the band that day during the show. Wearing nice sharp uniforms, they all seemed so happy, as though their lives were so together.

Seventeen at the time she walked into the recruiter's office, Master Sergeant Frank Kelsey told Beverley he couldn't talk with her about joining the Army without a parent or guardian present. Army regulations, he explained, required her grandmother to come in before he could talk to Beverley.

That was the last thing Beverley wanted—for her grandmother to have any decision-making power over her choice to be in the Army. But she had no choice. So she played nice and took Mama with her to the recruiting office. Mama grudgingly signed the paperwork giving her permission to join the Army once she turned eighteen.

Unfortunately, many things could happen in a couple of months. Beverley started seeing Kenney who had several girlfriends. Beverley knew one of his girlfriends, Teresa, because she lived right around the corner from Aunt Ida Mae's house.

Teresa didn't take too kindly to the idea that her man (he was twenty-one and she was fifteen) was seeing Beverley. They got into a fight, a good old fisticuff fight. When Beverley got the better of Teresa, Teresa's mother joined the catfight and slapped Beverley's glasses right off her face.

Nothing like fighting blind, Beverley struck out and pummeled the woman to the ground, forgetting to respect her age. She battered Teresa's mother so badly, it took three people to pull Beverley off the woman. On the run for three days following the altercation, Beverley was finally caught by the cops two days before Thanksgiving.

Because Teresa's mother had sworn out a warrant for her arrest, the police had to take Beverley to county lockup before a judge would see her. Locked up for six hours before her turn came to appear before the judge, Beverley thought her life was over and that she would become a statistic, joining her friends who were already in jail or prison.

Fortunately for Beverley, she had already signed up for the Army. The judge honored that with only one stipulation—if she decided to not go into the Army, she would have to serve time for the assault.

Beverley thought back to that as she and Janie finished packing her clothes. She couldn't wait to leave Aiken. Aiken was no longer a home or a refuge for her. She needed something different in her life and knew the Army could give her what she was seeking. When she went to Columbia for her physical and swearing-in in October, she met a totally different kind of people and freedom.

Beverley met people from places she had never been before—Florida, Alabama, Mississippi, Washington, DC, Connecticut, and other states. She enjoyed talking to these people and hearing about places other than boring South Carolina. She knew she would enjoy the experience of being in the military and being allowed to travel to places like Europe, Asia, Alaska, and Hawaii. When she returned to Aiken after swearing in to await her birthday and her boot camp, which started in March, she sullenly lived life, ready to leave for the last time.

Looking around the room she rented from her Aunt Ida Mae for the last time, Beverley closed the door on the life she had lived. She wanted to forget. She wanted something poles apart from what she was accustomed to. She wanted a new day and the Army was going to give her that.

As Beverley hugged her aunt and went out the front door of the modest house, she assured the feisty, old, gray-haired woman she would take care and call and write often. She loved this petite woman, her beloved Daddy's younger sister. She had taken Beverley in when she couldn't spend another day in the house with her grandmother.

Running down the steps to Janie's car waiting to take her to the bus station, she glanced over her shoulder at the house where she had spent her last six months in Aiken. Quickly waving her hand before ducking into the car, Beverley realized how much she would miss her aunt and most of the rest of her family.

But now was the time to look forward. Today was the first day of the rest of her life.

The Baby Chronicles

FIFTY-TWO

T his was it! This was the day in each eternal stream that each of the four young women—Beverley Scott, Margarette Ann Wells, Emmaline Ruth Johnson, and Joyce Renee Jones—would enter the United States Army and train to become United States Army soldiers.

Time stood still as each of the young women repeated the oath of enlistment that had been repeated by thousands, hundreds of thousands, of other soldiers before them.

"Attention!" commanded the various Enlistment Officers. Please repeat after me . . . I, state your name . . .

I, Beverley Scott . . . , October 14, 1976
I, Margarette Ann Wells . . . , April 21, 1977
I, Emmaline Ruth Johnson . . . , June 19, 1977
I, Joyce Renee Jones . . . , June 20, 1978

. . . do solemnly swear or affirm that I will support and defend the Constitution of the United States against all enemies, foreign and domestic; that I will bear true faith and allegiance to the same; and that I will obey the orders of the President of the United States and the orders of the officers appointed over me, according to regulations and the Uniform Code of Military Justice. So help me God.

As the last words were repeated by the newly enlisted United States Army soldiers, each young woman considered the path she had taken on this very day in her life.

Beverley

I *can't believe I've done this*," Beverley Scott thought to herself.

Here she was . . . seventeen years old and away from home almost for the first time! She debated on whether she should call anyone to let them know what she had finally accomplished. Then she thought better of it. After all, the only people who cared about her enlisting in the Army already knew what she was doing. The only one who she really wanted to talk to about her decision, her Daddy, Otis Scott, was dead.

Beverley left the room with the others she had recently become acquainted with at Fort Jackson, South Carolina Military Entrance Processing Station. They all congratulated each other on enlisting and made plans to enjoy their last bit of freedom before entering boot camp. Because of her age, Beverley would be forced to return to Aiken until March 9, 1977 when she could officially enter boot camp. She hated the thought of returning to her place of torment.

Beverley walked into the room she shared with seven other young women from various states on the East Coast. She enjoyed the camaraderie they shared during the few days they had come to know each other. She looked forward to maybe sharing basic training with at least two of them since the others would be sent to basic during the next cycle of training as part of the delayed entry program. Today was a day of firsts and Beverley looked forward to a new life that would take her to where she wanted to be—away from South Carolina, perhaps to a place where she and Roxy could build a life together.

Margarette Ann

Margarette Ann Wells smiled to herself as she looked at the enlistment papers in her hands.

"This is something *he* will never be able to take away from me," she scoffed, looking at the paperwork again for about the hundredth time. She had just repeated the oath of enlistment with fifty-five other new soldiers and was about as happy as she could be considering the journey she had taken to get to where she was today.

Margarette Ann thought back several days to the day she left home for the first and also the last time. She bitterly considered whether she should call home or not and thought better of it. She really didn't want to hear Albert's voice no matter how much distance there was between the two of them. She'd had enough of him in her life. She refused to allow him to ruin the moment of her greatest triumph since leaving home.

Instead, she called her cousin Jerry who had taken her to the airport. She hadn't spoken with him since their drive to the airport. Margarette Ann wondered what changes had been made in her family since he went back and revealed the revolting secrets she had shared with him, with anyone, for the first time.

"Jerry, it's me. I did it," Margarette Ann stated in her somber voice. In all their years of growing up together, Jerry could never remember her being excited about anything. Today was no different.

"Hey, cuz! Congratulations!" Jerry shouted into the phone, hoping to help her become a little more excited about her accomplishment. Out of all his girl cousins, Jerry admired and loved Margarette Ann just a little more than the others. From the time they were all cutting teeth, they had played and become close. Not just because of the blood ties, but because they all shared a real closeness.

"Thanks, Jerry! I appreciate you being there for me," Margarette Ann returned, trying to lighten her voice just a little but unable to since she didn't know the status of her siblings and parents back in Ohio.

"Margarette Ann, a lot has already changed in your house," Jerry shared. Social Services had stepped in and removed her siblings. They were temporarily with her mother's parents. The judge would decide in about a month or so whether the courts would leave them there or not.

Tears of joy and sadness rolled down Margarette Ann's face as Jerry shared everything. Now, she was sure her brother and sisters would not have to endure what she endured for much of her still young life. Maybe there was a God.

Margarette Ann thought back to how Jerry had cried as he drove while she shared with him the things her father had done. At one point, Jerry pulled over on the side of the road to vomit. He was so disgusted with what Margarette Ann told him. She shook her head in disgust as she walked to the room she shared with other young women who were entering Army basic training.

Margarette Ann knew this was going to be a difficult time in her life, this basic training she had to endure. She didn't care. She wanted this. She needed this to happen in her life. Maybe, just maybe, she thought to herself, she would be able to forget about all she had gone through as she forged a new life for herself in the world. She was determined to move forward. Nothing would stop her.

Emmaline

Emmaline Ruth Johnson grinned into the telephone receiver as she spoke to her mother.

"Mama, I did it! I'm in the Army!" she shouted into the receiver.

Emmaline was ecstatic! Finally, she had done the one thing everyone in her family in Charlotte had told her she couldn't and shouldn't do—join the Army. She was on her way to doing something none of her other family members, male or female, had done. She would have bragging rights on this.

"Honey," Maybelle replied through the shared laughter, "I am so proud of you!" Tears welling in her soft brown eyes, Maybelle wished her beloved Alton could be there at that particular moment to share in the joy of their daughter. Oh, how she missed him!

"Mama, we start training tomorrow," Emmaline continued excitedly. "We have our uniforms and everything! Mama, some of this stuff is sooo ugly," Emmaline dramatized, laughing as she shared with her mom how some of her new friends looked as they paraded in the barracks halls wearing different items of the uniforms.

Maybelle laughed with her daughter as she described the uniforms in detail. Looking around herself in her kitchen, she knew that life would not be the same without their Emmaline around the house. However, she was willing to forego her daughter being at home so she could find her place in the world, and prayerfully, in God.

Maybelle acknowledged that life had not been the best for Emmaline Ruth Johnson. She had been rejected, put down, and all together pushed out of Charlotte because of the way friends and family had treated her. Although Maybelle felt sadness in her heart, she knew that her daughter had made the right and only decision in this season of her life.

"Honey, enjoy the journey," Maybelle advised her daughter as they prepared to hang up.

Maybelle had much to think about now. Emmaline had asked permission for her younger sister to come and live with her once she received her permanent assignment. Maybelle thought it would probably be a good idea, but she would think on it. She pondered on the request to see what Alton would have decided had he been there. Maybelle wanted the best for her children. If that meant they needed to leave Charlotte, then so be it.

Joyce

Joyce Renee Jones grinned as she completed the oath of enlistment. She was more excited than she had ever been in her entire life. She was finally going to fulfill her dream of getting away from home, family, and friends so she could go and do what she wanted to do. The Army would allow her the opportunity to travel to many places in the world she would otherwise not have been able to visit.

Joyce looked down at the uniform she wore. Goodness! This had to be the drabbest shade of green the Army could have come up with! Olive green with only the black of the nametag and the army tag to give it any contrast. And these boots! What could the designers possibly have been thinking when they came up with these uniforms?

It's a good thing I'm female, JoJo thought to herself. At least the female uniforms were more contoured to the female body. They even allowed them to show a little leg every once in a while if they wore the skirt. And then there was the ugly mint-green skirt set. Boy, was that ever ugly!

But she didn't care. She was here, exactly where she wanted to be at this time in her life. She knew her entire family was behind her. Her parents had to be the proudest people on the face of the Earth. She was cool with that. Joyce knew she had given them a lot of heartache over the past five to seven years. She was determined to make it up to them.

Kingdom of Darkness . . .

"I will wreak havoc on these four," satan threatened, observing each young woman in her time continuum. He went from one to the other as he hissed and cursed in the atmosphere above each of the four young women he had watched from the moment of their creation. He knew that Almighty God had plans for each of these women. He was determined to cause them to walk on the side of darkness before it was all over.

Kingdom of Light . . .

Almighty God observed Lucifer stalking from one time period to the next, threatening those who would be called by the name of the Most High God. He knew the plans of the devil and would allow certain things to happen. But there was no stopping the plans of God for these four young women. He had determined that these four would serve not only in the Army of the world but the Lord's Army. He had orchestrated it and it would happen.

These are His babies. And these are their chronicles.

ABOUT THE AUTHOR

Beatrice Bruno is the author of several motivational/inspirational titles that include *How to Get Over Yourself, Get Out of Your Own Way, and Get What YOU Want Out of Life!* Beatrice is an Army veteran and former (but always and forever) drill sergeant.

Beatrice is an ordained gospel minister and life and writing coach who loves showing folks how to get over themselves and let go of the PAST.

Now, having written her first novel, Beatrice is spreading her wings as a novelist and creating the series, *The Baby Chronicles, Volume 1,* which includes the *GI Josephines* (Volume 2) and the *Soldiers of the Lord* (Volume 3).

Hang on to your hats as you follow the escapades of Beverley, Joyce, Margarette Ann, and Emmaline from before birth until . . . well, you'll just have to read the series to see where it all ends!

A free eBook edition
is available with the
purchase of this book.

To claim your free eBook edition:

1. Download the Shelfie app.
2. Write your name in upper case in the box.
3. Use the Shelfie app to submit a photo.
4. Download your eBook to any device.

Shelfie

A **free** eBook edition is available
with the purchase of this print book.

CLEARLY PRINT YOUR NAME ABOVE IN UPPER CASE

Instructions to claim your free eBook edition:
1. Download the Shelfie app for Android or iOS
2. Write your name in **UPPER CASE** above
3. Use the Shelfie app to submit a photo
4. Download your eBook to any device

Print & Digital Together Forever.

Snap a photo

Free eBook

Read anywhere

Printed in the USA
CPSIA information can be obtained
at www.ICGtesting.com
JSHW022211140824
68134JS00018B/998